FIGHTER IN LINGERIE

LINGERIE #14

PENELOPE SKY

Hartwick Publishing

Fighter in Lingerie

CONTENTS

1

CARMEN

I SOLD my soul to the devil.

The second I was his, he claimed me so thoroughly I could barely breathe. His hold was tight, gripping me so my lungs couldn't expand with my deep breathing. He didn't touch me, just gave me his fierce expression before he walked out.

Then he ordered me to grab my things.

I spent the evening packing all the essentials. I grabbed my clothes, makeup, hair supplies, birth control, my favorite shoes and boots, and everything else I would need on a daily basis. I suspected I would come back to my apartment from time to time, just in case someone stopped by to see me.

I couldn't just move out.

I placed my luggage in the doorway then opened another bottle of wine. It was almost midnight and I was usually in bed by now, but my evening had been unusual.

Bosco, the owner of the city, came to my apartment and basically bought me.

Actually, he'd leased me for three months.

Now I would be his exclusively, fucking him every night and sharing his space like some kind of mistress. The idea of spending more time with him didn't upset me since I knew it had an expiration date.

But I feared he wouldn't honor our agreement.

What if he became more obsessed with me, and despite our original agreement, he would take it all back? He would hold on to me even tighter and refuse to let me go? There would be no escape from this madman.

I would be doomed.

His footsteps were audible on the other side of the door. He could announce his presence so easily, because every part of him was loud. From his heavy footsteps to his aggressive persona, his threatening vibrancy filled the air.

He stepped inside and surveyed the bags of essentials ready to be taken away.

I drank my wine at the counter without looking at him.

Bosco communicated silently with his men, and four of them stepped into my apartment and gathered my things. They moved stealthily, barely making a sound as they left the apartment and carried my belongings down the hallway and to one of the cars.

Bosco came to my side and pressed his chest into my shoulder. His arm hooked around my waist, and he looked down at me, a slight smile on his lips because he'd won the battle. His hand slowly moved up my back and neck until his fingers dug under the fall of my hair. He turned my face toward him, making me stare into his gaze. "This will be the best three months of your life. I promise you."

His smell and masculine presence immediately made me feel feminine, made me naturally want to submit to this strong man. My body constantly felt the pull of his gravitational field, wanting to be sucked deep inside and never released. "But will it only be three months?"

His eyes looked into mine, his gaze searing. "That's the deal we made."

"But will you honor it?"

He gave me that lopsided grin. "You don't trust me."

"Why would I?" I asked coldly.

"Because I've been honest since the beginning." His thumb brushed across my bottom lip. "I've never thrown you a curveball and I never will."

"That's not enough for me."

"Then what do you want?" he asked, still amused. "A contract? A notary?" He chuckled, thinking the suggestion comical.

It was better than nothing. "Yes."

He raised an eyebrow, his smile slowly fading. "You're serious?"

"Yes." Maybe it was a stupid thing to ask for, but if he backed out later, at least I had something to make an argument with. I could throw his signature in his face and prove that he was a liar—and had no honor.

The menace started to shine in his eyes, his heartless anger slowly rising. "In my world, you're only as good as your word. If you break it, people will lose respect for you. That's why I punish the men who cross me—because I have to keep my word. No one gets away with any crime. They all face the same fate. This is no different. If this is the deal we agreed on, I will fulfill my end of the bargain."

"Then you should have no trouble putting it in writing," I countered. "With a witness."

He turned quiet, slightly annoyed and slightly amused. "You think I'd bring anyone else into this? My personal life is private."

"You said you have a brother you run the casino with."

His silence was enough of an acknowledgment.

"I want him to be the witness."

He rubbed his fingers across the stubble of his chin, his eyes shining with disdain. "Will this really make you feel better?"

"Yes. Because I know you don't want to look like a liar in front of the only family you've got left." Regardless of how close they were, Bosco must care about the opinion his brother had of him. If he were a psychopath that wouldn't let me go, even though he promised he would, he'd look like an asshole. "It's accountability."

"Fine. If that's what you want, you can have it. But I'm disappointed you think this is necessary."

I gripped the glass in my hand, about to shatter it. "You threatened to kill my father if I didn't become your personal slave."

"I never said you were a slave. I just said you were mine—big difference."

"I see no difference," I said coldly.

"You'll be treated like a queen—that's the difference."

"Doesn't change anything," I said. "You gave me an ultimatum."

"And then you brought my mother into this." It didn't matter how quick the pace of the conversation was, he could keep up easily. He always fired back with an answer, his brain working at an impressive speed.

"It was the only option I had."

"But then you compromised. We reached three months—together."

"What else could I have done?"

He grabbed the glass from my hand and set it on the counter, keeping his eyes on me the entire time. He moved in closer to me, close enough that his breath fell on my skin. He made me rise on my toes because the tension settled over both of us like a cloud. He suffocated me with his presence, with his overbearing masculinity. "You could have pressed for your freedom. You used my mother against me, and you could have squeezed more out of me. We both know it. But you didn't. You settled for a compromise—because you wanted a compromise."

I turned to face him head on, shocked by the allegation. "So, you think I want this?"

"I know you do," he said confidently. "A woman like you only does something if she wants to. You want this. You want me—just not forever. You want to enjoy me, knowing there's a way out. You know I'm not the right man for you, but this alleviates your guilt. It's fine if you don't want to say it out loud. I can't blame you. But we both know that's the case." He pulled away abruptly, ending the conversation with the cold shoulder. "Let's go." He walked into the hallway without waiting for me.

I stayed at the counter and stared at the bottle of wine I didn't get to finish. A dread descended into my stomach because his analysis was right. A part of me wanted to be his woman, to keep this level of invincibility I'd become addicted to. I wanted good sex without having to find it. I wanted a man so powerful no other man could match him. But I also wanted to walk away…without taking any responsibility for the time I'd wasted. Would I say that to him? Never.

I'd take it to the grave.

BOSCO PULLED HIS SHIRT OVER HIS HEAD THE SECOND he was inside the bedroom. He tossed it on the back of the chair that faced the desk and moved about the room in just his jeans and belt. His muscles shifted and worked together, rippling under the tanned skin as he walked to the large closet against one of the walls. He pulled it open, revealing empty hangers on the bar where I could hang my clothes. "Help yourself." He walked into the bathroom, pretending all of this was normal, and shut the door to brush his teeth and wash his face.

I opened the first suitcase and started to hang my tops and jeans, but that's when I noticed the short cocktail dresses, pumps, and other clothing toward the right side of the closet. I stared at a black strapless dress and a pair of red pumps. There was also a piece of black lingerie hanging next to it.

None of that stuff was mine.

Did it belong to an old lover? Did he lie when he said

he didn't have a relationship? Had someone else ever lived here? Or did they simply leave their clothes behind and went home in his t-shirt?

I kept hanging up my clothes, doing my best not to give a damn what the story was. Whoever shared his bed before me was irrelevant. I didn't care, and I never would care. I set my shoes on the shelves then closed the doors, hiding the other dresses from view.

It was late, so I opened one of his drawers and pulled on one of his shirts he wore around the house. The material was something I'd never felt before, such soft cotton it was like wearing a cloud. Even though it was clean, it smelled like him, his cologne and whatever soap he used in the shower. If someone could capture that smell and put it in a bottle, they could slap the word masculine on it and have a new fragrance line.

I got into his large bed and set the alarm on my phone so I would be on time for work in the morning. Sometimes I had to get there early because I had shipments come in. At this time of year, it was too cold for the more exotic flowers to bloom, so they had to be imported.

Bosco emerged from the bathroom, finished with his nightly routine. He ran his hand through his hair as he approached the bed, sighing quietly like there was something on his mind. He grabbed his alarm on the nightstand and checked a few things before he stripped off all his clothes and got into bed beside me.

He usually slept in his boxers, so the fact that he stripped down completely meant he thought he was gonna get some.

Wasn't gonna happen.

He pressed his chest against my back and kissed the curve of my shoulder, his enormous erection pressed right in between my cheeks.

I wondered how many times he'd done that with someone else. He said I was the only woman he'd screwed without a condom, but was that a lie? He had an entire wardrobe in the closet—and none of it was mine. "I'm tired." Like an irritated wife, I dismissed him and closed my eyes, hoping he would back off and go to sleep.

"Then just lie there." He grabbed my arm and turned me over onto my back. "I don't mind doing all the work, Beautiful."

The nickname irritated me even more. How many times had he used that nickname in the past? "Well, I don't want it. Good night." I pushed him in the chest then turned over again, hoping the tension would fade as we drifted off to sleep.

He continued to hover next to me, looking at me with bubbling disappointment. His hand moved over my hip and down my thigh, subtly caressing me. He didn't turn me over and try again, but he couldn't keep his hands off me. "What is it?" His voice emerged deep and hostile, not seductive like it was a second ago.

"I'm tired."

He sighed quietly, annoyed by my answer. "I'm always honest with you. Be honest with me."

"Ha," I said sarcastically. "You're always honest with me, huh?" I sat up and looked at him over my shoulder. "Whatever you say, jackass." I lay down again, giving him the coldest shoulder I'd ever had in my life.

He dropped his hand from my hip. "Carmen, what is

it?" He pressed more firmly, only using his voice for authority. "Because you're mistaken about whatever you think happened. So, just tell me."

"I'm not mistaken," I said coldly. "Not everyone is gullible like the rest of your men. Not everyone will bow down to you just because you have money."

"People don't bow down to me because of my money," he said matter-of-factly. "They bow because of my absolute power. I can take away people's homes in a heartbeat. I can call off the police with a simple text message. I can overrule a court hearing after a short visit to the judge. They bow because I own every single inch of this city, from the sewers to the cathedrals. You're no different. Now, tell me what the problem is. When we came home, everything was fine. But something has set you off in the meantime. What is it?"

"Home?" I scoffed. "This is not home."

"It is—for the next three months." He grabbed me by the arm and jerked me onto my back again. This time, he pinned me down with his body, making me sink into the mattress. He pressed his face close to mine, his expression hardened with a look of rage. "I'm tired of your games. Tell me."

"I'm not playing games," I whispered. "You are."

His eyes flashed with hostility. "I've always admired you for speaking your mind. But now you're playing coy, and I don't like it. It's not your most attractive color. The only reason you aren't telling me is because you're embarrassed by it. And I don't like a woman who gets embarrassed."

Those words burned me to my core. I shouldn't be

offended by anything he said, not when I didn't care about his opinion. But that felt like a slap to the face. "I'm not embarrassed…" My throat shifted when I swallowed, slightly uneasy about the way he could read me so well.

"Then tell me so we can fuck and go to sleep." He moved off me, his dangerous eyes trained on me. They thudded with animosity, like he wanted to wrap his hands around my neck and choke me. The only thing keeping him back was his promise to me.

I moved out of bed and walked to the closet where all my things were stored. I opened the doors and turned on the lights inside, highlighting the dozen dresses and shoes that were there long before I opened the doors.

He was propped on one elbow, his thick arm chiseled with muscles. His biceps were distinct from his triceps. His shoulders were thick and round, and his arm practically looked like arm porn. He continued to wear the same cold expression, like the sight of those clothes meant nothing to him.

"One of your girls left these behind." I left the door open and crossed my arms over my chest, wanting to see the terror in his face.

But it never came.

"It seems like you've had more intimate relationships than you've let on…"

Slowly, a slightly lopsided grin stretched across his face. His eyes lit up with amusement, and all the anger that was once in his expression faded away.

I waited for an explanation, continuing to stand my ground. "Well?"

He chuckled as he rubbed his fingers across the stubble of his chin.

"Yes?" I pressed.

"I want to enjoy this a little longer…" His grin stretched wider, becoming a full-blown smile that was so handsome, I was irritated. His eyes shone with joy, like everything I said was innately pleasing to him.

The fear started to creep into my veins. Perhaps there was something missing, and I was so tired and stressed I didn't notice it. "Enjoy what?"

He chuckled again before he dropped his smile. "You're so damn jealous."

"I'm not—"

"Jesus Christ, it's sexy. Sexiest thing ever." He got out of bed and moved toward me, his muscles shifting as he made his way toward me. His thick arms hung by his sides, but once he was close enough to me, they reached out and grabbed me. He lifted me into the air and wrapped my legs around his waist as he carried me back to bed.

"Whose are they?" I demanded, my back hitting the sheets and my thighs falling apart as he conquered me like a tyrant.

He pulled my panties to the side and pressed his cock inside me with a smooth motion, grinning because I was wet like usual and there was no way to hide it. He sank until he was completely inside me, his balls tapping against my ass. "Yours." He kissed me softly, consoling me for my loss in the skirmish. He slowly thrust inside me, feeling every inch of my cunt with his long dick. "I bought those for you."

WHEN I WOKE UP THE NEXT MORNING, BOSCO HAD already left the bed. The sheets felt cold, and that was probably why I woke up five minutes before my alarm went off. I jumped into the shower and got ready for the day, doing my normal routine in the master bathroom that was bigger than my kitchen and living room put together. There were two large sinks and plenty of counter space, along with a shower that could fit twenty refrigerators.

This would be my life every day for three months.

I pulled on jeans, a gray sweater, and an olive-green jacket before I walked into the main area of the penthouse. My hair was in loose curls, and I wore earrings my mother got me for my twenty-first birthday.

Bosco was in the kitchen, wearing black sweatpants that hung so low on his hips that I could see the dramatic V embedded in the muscles of his eight-pack. His stubble was thicker than it was the night before, his hair growing quickly since he still hadn't shaved.

I wasn't sure what look I preferred more—shaved or not shaved.

He scooped everything out of the pan and put it on the two plates before he carried it to the dining table that was placed in front of the floor-to-ceiling windows. With his tanned skin and perfect physique, he looked too beautiful to be real. I'd never seen a man more in shape in my life. My brother and cousin were fit, but Bosco was something else. He was ripped to the point it seemed unreal.

He set two mugs of coffee on the table. "Hungry?"

I looked at the breakfast he made, salmon with

veggies. If I kept eating like this, I was going to be fifteen pounds lighter—and that wasn't a goal of mine. I never cared about my weight. Whether I was heavier or lighter, it didn't change my life too much. It didn't seem like men cared either. "Yeah." I didn't want to sound ungrateful that he cooked for me, so I sat down and grabbed my fork.

He sat across from me and ate quietly, scrolling through his phone. He didn't seem like the kind of guy to check his social media pages, so he was probably looking through emails or whatever villains did.

I had to admit that salmon didn't go with coffee —at all.

Without taking his eyes off his phone, he addressed me. "You look beautiful today." The words rolled off his tongue so easily. His masculine voice naturally made my thighs clench under the table. Even if I had no idea what he looked like, I would get off just to the sound of his voice.

"Thanks. You look beautiful every day." The words flew out of my mouth automatically, like a bird that took flight for the sky. It happened so quickly, I couldn't stop it, especially since it was over by the time I'd realized it happened.

He slowly looked up, his gorgeous blue eyes meeting mine. He didn't give me that smug smile that he wore when he won an argument. He held my gaze with pure sincerity, like those words meant something to him.

It was one of those rare times when I couldn't handle his intense stare, so I looked down at my food, embarrassed I'd said something so pathetic. It was impossible for me not to feel attracted to a man who looked the way he did, a handsome face with a perfect body to boot. If he were a normal man I'd met at a bar, I'd probably be so hung up on him. I'd probably imagine our life together before our second date.

He finally turned his gaze back to his phone, giving me some reprieve from his suffocating presence.

I kept eating my salmon, enjoying the taste but not loving it. "So, can I expect to eat fish every day for breakfast?"

"Unless you cook something yourself." He drank his coffee then licked his lips.

"You really eat this every day?" I asked incredulously. "What about your cheat day?"

He gave me a blank stare. "Does it look like I have cheat days?"

No. It looked like he did nothing but work out and drink protein smoothies. "Well, I can't live like that. I need some pancakes and bacon once in a while. Some cereal too. Chips and salsa. Spaghetti. Not fish or chicken and veggies all the time."

"Alright. Put it on the list on the fridge. My maid will pick it up for you."

I forgot that he had someone that cleaned up the penthouse in the middle of the day. I'd never seen her. "What's she like?"

"Who?"

"The maid."

He shrugged. "She's nice. I never see her."

"How is that possible?"

"Because she purposely comes when I'm not here. I want this house clean and the fridge stocked, but I don't want to make small talk with someone who works for me. When I'm home, I don't want to be bothered."

I shouldn't be surprised by his cold attitude toward his need for solitude. "I'll put it on the list, then."

He finished his plate then drank his coffee slowly, leaning forward slightly, and his reflection was visible in the glass. The individual muscles of his back shifted and bunched at the slightest movement.

"So, what is your schedule?"

He stared at me blankly, like he had no idea what that meant.

"You work late at the casino sometimes, but then you're up early every morning. I don't get it."

"I don't sleep much," he said simply. "I like to get my workouts done in the morning. If I don't, I won't complete them."

He had more discipline than an Olympic athlete. "I hate working out."

"You're lucky you're so damn beautiful that you don't have to."

"Like you aren't," I countered, shoving my foot into my mouth.

A smile crept over his lips.

I looked away, wishing I would just shut my mouth and be quiet.

2
BOSCO

I SAT in the back seat of the car while my driver took me to the casino. Carmen would be getting off work soon, but the crew of men I'd assigned to her would pick her up and take her back to my penthouse. If there was somewhere else she wanted to go, they would take her. If she wanted to go on a shopping spree with my cash, she could do that too.

Whatever she wanted.

When she saw those clothes in my closet, she became so angry. Visibly wounded and even a bit heartbroken, she died a little inside to think some other woman had my attention the way she did. She thought I had a more intense relationship with someone else, that I came inside a woman besides her. It ate her up inside, gnawed her to the bone.

It made me smile every time I thought about it.

She was jealous.

Out-of-her-mind kind of jealous.

Little did she know, I gave her size to my personal shopper and asked her to pick up cocktail dresses and gowns for her to wear to various events. I made appearances all over the city, not just at the casino.

And Carmen thought they belonged to someone else…cute.

Now, she was humbled by the truth, taking her hatred down a notch because of her humiliation. She seemed to open up to me a little more, trust me a lot more than she had before. Her mouth said things she regretted, that she thought I was a beautiful man.

I couldn't stop smirking.

I kept my eyes out the window, thinking about the gorgeous woman who would be in my bed for the foreseeable future. She was complicated, deeply layered with so many different emotions that she was far from simple. That was why I found her fascinating—because she wasn't brainless. Any other woman would have jumped for joy if I were obsessed with her like I was with Carmen. They would picture the life of power and luxury I could provide for them. They would make my properties into their castles. They would be proud of themselves for bagging a king.

But Carmen was a queen of her own kingdom—a ruler who didn't need a king.

That made her the sexiest thing in the world—because she didn't need me for anything.

Her attitude was refreshing because it was real. She said contradictory things all the time, because she was so honest. She hated me at times, but then she wanted to fuck me harder than she ever had before. I could read her thoughts so easily, like I was sitting across from her at a poker match.

I was grateful I'd happened to be passing that alleyway at that very moment.

I hardly walked anywhere, so it almost seemed like fate.

Maybe it was fate.

I arrived at the casino, passed through the quiet floor since it was still too early for anyone to be there. The hardwood floors were sterile because the cleaning crew combed every single inch of the place to make sure a single chip hadn't landed somewhere it shouldn't have and everything was accounted for. The cages were empty of the strippers, and the music was off. All the lights were on, so the casino looked totally different from how it did in the evenings.

Ronan's back was to me as he spoke to a few guys on the security team. He was dressed down in jeans and a long-sleeve shirt since he wouldn't be there later that evening.

We hadn't spoken since he'd stormed out of my office, and I knew the silence could last much longer. I approached him from behind, then dismissed the guys with a subtle wave of my hand.

Ronan turned around, knowing I was there because I was the only person who could get rid of five men so quickly. He still wore that pissed-off expression, that serious scowl around his eyebrows. He slid his hands into his pockets and squared his shoulders, tensed for a fight rather than a conversation. He didn't say anything, waiting for me to state what I wanted first.

I didn't even know where to begin. I'd never been good at these heart-to-heart conversations. Ronan was more sensitive than I was, slightly jealous that Mom and I had had a stronger connection than they did. I was the one who started this casino, and I was the reason Mom got to stop working as a dishwasher and a bartender. There was silent tension between us, something we'd both ignored for the last five years. "Everything you said was right, Ronan. I've never been the same."

We were the only people on that side of the casino, so no one could overhear us. He stared at me with the same startling blue eyes I possessed, both gifts from our mother. His attitude toward me hadn't changed at all over the week.

"You never truly appreciate something until it's gone…" My mom worked hard most of her life to provide for us, and I don't mean forty hours a week like most people. She worked two jobs and also made a home for us. She developed severe back problems from hunching over a sink for so long, in addition to anxiety and other issues. My biggest regret was she didn't have more time to enjoy the luxurious life I gave her. She was in her early fifties when she passed away—way too young.

Ronan stared at me, clearly unsure what I meant by that.

"I've never gotten over her death, even though it's been five years. I'm still bitter about it. If she'd gone to the doctor sooner, maybe things would have been different. What happened to her wasn't fair, that all she ever did in her entire life was work."

Ronan's anger started to dim like an extinguishing

candle. I never spoke this way, so he knew I was being transparent with him.

"I built a wall between us to mask the pain. I've shut down everything so I don't have to think about it. This numbness has carried over to every other part of my life. I've felt dead inside every single day since her funeral."

He continued to listen.

"You're right, Ronan. I'm an asshole—but I shouldn't be an asshole to you." I held his gaze easily because we were the same height. It was like looking into a younger version of myself. He was two years younger than me, so we were practically the same age.

Ronan crossed his arms over his chest and tilted his gaze toward the floor. He sighed deeply, taking his time as he considered what to say in response. "Honestly, I wasn't expecting any of that. I figured you would just ignore what I said, and we would move on."

"How could I ignore that, Ronan?" Was I really that out of touch with reality? Was I really that cold?

He shrugged. "You ignore a lot of things, Bosco. You're alive, but you're barely living. You control every aspect of everything, and you're so coldhearted about your decisions because you don't actually feel anything."

Maybe he was right. "You want to go get a drink somewhere?" The second I asked the question, I realized I hadn't tried to spend time with him once in the last five years. We didn't even celebrate Christmas together. I just saw him at the casino…and that was it.

"Yeah." He looked me in the eye, his expression softening. "Let's do it."

MY MEN CLEARED OUT THE FEW PEOPLE HANGING IN THE bar so we could have the place to ourselves. I frequented a few establishments in the area, so the businesses always knew how to handle my appearance. I always paid a service charge for the inconvenience they were causing to other customers, and since it was such a handsome price, the owners didn't care.

We sat at the bar, keeping an empty stool between us. I ordered a scotch. He ordered a Jack and Coke.

The TVs were off, and the music in the background was dimmed to my preference. When I glanced at the time on my watch, I knew Carmen would be returning to the penthouse at any moment. I wondered if she would call me and ask where I was.

Sometimes, she showed her jealousy. Sometimes, she showed her concern. Sometimes, she showed her strong attraction. In every instance, it made me feel more like a man than any other woman had.

Ronan wiped his finger along the rim when he was drinking, his eyes watching his movements.

Now that we were together, we should talk. It seemed like we were starting from the beginning, getting to know each other for the first time. "How's Giada?"

"That's over," he said quickly. "She could throw her legs behind her neck, but the sex went stale pretty quick."

Sex with Carmen wasn't remotely close to being stale. It seemed like it'd just started. "Did she take it well?"

"No," he said with a sigh. "Most of them don't."

I drank from my glass. "When you tell them it's never

gonna go anywhere, it seems to make them want you more."

"Unfortunately. So, what about your woman?" He lifted his gaze and looked at me.

I had told him about the other women I'd screwed, but sharing the details of Carmen's perfect body seemed wrong. Confiding our intimate moments, like her dirty talk and the way she was so wet for me seemed like a huge invasion of privacy. I never considered myself to be a gentleman, but I wanted to be a gentleman for her. "I'm still seeing her."

"How long has it been?"

"A month."

"Wow." He raised his left eyebrow. "That's a really long time."

Not really. But for me, that was practically an eternity. "It's strange because it seems like it's only been a week."

The corner of his mouth rose in a smile. "Time flies when you're having fun."

It'd definitely been flying.

"So what is this?" he asked. "You said it was just a fling, but it doesn't seem like it."

I wanted to shut down the conversation because this wasn't a subject I was excited to share. But since I had a lot of making up to do, I had to start somewhere. Carmen wanted to draft that stupid contract to ensure her freedom, so Ronan would have to be aware of the relationship at that point anyway. "It's more than a fling. But not much more."

Ronan stared at me like he wanted me to elaborate. "She must be incredible to keep your attention this long."

"She is incredible." I blurted out the truth without missing a beat. "One hell of a woman. She tells me off one minute, then she's all over me the next. She's got a fiery attitude that makes her innately alluring. She doesn't put up with bullshit—not even from me."

Ronan raised an eyebrow as he looked at me.

"What?" I asked, unsure why he was surprised by my words.

"It's interesting…"

"What?"

"Not once did you describe her physical attributes. All you said was she was an amazing woman because of who she is…" His smile widened. "Definitely seems like more than a fling now."

I didn't even notice the way I described her until he pointed it out. "I respect her. I'm not ashamed to admit that. She's different from the other women I meet. Instead of being obsessed with my money and power, she's indifferent to it. She's independent and self-sufficient. She doesn't need a man for anything because she can provide everything herself. It's…sexy."

"That is sexy," Ronan said in agreement. "I haven't met a woman like that. Well, besides Mom."

Our mom had been the same way, hustling to give us a better life. She worked her ass off to make sure we had what we needed. She paid all the bills, got us through school, and she never needed a man for help.

I'd never noticed the similarities until now.

Maybe that was why I was drawn to Carmen so much —because she had my mother's spirit.

"But she hates you?" Ronan asked.

"She did. I don't think she does anymore. She was just using me for sex in the beginning. Now everything is more intense." I persuaded her to be mine for the next three months, but if she really wanted to be free, she would have fought harder. I knew it, and she knew it. "We've actually negotiated an agreement…"

"What kind of agreement?"

"She's mine for the next three months. After she does her time, I'll let her go."

"Let her go?" he asked, an eyebrow raised. "That sounds sinister."

"Well, you know me…"

"What does that mean? You're forcing her?"

"No, not at all." When I ignored her, she couldn't stand it. She called me in the middle of the night because she missed me. "She just doesn't want anything serious to happen because I'm not right for her. She wants to find a husband and have a family. So she wants to walk away when the three months are over."

"Sounds like she wants to make sure she doesn't fall in love with you."

He hit the nail right on the head. I saw the way she fell into me, but then abruptly pulled back because she got too close. She put up her walls, and sometimes they came down slowly. But when she realized they were missing, she quickly built new ones. She was stubborn in her decision that I wasn't the right man for her. She wouldn't change her mind, so she needed an escape plan. That's what the contract was really about. I lifted my glass and nodded to him. "Exactly."

I CAME HOME A COUPLE WEEKS LATER AROUND midnight, expecting Carmen to be asleep since she worked early in the morning. I wasn't down at the casino all the time, but now it felt like an eternity when there was a beautiful woman living in my penthouse.

The elevator doors opened, and I stepped inside, shedding my black coat and hanging it on the coatrack along the wall. My tie was already undone, and the buttons of my suit were unfastened. I smelled like strippers, cigars, and booze. My clothes were always dry-cleaned after I wore them so the smell wouldn't carry over into my home.

When I stepped farther inside, I noticed the glow of the TV hitting the couch. The sound was so quiet, it was practically on mute. Looking like the sexiest thing in the world was Carmen, wearing one of my gray t-shirts as she lay on the cushions. Her knees were bent toward her body, making her shirt rise up and reveal her perky ass and amazing thighs.

I watched her for a moment before I slowly walked toward her, making sure my shoes didn't tap too loudly against the hardwood floor.

She must have only partially been asleep, because her eyes opened and immediately darted to my face. Instead of being frightened by my frame leaning over her, she slowly sat up and pulled her hair out of her face.

I watched her with my hands in the pockets of my slacks, unsure why she was sleeping on the couch instead of in the enormous bed with sheets that cost more than an average car payment. I grabbed the remote and turned off the TV before I leaned down and scooped her up into my arms. I cradled her against my chest as I carried her into the bedroom.

Her arms circled my neck, and she leaned her cheek against my chest.

"Why were you sleeping on the couch?" My knees hit the bed, and I lowered her to the mattress, my body rolling with hers slightly until her back hit the sheets. My hands pressed into the bed on either side of her as I held myself over her.

My shirt was baggy around her frame, but it rose up over her stomach and revealed a small amount of her piercing. She had an hourglass figure, big tits with a curvy waist. Her long legs were even better, going all the way up to her chin. She could wear a plastic bag, and she still would be the sexiest thing in the world, the most beautiful woman to lie in this bed. Her eyes were red and puffy like she hadn't gotten any sleep despite how tired she was. "I was having a hard time sleeping."

"So you thought a couch would be better?" I asked, a hint of sarcasm in my voice.

"I thought watching TV would help."

"There's a TV in here."

She grew frustrated with my interrogation and turned on her side. "Let's have sex and go to bed." She turned on her side and pulled the sheets to her waist, clearly tired.

I let her be and shed my clothes, putting them in the special hamper so my maid would make sure they were properly dry-cleaned. My shoes were tossed in there as well, so they would be buffed and shined. After washing my face and brushing my teeth, I came back to bed.

She was out.

Her chest rose and fell deeply, the sound of her breathing slightly audible. Her entire body was relaxed like she'd been sleeping for the last few hours.

I lay beside her, naked because I assumed I would get some action before bed. I could still get it anyway if I wanted it, but seeing her sleep so soundly pulled at a heart I didn't have. I lay beside her and stared at her back, watching her hair stretch across her pillow and reach onto mine.

I moved closer to her and spooned her from behind, my chest pressing against the t-shirt across her back. My arm hooked around her waist, and I pressed my face into the back of her hair, breathing in her scent mixed with mine.

She shifted slightly underneath me, getting more comfortable even though she was fast asleep.

I closed my eyes, and before I knew it, I was asleep.

———

I WAS AWAKE BEFORE SHE WAS.

I usually woke up with the sun regardless of how late I went to bed. I'd never been a big sleeper, something that drove my mother crazy when I was growing up. I didn't consider myself to be an insomniac; I just didn't need sleep like everyone else.

I made breakfast then used my laptop to check on a few things. I was meticulous about my security, making sure all my accounts were properly managed and the security footage from the night before was clean. I hired men to take care of that, but I also micromanaged my world, making sure they didn't overlook anything. Whenever someone missed their membership dues, there was no grace period. If anyone didn't pay on time, their membership was permanently revoked—no exceptions. To this day, I'd never had a problem with someone not paying, so the system worked pretty well.

Her bare feet tapped against the floor as she came into the kitchen. I left half of my breakfast in the pan if she wanted to eat it, but when I heard the cupboard open and shut, along with the fridge, I knew she'd decided to have something else.

She joined me at the kitchen table, carrying a bowl of cereal. She looked tired because she didn't get a full night of sleep. Her hair was still a mess, and she wiped the sleep from her eyes.

I watched her, ignoring all the invoices on my laptop. Whether she was caked in full makeup or she wore nothing at all, she was still hypnotizing. Other women could never pull that off, but she did it flawlessly. I shut my laptop because I decided she was far more interesting than work.

She ate a bite of her cereal before she looked at me. "I'm not eating fish again."

The corner of my mouth rose in a smile. "Not everyone is crazy about seafood."

"No, I love seafood. Just not for breakfast—every day." She dug into her bowl and kept eating. "I need carbs. How do you work out and function without them? I'd be sluggish all day."

"You get used to it." It was all worth it when Carmen

pulled me deeper into her, coming around my dick while her nails sliced into my muscles. She loved my body, was as obsessed with it as I was with hers.

"I'll pass." She kept chewing, eating the processed cereal along with the milk.

I couldn't remember the last time I had cereal. It was probably when I was a child. "Did you still want to do that contract?" I was a man of my word, so I wasn't worried about upholding my end of the bargain. It didn't make a difference to me whether we did this or not. It was completely up to her.

She looked down at her cereal again. "Yes."

I wasn't sure if I should be happy or annoyed. "Alright. Ronan will do it."

"When?"

"I'll talk to him tonight. See if he's available."

"You have to work again?" she blurted, her head rising to meet my eyes.

I detected the disappointment in her voice. When a woman was needy, it was the most annoying thing in the world. But coming from her, it was the sexiest thing ever.

She quickly looked away, trying to hide her confession. "You don't normally work two nights in a row…that's the only reason why I'm asking."

"No, it's not." I called her out on her bullshit. "And I'm glad it's not."

She flicked her gaze up to meet mine, and just like she usually did, she adopted her brave look, her fire burning to the surface to combat my coldness. Anytime she was challenged, she rose to meet her enemy. She did the same now, hiding her embarrassment instantly.

"Yes, I'm working tonight. Come with me."

"To the casino?" she asked, like that was the craziest suggestion I'd ever made.

"Ronan can do the contract in my office, and I can show you around." I could have her on my arm, wearing a beautiful skintight dress so she would look like a trophy I'd earned. Wearing my diamonds and heels that cost ten thousand euros, she would look like the queen that she was.

And everyone would know I was her king.

"Uh…I'll pass."

I pushed the laptop away, my eyebrow rising. "I apologize for making you think you had a choice in the matter."

Her eyes flashed in anger. "I don't want to go, Bosco. I'm not meant for a world like that."

Carmen wasn't scared of anything, except for me and my underworld. "You underestimate my power. You can't grasp it because you can't understand it. There's nowhere you can go, including the casino, where you aren't safe. You're coming with me—and you'll enjoy it."

She held my gaze but didn't challenge me, understanding she would never win any of these battles.

"You gave me your complete cooperation for three months," I reminded her.

"You're confusing cooperation with obedience. They're completely different."

I stopped myself from smiling, always impressed by her quick intelligence. "Why don't you want to go?"

"Why?" she asked incredulously. "You said all the members are criminals, murderers, thieves, rapists… Do I need to continue? Why would I want to be in the same room with a bunch of men I despise?"

"Because there are a strict set of rules that comes with their memberships. No one is armed. There is no violence. The dancers are off-limits. I run a very tight ship, and if anyone steps out of line, they'll face the consequences. But no one steps out of line, so there's nothing to worry about."

She still wasn't convinced, judging from her hesitation.

"Beautiful."

She sighed the second she heard the nickname.

"You have nothing to be afraid of. I promise."

"Do you bring other women there?"

I wanted to pretend I didn't so we wouldn't have to talk about it, but my commitment to honesty forced me to tell the truth. "Often."

"And they were fine with it?" she asked, not a hint of jealousy in her voice.

"Most of the women I bed *want* to go to the casino. They want the whole experience, my money and my power. The underworld excites them. My authority excites them. They know they're untouchable under my arm."

Her shoulders lost their tension when she heard that reassurance. "After being in that alleyway with those four men, I guess I'm a little paranoid…" It was the first time she'd admitted that night shook her up. She'd brushed it off like it was nothing, keeping up a brave front. I knew it bothered her, and now she was being honest about it. "I just don't want to be in that position again." When she looked at me, there was a hint of sadness in her eyes, like the memory still disturbed her.

I never wanted her to feel like that again. I would never let anything happen to her—ever. Even if she wasn't mine, I would cover her in my invincibility. "Let's not forget who chased those men away—with just a few simple words."

She set her spoon down and kept looking at me.

"As long as you're with me, you never have to worry about a thing. I don't know how many times I can say it, how many times I can prove it." I was the most powerful man in this city, and that was something I didn't need to say once—especially not more than once. She was a descendant of a powerful family that had a respectable reputation. The Barsetti brothers were formidable opponents, but frankly, they were nothing compared to what I had. Maybe if they'd stayed in the business, things would be different, but now they were two simple men with simple lives.

Carmen didn't press her argument because she didn't have one. "Alright."

"We'll leave when you get off work." I carried my dishes to the sink then walked into the bedroom and to get ready for my workout. I pulled on a pair of running shorts and a white t-shirt. I wore different shoes for running and for lifting, so I started with the running shoes first.

Carmen walked in a moment later, her long legs peeking out from under my t-shirt. She watched me sit at the foot of the bed and tie my laces.

I sat up straight and met her look, unsure what she wanted to say next. There was nothing she could do to change my mind about my decision. She was my property now, and I could do whatever I wanted.

She walked toward me and stopped when she stood between my knees. Then she lowered herself to the floor and pulled my shirt over her head. Plump tits were revealed, along with perfect nipples. She had a large bust in comparison to her small rib cage. She was petite everywhere else, except for her perfect rack and beautiful ass.

She grabbed my shorts and boxers and pulled them down, revealing my throbbing cock. I was hard for her at any time, so whenever she was ready, so was I. She ran her hand through her hair and pulled it from her face. Her tongue swiped across her lips before she lowered her mouth to my head. She opened her mouth wide and took me in deeply, pushing me to the back of her throat.

I closed my eyes and moaned, my hand digging under the fall of her hair. I could feel her pulse in her neck, feel the muscles of her throat work to take me as far as she could. Now I didn't care about my workout. I didn't care that she needed to get to work. All I cared about was that pretty mouth tight around my dick.

I hadn't asked her to do this. She fell to her knees on her own, pleasing me just because she wanted to. It was like the first night we were together, when she blew my mind with her confidence. She gave as much as she received, was amazing in bed—the best I'd ever had.

Her hair was all over my thighs as she moved, her tits dragging against my legs as she moved up and down. Her nails dug into me, and I loved the way she cut me without caring if I bled or not.

When I was soaking wet, she pulled her mouth away and scooted closer to me, cupped her tits in her hands, and pressed her cleavage line around my cock.

I moaned again, loving her slippery flesh against my dick. She had the perfect rack for a tit-fuck, and I'd been enjoying her mouth so much I hadn't even considered that. My hands replaced hers, and I guided her body up and down my length, enjoying the way we slid together so smoothly.

She looked me in the eye, her lips parted as she breathed deeply with me. Her hands gripped my thighs, and she raised and lowered her body, sliding up and down my length from the head to the base.

I could have stared at the way my dick slid through her cleavage, but I was more entranced by her beautiful face. She had tits built for a man's hands, so I held on to them tightly as I slid through the warmth of her tits. "I love your tits, Beautiful."

"I love your cock, Bosco."

A quiet moan came from the back of my throat. I pulled her closer to me then kissed her, my lips moving against her soft ones slowly. My feet pressed against the floor, and my hips bucked up and down, sliding through her saliva-soaked tits.

Her kiss was as good as her tits and pussy. Kissing had never been erotic for me, just a quick form of foreplay. But I loved kissing this woman, feeling our tongues swirl together. I loved sucking her bottom lip into mine and feeling her breath fade away. I loved swallowing her moans, loved devouring her in so many ways. "I'm gonna come, Beautiful." No other woman tested my endurance the way she did. I could control my load during sex because I'd had so much practice, but this spontaneous move caught me off guard. Her tits made my knees weak, and watching this woman both hate me and want to please me turned me on.

"Come on my tits." She spoke into my mouth as she kissed me, her hands gripping my muscular thighs.

"Fuck." When I sucked her bottom lip into my mouth, I lost my reserve. I squeezed her tits tighter and came, exploding onto her chest and underneath her chin. I kept kissing her as I moaned, enjoying an orgasm so good it was even better than coming inside her. My cock kept pumping until every single drop was released. I exploded all over her, coating her tits with my come.

She pulled away and looked down at herself, her body decorated with my seed. There was a noticeable line from her chin all the way down to her cleavage. Startlingly white and thick, it was one of the biggest loads I'd ever unleashed. She dragged her fingers down the stream and smeared it across her fingertips.

Then she brought it to her lips and sucked it away.

Jesus Christ.

Instead of enjoying my slow descent from my high, I grabbed her hips and threw her on the bed. I dragged her to the edge so her ass hung over the end of the mattress. Her panties were gone, and her thighs were wide apart.

It was my turn to be on my knees. It was my honor to please her.

And I did.

3

CARMEN

WHEN I STEPPED out of the elevator, Bosco was sitting on the couch in his black suit, his knees spread and his shiny watch catching the light from the TV. He leaned against the back cushion as he looked at his phone, typing a message with his thumbs. His chin was cleanly shaven, and the cords on the backs of his hands tensed and shifted with his movements. When his eyes lifted to meet mine, it seemed like time had stopped.

Deep blue and brilliant, his eyes were so cold they were actually hot. He looked exactly the same as he had this morning, aroused and possessive. As if the last eight hours hadn't passed, he seemed to pick up exactly where we left off. "I'm ready when you are."

I stood in the center of the living room, forgetting to move because his stare was strong enough to keep me in place. I wasn't sure what I expected from him, and the longer I stood there, the more obvious I made it that I wanted something from him.

Like a kiss.

My legs finally moved, and I walked into the bedroom. A black and gold dress had been placed on the bed, along with the heels he wanted me to wear. A necklace of real diamonds was beside it, along with earrings that were worth more than a new car.

Everything was beautiful, far more beautiful than anything I'd ever worn in my life. I would walk into the casino wearing hundreds of thousands of dollars. I stripped off my casual outfit of jeans and a sweater and pulled on the short dress. It reached slightly past my thighs, clinging to the deep curves of my waist, and stretching across my bust. It had a deep cut in the front, showing a cleavage line Bosco would stare at often. The earrings and necklace came next, followed by the heels.

When I looked in the mirror in the bathroom, I fixed my hair and refreshed my makeup, knowing Bosco would want me to look my absolute best. I walked back into the living room, my heels tapping against the hardwood floor as I made my entrance to Bosco.

He was on his phone again, and this time, he slipped it into his pocket before he looked at me. His gaze didn't change at first. He still wore that indecipherable poker face, making him impossible to read. But once his eyes settled on me, they immediately changed. He took in my appearance with approval along with surprise. His eyes scanned my body, starting from my long legs in my heels, over my hips, and to my face and hair. He examined the jewelry I wore, the outline of my chest in the material, and then the lipstick color on my lips.

He rose to his feet and slowly approached me. His

hands unbuttoned his jacket before he went to the belt around his waist. He undid it then unfastened his slacks. His pants slid down his legs and fell to the floor, his enormous cock on display. "Bend over."

"You must like it, then." I moved into his chest and pushed his jacket over his shoulders so it fell to the floor. I moved to his mouth to kiss him.

He refused to give me his mouth. With a searing look in his eyes, he looked so turned on it seemed like he was furious. His hand wrapped around my neck, and he squeezed me harder than he usually did. "Bend. Over."

WE SAT IN THE BACK SEAT OF HIS PRIVATE CAR, watching the city lights pass through the window. My legs were crossed, and I could feel the weight of his come sitting inside me. Some of it had seeped into my thong, and I could feel it against my pussy lips every time I moved. The second he finished, he ordered for us to leave —and refused to let me clean up.

Aggressive, possessive, and territorial, he turned into a testosterone-driven man who exuded more masculinity than I'd ever seen. Like he turned into a wild animal that only understood carnal instincts. Or a caveman who only understood a few simple ideas like sex, food, and violence.

He looked out the window and didn't touch me. His hand didn't rest on mine like it usually would. His mind seemed to be elsewhere, probably thinking about all the aspects of his casino.

I was still nervous because I had no idea what I was

getting myself into it. When Bosco told me I would always be safe at his side, I believed him. Even if someone wanted to take him out, they had very slim odds of success. But that didn't defeat my anxiety. I brushed off my incident in the alleyway on the outside, but on the inside, it terrified me. The barrel of the gun had been pointed right between my eyes while the rope was bound around my wrists. It didn't matter how hard I fought, there had been no escape. I'd always considered myself to be strong and quick, but when faced with four men, my skills were useless. It was the most humbling experience of my life— because I realized how weak I truly was. If Bosco hadn't been there, I would have been trafficked until my family figured out how to rescue me.

My hand moved to his, and I held it, not for him, but for myself. Bosco was the only man who could have walked into that alleyway unarmed and made a demand. He was my superhero, and even though he wasn't a good man, he was good to me.

He turned my way slightly, his dark gaze settling on me.

Something about his touch comforted me, reminding me of the power in his veins that circulated with his blood. I never wanted to be dependent on a man for anything, but I found myself thriving in his shadow, getting high off the invincibility he gave me. I didn't realize how attracted I was to power until now.

"Beautiful?" His voice escaped as a masculine whisper, his tone washing over me like the incoming tide from the ocean. He must have detected the emotion in my heart because he kept looking at me, pressing for an answer to a question he never asked.

"It's nothing…" I pulled my hand away and looked out the window.

He reached for it again and held my hand on my thigh. His thumb gently brushed over my knuckles as he turned his gaze out the window.

After another ten minutes, we pulled up to a tall building with no lights. From the outside, it looked abandoned. There were no cars anywhere. The buildings surrounding the area looked abandoned too. It seemed like the bad side of town, except there were no homeless people or thugs walking the sidewalk.

A large door on the side of the building opened suddenly, and the car drove inside until we were in an underground garage. We pulled through another door until we came to a private sector where there were no other cars. The car stopped in front of an elevator guarded by a dozen armed men.

Now my heart was racing.

Bosco seemed calm as usual.

One of the men carrying a rifle opened my door while the driver opened Bosco's door.

I didn't move for a second, uncomfortable by the enormous gun the man held in his hands. When he backed up, I stuck one leg out then pulled myself up. Bosco reached me and took my hand. He gave a slight nod to his men as he walked to the elevator.

The doors opened for him without pressing a button, and he pulled me inside. The elevator car was lined with red. The tile was red, and the walls were the same color. The buttons on the wall seemed to be made from solid gold. The elevator shifted before it began to rise.

Like we were attending a fancy party, he grabbed my arm and hooked it through his. His free hand moved into his pocket.

I gripped the inside of his arm, my other hand resting on his forearm. I was nervous in a way I'd never been before. Before I met Bosco, I was calm and free-spirited. I never worried about anything because there was nothing I couldn't handle. Now the adrenaline had spiked, and it seemed like I was in perpetual danger.

The second the doors opened, we were greeted by loud music, cigar smoke, booze, and flashing lights from the girls dancing from the ceiling. The sound of constantly moving chips filled the background. The floor was covered with red carpet, and poker tables were spread out everywhere.

Bosco stepped inside, moving like he owned the place, which I guess he did. There was security everywhere, men dressed in all black who looked at Bosco as he passed. They kept their positions along the wall, following both of us with their eyes.

Every seat was taken by a man of the underworld. Topless women carried trays of drinks around, and some of the men looked up to stare at their racks, but most of them were too involved in the game to care.

As Bosco took me deeper into the casino, the music became louder. Men looked up to see him pass, and sometimes they looked at me too.

Bosco seemed indifferent to everyone in the room.

We reached a table positioned slightly farther away from the others. The lights were lower there, and there were two vacant seats at the table. A dealer was there along with two other men.

A man appeared out of nowhere and pulled out the chair. "Will you be joining, sir?"

"Yes." Bosco took a card out of his pocket. "Two hundred."

Two hundred what?

Bosco pulled out the chair beside his and took my hand to help me sit.

I lowered myself into the chair, doing my best to appear calm the way Bosco did. There was a lot going on, from the topless waitresses to the naked woman dancing in the cage just a few feet away.

The men at the table didn't look at me, didn't acknowledge my existence at all. They had women at their sides. One guy had two, actually. The women smothered the men with affection, like they were constantly working for their attention.

Bosco sat beside me, and the chips were placed in front of him. An ashtray was placed beside him along with a lit cigar. Two men catered to his every need, positioning a glass of scotch next to the cigar.

Bosco turned to me. "What would you like to drink, Beautiful?"

I was a little stunned by all the attention he was getting, having a group of men wait on him like he was some kind of emperor. "I'll have the same."

"Scotch on the rocks," he ordered.

The men left to fetch the drink.

Bosco turned toward me and pressed his lips to my ear. "Never order from the waitress. Only order from my men." He pulled away and nodded to the dealer, who started to deal the cards for the game.

I didn't get a chance to ask why.

The men brought my drink a moment later. "Cigar, miss?"

"Uh, no thanks," I said quickly. "I don't smoke."

The round started, and the men exchanged their cards and examined their hands. Bosco took a drag from the cigar then let it sit in his mouth as he examined his hand.

I didn't look at his cards, afraid I would give him away by accident.

More chips were piled into the center as the men raised their hands.

Bosco had never looked calmer, like this high-stakes game was how he spent his time relaxing.

The women kept pressing up against their men, practically sitting on their laps.

I sat in my chair and remained still, watching the game and feeling the tension rise.

Bosco let the smoke out of his mouth and nose before he set the cigar back in the ashtray.

I'd had no idea he smoked since I never smelled it on his breath. That was probably why he brushed his teeth every night before bed, to get the taste off his tongue. I wasn't a fan of smoking, but I didn't mention my opinion during a time like this.

When it was one of the other men's turns to raise or fold, Bosco directed his gaze on me. He gave a subtle tap to his thigh, commanding me to get closer to him.

I knew what he wanted, for me to smother him the way the other women did their men.

I wasn't sure if that would distract him, but obviously, nothing was going to distract a man like him. I moved into his side and hooked my arm around his elbow. I pressed into him, feeling his muscular side against my body. My chin rested on his shoulder, and I ignored the smell of the smoke that filled the room. Most of the men were smoking, not just Bosco.

The man folded, leaving three men in the round.

Once Bosco had my affection, he kept playing. Another man folded, leaving Bosco and one other man. The chips were piled even higher in the center, and then the cards were laid down.

The man had four queens.

Bosco had a royal flush.

"Bosco wins the hand." The dealer pushed the chips toward him. "Congratulations, sir."

Bosco snapped his fingers, and one of his men organized the chips into a special case.

The other men were visibly irritated and their women rubbed their shoulders, but they didn't leave the table.

"Another round, sir?" the dealer asked.

Bosco nodded. "Another."

When Bosco was finished, we left the table, my arm hooked through his like he preferred.

"How much did you win?" I asked, unsure where he was guiding me. We passed more tables that were filled with terrifying-looking men. Some were dressed nicely the way Bosco was, but others had tattoos on their necks and faces. But they weren't handsome the way Griffin was. They reeked of hostility.

"Five."

"Five dollars?" I asked blankly.

He smirked as he stared ahead. "Five million."

Oh shit. I just witnessed a high-stakes game without even realizing it.

Bosco kept walking, reaching a back set of elevators that were guarded by more security. They all had serious artillery, enough to handle any kind of attack. There was a man standing there dressed in a navy blue suit with a gray tie. He had the same dark hair as Bosco and the same gorgeous eyes. With a similar facial structure and build, he looked so much like Bosco, there was no doubt who he was.

Ronan Roth.

Ronan gave his brother a slight grin when he approached, a silent conversation passing between them. He hit the button on the elevator then shifted his gaze to me. "It's lovely to meet you." He extended his hand to shake mine. "I'm Ronan, Bosco's brother."

I shook his hand. "I know. You guys look so much alike."

Ronan grinned. "But I'm more handsome, right?" He winked then turned to the elevator.

Now I knew they had similar personalities too.

Bosco wrapped his arm around my waist and escorted me into the elevator. "Carmen has high standards, so I wouldn't bother, Ronan."

We gathered in the elevator, and the doors shut.

Ronan stood with his hands in his pockets and leaned against the opposite wall. The elevator shifted and started to move down. "They can't be that high. I mean, come on." He nodded toward his brother.

Bosco stared him down with a cold expression.

Ronan smiled, like he enjoyed teasing his brother. "Seems like I hit a button."

"That's the difference between you and me," Bosco said, his voice cold. "I don't have buttons."

Ronan dropped his grin, and the teasing stopped.

We moved farther down until we finally came to a stop. The trip was long, so it seemed like we went underground. "Where are we?"

"The office is below ground," Bosco said. "Has a specific satellite feed for the servers."

I had no idea what that meant.

The doors opened and revealed a short hallway before stone steps.

Bosco held me against him. "Shoes off."

I slipped them off, knowing I didn't want to walk down those steps in the sky-high heels, even with his strong arm around my waist.

Bosco went first, holding my hand and making sure I got down the narrow passageway in one piece. He took me through the doorway into a sleek office. The desk and furniture were black, and the couches were leather.

There was a laptop on his desk, along with a private bar.

"How did you get all this furniture in here?" I asked.

"It was built in here." Bosco poured three glasses of scotch and set them on the table. He opened a drawer and pulled out a stack of paper before he tossed it onto the table. "Here's the contract." He pulled a pen out of his pocket and set it on top. "Let's do this." He sat on the leather couch and stared at me, waiting for me to join him.

I took the seat beside him and crossed my legs.

Bosco didn't touch me, turning serious like this was a business meeting.

Ronan sat across from us, grabbed the contract, and then crossed his legs. Like his brother, he wore a flashy watch on his wrist. He had corded veins like Bosco, the same chiseled jawline too. They were both equally beautiful, but Bosco was a little more unfriendly on his exterior. Ronan flipped through the pages. "It basically says you're required to live with him for the next three months. Well…the next two and a half months since two weeks have already passed. He has full authority in your ownership, making all decisions. When the time period comes to an end, all rights are restored to you, and Bosco must respect every decision you make." He closed the contract and placed it in front of me. "A little excessive, but not surprising."

I could tell his brother was a lot different, far more playful and less intense. "I'm not a fan of the ownership part."

"It's what we agreed on," Bosco said coldly. "If you want me to fulfill my end of the bargain, you fulfill yours."

I turned my stare on him. "You already have me, Bosco. You don't need to rule me with an iron fist."

Ronan grinned. "Well said, sweetheart."

"Don't call her that." Bosco's threat shattered the calm in the world. He directed his angry gaze on his brother. "You address her as Carmen and nothing else."

Ronan turned to me and grinned. "In case you haven't noticed, he likes you a lot."

Bosco gave him a deeper look of hostility. "Ronan."

He raised his hands in the air in the form of surrender. "Just stating the obvious, Boss."

"Boss?" I asked.

"It's short for Bosco," Ronan explained. "I'm not referring to him as a boss. Nor will I ever."

There was obviously an element of competitiveness between them. I could feel it in the room, the way their levels of testosterone continued to rise. I grabbed the contract and flipped through it. "I agree. It is excessive."

Ronan grinned. "I like her."

Bosco ignored him.

"You can't tell me where to go." I grabbed the pen and scratched that line out. "I can do whatever I want. I'm not running home for curfew like a child. I have a life."

Ronan nodded in approval. "It's nice seeing someone stand up to him."

"I'm not standing up to him. Just making my demands." I set the contract down and signed the bottom. "My brother is getting married next weekend, so I'll be gone during that time."

Bosco's head snapped in my direction. "What did you say?" Venom was heavy in his voice, like I'd just threatened him.

"My brother is getting married next weekend." I held his gaze without backing down.

"Where?" he asked, clearly annoyed I hadn't mentioned this before.

"My brother's house. He lives in Tuscany, a few miles from my parents," I answered.

Ronan's eyebrows rose off his face, and he could barely contain his smile, knowing his brother was going to go ballistic.

Bosco didn't contain his rage, not even in front of his brother. "And why would you need to stay there?"

"Because we'll celebrate the night before, the night of, and then have breakfast together the next morning. That's what we've done for every other wedding in the family. It's a whole weekend thing." That shouldn't be surprising, considering we were an Italian family who loved any excuse to drink and celebrate.

"No." Bosco was too angry to say anything else. "You can come back and sleep with me every night. You can drive there in the morning."

I didn't mind sleeping with him, but I didn't like being told what to do. At all. "Asshole, my brother is getting married, and I'm spending time with my family. I don't give a damn if you don't like it. Get over yourself." I rolled my eyes then gave him the cold shoulder.

"Damn…" Ronan was enjoying every second of this. "That was hot."

I wasn't putting on a production for his brother's sake.

I was standing up for myself because I refused to let Bosco take this away from me. "I'm really close to my family, and I'm looking forward to this. It's nonnegotiable."

Bosco rested his fingertips against his lips, considering my words with a hard gaze. "Then we add three days to the contract. That's the best compromise you're getting from me."

Ronan shifted his eyes back and forth as he listened to us.

That seemed fair. "Fine."

Ronan made the note on the contract. "He's treating your time like money…every little thing counts."

"Shut up, Ronan," Bosco ordered. "You're here to witness this, not give your two cents."

"Fine," Ronan said. "I'll just give you my two cents when she's not around."

Bosco didn't argue with that. "Anything else you want to tell me?" He turned his eyes back to me.

"No." I didn't have any other plans during our relationship.

Bosco grabbed the pen then added his signature. "Then we're finished here."

"You want a copy?" Ronan asked me.

"No." I didn't want to remember the moment I signed my soul over to the devil.

Ronan carried it to Bosco's desk and put it in a drawer. "I'll make sure my brother keeps his word. He's a stickler for rules, so there shouldn't be an issue. But if there is, I'll be on your side." He stood in front of the desk with his hands in his pockets. He looked at his brother. "I'll leave you two alone." He turned to the doorway to walk out.

Something must have been going through Bosco's mind because he stood up and followed his brother to the doorway. "Ronan."

Ronan turned around and gave his brother a serious look.

Bosco sighed, like he was restraining himself from some source of anger. "I'm sorry for barking at you. Not sure what came over me."

I raised an eyebrow, shocked Bosco actually apologized for something.

Ronan grinned then tapped him on the shoulder. "I know you're working on it. And I know you can't see straight when it comes to this woman, so I'll cut you some slack. Besides, I was giving you shit." He winked then walked out.

I turned my head to the desk, and that's when I noticed the picture that was sitting there. It was a picture of Bosco and Ronan along with an older woman. Judging by the color of her hair and eyes, it must be their mother. With a beautiful smile and tears in her eyes, she looked happy surrounded by her two adult sons.

I immediately forgave Bosco for being an asshole because the picture made my heart soften. He had a heart underneath all that aggression. It was there, even if no one could see it. Then he'd apologized to his brother in front of me, which was another curveball.

Ronan left then Bosco moved to the couch across from me where his brother had been sitting. He massaged his knuckles like he'd just punched someone. He stared at his hands as he hunched forward, his jaw clenched.

"Is that your mother?"

He didn't look at the picture. "Yes."

"She was beautiful."

"I know." A hint of pride was in his voice, buried deep under his anger. "That was taken a year before she died."

I stared at the picture again before I turned back to him, watching him stare at his hands. "What happened that day? A birthday? A holiday?" I couldn't tell what time of year it was because it was a close-up, but she seemed emotional in the picture.

"Ronan and I bought her a new car for Christmas. She used to drive this beat-up piece of shit, so we got her her dream car. A brand-new Mercedes." He finally lifted his gaze and looked at the picture, the emotion absent from his eyes. "I don't think she cared that much about the car, just the fact that we got it for her."

"It's the thought that matters, not the gift."

He nodded. "I still have it. It's in the garage. Didn't have the heart to sell it."

He seemed so cold most of the time that I forgot he had a huge heart. He rarely showed it. If I hadn't known about his mother, I might never have realized it. "I'm sorry she's not here anymore. I can tell you miss her."

"Every day." There was a hint of shame in his voice. "She could have abandoned us too, just the way our father did. She never did. Life was hard, but that didn't stop her from being happy. Even though money was always a problem, I never felt unloved. She was a remarkable woman, and the world is worse off without her."

Listening to him brought tears to my eyes. I couldn't imagine my life without my parents. They were the greatest parents in the world. There was never a time when I didn't feel loved. "You love your brother too."

He nodded. "We've had our problems."

Since he was opening up to me, I pushed the envelope a little further. "What happened?"

He grabbed the glass of scotch in front of him and took a long drink, stalling as he considered what his answer would be. He licked his lips quickly, in a sexy way only he could pull off. With his elbows resting on his knees and his weight shifted forward, he looked at me. "Ronan didn't do anything. I'm the one who fucked everything up." He brought his hands together, both of his palms flat as he lined up his fingers. "When Mom died, I just shut down. Her death gnawed at me because there was so much regret. She told me she'd been feeling pain for a few months, but she brushed it off as nothing and never went to the doctor. Only when it got really bad did she see someone. By then, the cancer had spread, and there was nothing that could be done." He shook his head. "I always wonder what if… What if she'd been seen sooner?"

My heart ached as I listened to this, listen to this strong man show his weakness.

"She and I were really close, so losing her just made me shut down. I turned cold to everyone—including my brother. We stopped spending time together, and I just… cut him out. The only time I saw him was at work, and I kept pulling away. He called me out on it a few weeks ago. I thought about it for a while and realized he was right. I've been so angry at the world because of what happened… But I need to get over it. It's been five years. I shouldn't be this bitter and this angry. My mother would be disappointed in me for letting it affect my relationship with Ronan. So I've been working on it, trying to talk to him, be less of an asshole…"

I watched him from my spot on the leather couch, my scotch untouched because all I cared about was him. We were hundreds of feet underground, so we were completely alone. No one could bother us down here. No one could hear his secrets.

"I've come to realize that it's nearly impossible for me not to be an asshole."

"That's not true." The words flew out of my mouth automatically.

He lifted his gaze to look at me. "It is."

"You're an asshole sometimes, yes. But not all the time. You can be a good man when you want to be. I've seen it with my own eyes. Don't be so hard on yourself."

He held my gaze, his look still cold. "I just made you sign a contract, claiming my ownership."

"You didn't make me do anything, Bosco. I'm not a woman you can make do anything." If I really wanted out of this, I could walk away. Bosco was a formidable man, but he wasn't evil. Even though I'd signed the contract, I could still get out of it. But at least now he knew I wanted this relationship to end for good in two and a half months. This was a fling with an expiration date, and I wouldn't change my mind.

The corner of his mouth rose in a smile. "I'm a hard man who makes hard decisions every day. I never lose any sleep at night because of it. But I've been too hard on Ronan. I've treated him like one of the other men…like he doesn't matter."

"We all lose our way sometimes."

He nodded. "I'm still lost. Now I'm trying to find my way back." He was a transparent man, so secure in his masculinity that he didn't care what he shared with me. His vulnerability didn't take anything away from his strength. He would still walk through that casino with the power of a king, even if he wore his heart on his sleeve. He was a fascinating man, far more complex than I realized.

"Ronan loves you. I can tell just by watching the two of you together."

"Yes…I'm very fortunate."

"And he knows you love him too…because you just showed it."

Bosco leaned back against the chair, his knees spread apart and his shoulders broad. With his elbow propped on the armrest, he rested his fingers over his lips, watching me closely. It seemed like his sensitive side had faded away, and now he was aggressive once more. "You'll be on your family's property for the wedding?"

"Yes. The wedding is at Carter's, but I'll be staying with my parents."

"I won't be able to have my men follow you there."

I stopped myself from rolling my eyes. "Which is perfectly fine. There's no safer place in the world than with my family."

"Correction," he said. "The safest place in the world is by my side."

I didn't deny that because it was probably true. "So, where are we, exactly?"

"Two hundred feet below ground."

"That's a little scary...what if the elevator shuts down?"

He shrugged. "I'll let you know when that happens."

"Why do you have it this way?"

"All my files and data are securely stored. If someone gets on that elevator other than Ronan and me, it's supposed to crash down to the bottom."

That was a gruesome death. "I'm sure you've thought this through, but if someone really wanted to kill you, couldn't they just wait until you went down here and then cut the wires in the elevator so you could never get out?"

He kept the same expression, so the suggestion must not have been surprising to him. "No one knows what's at the bottom of the elevator—except Ronan. No one knows how deep it goes. My men only know what they need to know to do their jobs."

"How do you keep them so loyal?" They behaved like dogs eager for a treat.

"They're paid very handsomely. And it's a relatively safe job, so they know they'll go home to their families at the end of the day."

"Safe?" I asked in surprise.

"I've been in charge for a decade now. There've been no issues. And everyone wants to play for the winning team, especially when I have fifty men working for me at any given time of the day. That's a lot of support. If there were only a dozen, that would change the game."

"So you basically have a whole army?"

He nodded. "Yes. That's a good way to put it."

I'd never asked him how old he was. He seemed to be

my brother's age, but judging by how grizzled he was, he might be a little older. "How old are you?"

"Seven years older than you."

"So you know how old I am?"

"I know everything about you," he said with a smirk. "Everything that's public record, at least."

"You're thirty-two, then."

"Yes. I'm probably old in your eyes."

"No." I liked older men. I always assumed I would settle down with a man around his age. My father always encouraged it, said a man needed to live more life than a woman to understand what he wanted. A man also needed to be older before he had children, because they never seemed to be ready for fatherhood. "How old is your brother?"

"Thirty."

"You guys look so much alike."

"I hope you don't really find him more handsome." He gave me a lopsided grin, telling me he was joking.

"No." I smiled back. "You're the most handsome man I've ever seen." Once the humiliation hit me like a train, my smile disappeared and I regretted my choice of words. Dumb compliments like that were constantly rolling out of my mouth lately, and I felt stupid every single time. It was obvious he was obsessed with me, but it was becoming more obvious that I was obsessed with him.

His grin disappeared, and he gave me a serious expression, without a hint of gloating. He didn't smirk in arrogance like he usually did. He took my comment seriously but not with victory. It was difficult to tell if it meant something to him or meant nothing at all. He leaned back against the couch then tapped his thigh, quietly commanding me to move to his lap.

Normally, I would have denied an invitation like that, but he looked so handsome in that moment, his hard jawline chiseled from stone and his shoulders broad. He had muscular thighs that were comfortable to sit on, and his enormous dick was outlined in the front of his slacks, making a bulge so defined, it left very little to the imagination.

I left the comfort of the leather couch and moved to his lap, straddling his narrow hips and letting my center rest against the base of his thick shaft. I leaned forward against his chest, feeling like I was propped against a concrete building. My dress popped up over my ass because it was too short to cover my rear at an angle like this.

He pulled me closer to him until our foreheads were pressed together. He didn't kiss me, just sat there with me. His fingertips brushed against the soft skin of my cheek and neck, feeling my strands of curled tresses. Sometimes his eyes flicked down to my lips, staring at the red shade I had painted across my mouth. A hint of cigar smoke was on his breath, but I actually liked the smell, probably because it mixed with his cologne and soap. I could still feel how hard he was underneath me, but he didn't pull down my panties to take me in his office.

He grabbed both of my hips and squeezed them. "I'm madly, deeply, blindly obsessed with you. When our time together ends, it's gonna be hard for me to let you go. I will because I made you a promise. But trust me, it's gonna be the hardest thing I've ever had to do."

When I woke up the next morning, my back was against the couch, and Bosco was pressed against my chest. I'd been wrapped in his suit jacket and his collared shirt so I would stay warm through the night. My dress was somewhere on the floor, and my heels were nowhere to be seen. Bosco was completely naked, unaffected by the cold. His arm was wrapped around my body, and he'd offered his shoulder as a pillow for me to use.

My eyes opened slowly, expecting to see spots of sunshine enter through the windows. The lighting was exactly the same because we were deep underground. Only the lights on the ceiling cast any illumination. There was no way to figure out what time it was.

I hoped I could still make it to work on time.

Bosco stirred when I did. He was usually up at least thirty minutes before I was, without the need for an alarm. I hoped that meant he was awake at his usual hour, and we both hadn't slept in.

He peeled away my clothing and kissed my shoulder before he kissed me on the mouth. "Morning, Beautiful."

I grabbed his right wrist and looked at the time, grateful it was only six in the morning. "We didn't oversleep, thankfully."

"I don't know how to oversleep." He pulled more of the clothing away so he could kiss the area between my tits and trail his mouth down my sternum. He moved his lips over my rib cage, kissing me until he reached my belly button. "And why would I want to sleep when I have you beside me?" He positioned my back against the couch before he hiked my leg over his shoulder. He folded my body underneath him so he could thrust his cock inside me. I was still full from the come he'd dumped inside me the night before, so he must be sliding through it at that very moment.

Morning sex was the best because everything felt so good right when I woke up. It was so much easier to get off, especially when he pounded into me right away. At night, I liked to make it last a long time, but first thing in the morning, we both had things to do so it was usually quick.

But amazing.

He fucked me good and hard, driving me into an orgasm instantly. I clawed at his back as my pussy clenched him tightly, moaning into his neck even though I could be as loud as I wanted down here.

He came the second I was finished, like he could have released any moment once he was inside me. He filled my pussy with a groan, adding more to the pile he'd made the night before. "Perfect pussy." He stayed inside me until his cock softened before he slowly pulled out, dripping come in between my inner thighs.

He pulled on his boxers, slacks, and socks before he got his shoes on and tied the laces.

"What do you think is going on up there?"

"The casino will be closed. A new security team will be waiting by the elevators."

"I'm surprised they didn't check on you."

"They know to come only when I call."

I stripped off his clothes and put mine back on. "But what if I tried to kill you?"

He scoffed, like that was impossible. "I'd like to see you try. It would probably make me want you more." He buttoned up his shirt then pulled his tie through the collar.

I slipped on my heels then walked into the bathroom to see my makeup in the mirror. I looked like a nightmare. My mascara was smeared to the point it looked like those black marks American football players wiped under their eyes. My lipstick was all over the place too, reaching past my mouth and up my cheek. "I look terrible." I quickly washed my face in the sink, preferring no makeup to this clownish look. I walked back into the room.

Bosco got off the phone and shoved it into his pocket. "You're the kind of woman that looks beautiful with or without makeup. So even when it's not perfect, you still are." He gave me that handsome smile, just a hint of a true grin. He put himself back together like he hadn't spent the night sleeping on a couch. The only indication he'd been fucking me all night was his messed-up hair. When he was on top of me, I liked to fist it pretty hard, feel those short strands between my fingertips.

"You always know the right thing to say."

"Yes." He grabbed my hips and gave me a soft kiss on the mouth. "The truth."

Vanessa came into the shop around lunchtime, her belly a little bigger than before. "Hey, I feel like we haven't talked in forever."

The last two weeks had flown by quickly. I'd packed up my things and moved in with Bosco without looking back.

We'd been sleeping and fucking around the clock, sharing dinner and breakfast if we were at the penthouse at the same time. "I know. How's the baby?"

She rolled her eyes. "The baby is fine. The question is, how are you? What happened with Bosco?"

Bosco told me to lie about our relationship, and I'd agreed to it. We could enjoy our final three months together without having to worry about any interference. But the idea of lying to Vanessa made me sick to my stomach. She was my best friend, and it didn't feel right to make up a story. But since that was what we'd agreed on, I stuck to the plan. "I ended things. He took it hard in the beginning, but he let me go."

"Really?" she asked in surprise. "Wow, maybe the guy wasn't that bad, after all."

It was getting harder for me to remember that he was a bad guy, not a good one. "Yeah…there are definitely worse men out there."

"Well, problem solved. You wanna get lunch?"

"Sure." I locked up the shop, and we went to our favorite cafe. We ordered our food then sat at a table near the window. Vanessa would normally order a coffee at lunchtime, but since she was pregnant, one of her favorite things had been taken away. But she certainly made up for it by eating more calories.

"How's Griffin?" I asked.

"It's taken some time for him to get used to a slower career. He says it can be boring at times. Not much action going on."

"Well, I'm sure producing and shipping wine is nothing like killing people," I joked.

"But he says he enjoys spending time with our fathers. They're a lot more laid-back than he realized."

As long as the Barsetti men weren't threatened by you, they were pretty easy to get along with. "That's good. Griffin had to put up with a lot of bullshit from both of them." My father flipped out when he saw Griffin just talk to me.

"Yeah, I think they're putting that behind them, finally." She finished half her sandwich quickly, scarfing down her food quicker than usual. "This baby is definitely a boy. He needs to eat like Griffin does, which is constantly."

"You really think so?"

"Oh, I know so." She chuckled. "Griffin eats nonstop."

"Because he weighs two hundred and fifty pounds— and that's all muscle."

"Which makes me think this is his son."

"God, you're gonna have to give birth to that." She would have to shove a smaller version of Griffin through her little opening, and it might rip her clean in half.

"I know," she said with a sigh. "But I'm talking the drugs. No doubt about that."

"I'd do the same."

When she finished eating, she changed the subject. "I know this is weird, but I had an idea…"

"What's weird about it?"

"Well, I was thinking about your love life and how it hasn't been going well lately…"

My love life was a train wreck. But my sex life had never been better. When Bosco was gone, I would compare every man to him, and of course, I would never be satisfied.

She paused before she continued, like she wasn't sure if she should say it. "Remember when I dated Antonio for a bit?"

"The hot painter?"

"Uh-huh."

"Yeah. What about him?"

"Well, not only was he handsome, sweet, and charming, but he's successful, romantic, and passionate. He's pretty much got the whole package. I can't attest to his skills in the bedroom because I never even kissed him, but…what if you guys went on a date?"

"You want me to go out with your ex-boyfriend?" I asked incredulously.

"He's not my ex-boyfriend," she said sternly. "He can't be counted as an ex if I've never kissed him. But he was a wonderful guy. If Griffin had never existed, I would have fallen for him."

"Because you two are the same person. He and I have nothing in common."

"What are you talking about?" she asked incredulously. "You're both small business owners, and you're both artistic. He could paint your flowers. It wouldn't hurt, right? You already said you think he's hot."

I wasn't interested in dating anyone right now, not when I was in a committed relationship with Bosco. Even if it had an expiration date, I was loyal until the end. "I don't think that's a good idea. What if we got serious? Wouldn't be weird for you and Griffin?"

She shrugged. "Maybe in the beginning, but that would fade. Griffin wouldn't care either."

I raised an eyebrow.

"He wouldn't," she repeated. "I married him. I chose him. He has nothing to be threatened by."

I knew I was just looking for an excuse.

"Just walk in there and ask him to dinner. What's the worst that could happen?"

Bosco could murder him. "Uh…"

"Since when did you become this person who over-thinks everything?"

I couldn't stand this any longer. I didn't want to keep lying to Vanessa, even if I'd told Bosco I would. She would keep my secret, and I didn't want to lie for the next three months and make up excuses for why I wouldn't date the guys she recommended. "Don't get mad… I lied before."

"Lied about what?" she asked.

"Bosco."

Both of her eyes widened.

"I'm still seeing him."

"Oh my god…so he wouldn't let you go."

"No, not exactly. I told him I wanted to break it off, but he convinced me to stay." That was putting it mildly. I glanced around the café, wondering who was working for Bosco. They all looked like regular customers who were living their lives. "We agreed to three months. Then we'll go our separate ways for good."

Vanessa stared at me in disbelief. "Wow…are you sure that's a good idea?"

"Of course it's not," I said bluntly. "But we've agreed to it. When it's over, it's over."

"And you think he'll really honor it?"

I nodded. "I know he will. We signed a contract, and his brother witnessed it. And he told me so."

Vanessa shook her head slightly. "I'm not judging you, Carmen. I mean, I ended up falling in love with a man who kidnapped me and almost killed me. He's a natural-born enemy to our family. But if this guy isn't the man you want to love, I would get out now. Three months is a long time. You might feel differently about him at the end than you do right now. You saw everything I went through with our family to keep Griffin. It was totally worth it, and I would do it again in a heartbeat…but it was the hardest thing I've ever had to live through. There's no way your father will ever like Bosco. My father won't either. Griffin hates him."

"Griffin hates everyone."

She rolled her eyes. "He's not a good example. But you know what I mean. If you get too involved with a man so dangerous, who knows where you might end up? When you get in too deep in a relationship, it's nearly impossible to get out. And Bosco might change his mind at any time."

"He won't," I said firmly.

Vanessa didn't challenge me again. "If this is what you want, I won't try to talk you out of it anymore. I hope everything works out in the end. I don't want you to get your heart broken—and it seems like that's the only way this ends."

"I can't get my heart broken if I never fall in love with him."

"Carmen…" She sighed, giving me a look of pity

she'd never given me before. "I know you better than you know yourself. You treat men like business transactions, something I've always admired you for. When something isn't working, you don't hesitate before you ditch them. You're so smart and pragmatic. But with this guy…you aren't being smart or pragmatic. You continue to stay even though it's not working. That can only mean one thing… that you've already started to fall for him."

4

BOSCO

I WAS on the couch when Carmen came home from work.

Drake had already told me about her conversation with Vanessa, that Carmen decided to tell her about our relationship even though we'd agreed to keep it a secret. But that didn't upset me, not after Vanessa accused her of falling for me.

That information shouldn't make me happy, not when it didn't change the course of this relationship. Carmen didn't confirm it either, so there was no proof she felt that way anyway.

Carmen set her purse on the table in the entryway then pulled off her black pea coat and hung it by the door. Over the course of our time together, she'd made herself at home, leaving her coats on the rack and her favorite boots by the door.

She walked into the living room and stared at me, her guard up as she crossed her arms over her chest.

I rose to my feet and looked at her, standing in my

black sweatpants that hung low on my hips. I gave her a look that confirmed her suspicion—that I knew everything.

"I understand you have your men trail me everywhere, but it's unacceptable that you eavesdrop on my private conversations." She flashed me a fiery look that made her look angry, but also beautiful. "I don't overhear your intimate conversations with your brother, so it's unfair that you listen to mine."

I didn't deny her allegation. "I thought we agreed to keep this private."

"I know, but I couldn't lie to Vanessa. She's my best friend. And she's gonna keep trying to set me up with different men. It's a lot easier to tell her I'm seeing you instead of making up a bunch of excuses all the time. She would get suspicious after a while anyway and probably would have figured it out on her own."

"You trust her?"

She didn't flinch. "With my life. She would never say a word to anyone."

"I hope you're right. Because I would hate to hurt the people you care about."

Her eyes flashed like an atomic bomb had just dropped. "That shit ends now. Make another threat against my family, and I'll walk out and not come back. I don't give a damn about that stupid contract." She pressed her finger into my chest and poked me hard. "I will put you in the ground, asshole. I'm not kidding." She smacked her palm against my chest, hitting me with barely enough force to even register the sensation.

Truth be told, I didn't even want to hurt her family. I just wanted to keep her in line. "Alright."

"Alright what?" she pressed. "Does that mean you'll stop?"

I nodded. "I'll stop. I have no ill will toward your family."

She breathed a sigh of relief, that confession meaning the world to her.

"But make no mistake, if they ever become a problem, I'll be forced to do something. I know you don't want to hear that, but I have to be honest with you."

She gave me a heated look again.

"I'm sorry," I said gently. "As long your family never finds out about me, I'm sure nothing will ever happen. If you trust Vanessa, then I'm sure everything will be fine."

"I do trust her."

"Then let's not worry about it." I used to not care about making her angry, about threatening to hurt the family she loved so much. But now I hated myself a little bit more every time I dropped those kinds of threats.

"No more eavesdropping." She crossed her arms over her chest as she stared me down. "It's a huge invasion of privacy, and I think it's below you to cross that line. If you want to have months of amazing sex, that needs to change."

"Fair enough," I said. "I'll make sure it doesn't happen again."

She was visibly surprised I gave in so easily.

"My attention was never to eavesdrop on you. Drake told me about your first conversation with Vanessa because he thought it was important, but I never asked

him to do that. Now he's been doing it ever since…
because I didn't ask him to stop."

"That doesn't make it any better, Bosco." The fire in
her eyes turned to ice. "I demand the respect I deserve. I
want to tell my best friend about my life without worrying
about you listening. I shouldn't even have to ask."

She made me feel like shit so easily. Only a truly
powerful woman could do that. "You're right. It's over."

Her eyes shifted back and forth as she looked into
mine, searching for the sincerity in my gaze. But she didn't
need to look because I was always honest with her. If I
wanted to keep spying on her, I would just tell her that.
"Okay." Slowly, the anger faded away. Her eyes didn't look
so belligerent, and her body physically relaxed. Her arms
lowered to her sides, and she took a deep breath, like she
was truly relaxed.

Even though I was desperate to touch her, I moved my
hands into the pockets of my sweatpants. She wasn't
angry anymore, but her aura of hostility still burned
bright. "I'm gonna make dinner. Would you like some?"

She sighed. "Fish?"

I grinned. "Chicken."

"What if we order a pizza?"

I couldn't remember the last time I had pizza. "You
can order anything you want, Beautiful. But I'll pass."

She rolled her eyes so hard it seemed like they might
get stuck in the back of her head. "You need to live a little.
One day, all of this is gonna be over, and you're gonna
regret not eating more pizza and drinking more beer."

"Or maybe I'll live longer because I don't eat pizza
and drink beer."

She shook her head. "That's not a life worth living, if you ask me."

I chuckled, loving how real she was.

"Being around you makes me feel fat."

"I don't see how that's possible." I looked her up and down. "You look perfect."

"You're the one with the perfect body," she countered. "You have like six percent body fat or something?"

"Yeah. Probably." I didn't know how to be humble about it. "But trust me, men don't want a woman with six percent body fat."

"And what do they want?" she challenged.

Carmen. Every man in the world wanted Carmen. "A woman with tits, curves, and an ass."

"That doesn't sound like a lot of criteria."

"Because it's not. Men are pretty simple." There were a lot of beautiful women out there, but Carmen's fire is what attracted me to her the most. If I saw her in a bra, I probably would have thought she was sexy and got hard at the sight of her, but that wouldn't necessarily have caught my attention. It was watching her fight off four guys fearlessly that made me stop in my tracks. It was her demand for respect that made me drop to my knees. Those were qualities that had nothing to do with the size of her tits or the perkiness of her ass.

"Well, how about you ditch your strict diet and relax for once? Let's have pizza and beer tonight."

I shook my head. "You're a terrible influence."

"Like you aren't?" she teased.

We were both terrible for each other—but in very different ways. "Alright, let's do it."

The light brightened in her eyes as the excitement hit her. "Really?"

I nodded.

"Wow. I can't believe this is actually happening. My hands are shaking." She pulled out her phone to order the food.

I took her phone from her hand. "My address isn't in public records so you can't order anything."

"Not in public records?"

"It doesn't exist."

"How is that possible?"

I wouldn't bore her with the details. "Tell me what you want, and one of the guys will pick it up." I never ordered out, so the security team would have a new mission to complete. At least it would give them something to do.

"This is gonna be the best night ever. Pizza, beer, and sex."

I watched the brightness in her eyes, the way she got excited over something so simple. The other women I screwed wanted a trip to Paris on my private jet and a private, five-star meal at the Eiffel Tower. All Carmen wanted was a casual night in—with me.

SHE DRANK THREE BEERS IN HALF AN HOUR AND devoured half the pizza on her own.

I only had a few slices.

She ran laps around me, handling her beer better than most women. I saw her drink scotch, and it never went to her head. She could even finish a bottle of wine by herself and still hold her own in an argument.

Must be that Barsetti blood.

"That was the best meal I've ever had. So much cheese. There's no such thing as too much cheese." She finished off her fourth beer.

She was entertaining, sitting across from me in just my t-shirt while she ran her fingers through her hair in such a sexy way. "You act like you've never had pizza before."

"Well, I've been here for almost three weeks, and I've never seen you eat a decent meal."

"We have different definitions of decent." My meals were nutritionally rich, low in fat, and low in carbs. She wanted to eat pizza and pasta all the time. As a woman, that was fine, but curves on a man weren't sexy.

"You don't even have a cheat day. It's weird."

I shrugged. "I've been in this routine for a long time."

"You have a super-hot body," she blurted. "But if you ate pancakes for breakfast once a week and pizza for dinner, would you really be that much less hot?" She tipped back her beer again, which was empty.

Now I knew she'd drunk too much. I pulled the glass away from her and made sure she wouldn't have anymore. But I liked drunk Carmen. She was more candid than usual, and her openness was sexy. She called me super-hot without being remotely embarrassed about it. Most of the time, she regretted her compliments the second they were out of her mouth. But now, she didn't think twice about them.

"Can I be honest with you?" She leaned farther toward me, tucking her hair behind her ear. She had a lazy look in her green eyes, the alcohol making her inhibitions lower even more.

"Please." I set my beer to the side and leaned toward her, our hands almost touching in the middle. I was still in my sweatpants, my chest bare for her to see.

"Alright." She looked down for a second before she looked up again. "I want you to stop smoking cigars."

The request caught me off guard, so I didn't say anything right away. Of all the things she could say right now, my smoking habits seemed to be at the bottom of the list.

"Smoking a cigar is like smoking seven cigarettes. It's terrible for you. Do you realize how likely you are to develop lung cancer just from smoking? As well as other health complications."

I stared at her blankly, aware of all the warnings she gave me.

"I don't like it," she said. "I know I have no right to tell you what to do, but…" Her hand reached for mine. "But I don't want anything to happen to you." She squeezed my hand, the concern in her eyes the sexiest thing in the world.

I interlocked our fingers and stared at her across the table.

She stared back at me as she waited for an answer. "So?"

"You want me to quit that badly?" I couldn't keep back my grin, turned on by the way she cared about me. In the beginning of our relationship, she wouldn't give me the time of day, but now she was nagging me about my health like a wife.

"Yes." She brought my knuckles to her mouth and kissed each one slowly, seductively. She kept her eyes on me the entire time, pulling at my will with those green eyes.

I'd never even considered quitting until now. "Alright."

"Really?" she whispered.

I nodded.

"Even after I leave?"

I hated thinking about the moment when my men would carry her stuff back to her apartment and we would say goodbye. I'd never wanted a woman the way I wanted her. Maybe in a few months, I would get bored of her like all the others, but something told me the exact opposite would happen. I wasn't a man falling in love, but I was a man falling deeper into this intense obsession. "If that's what you want."

"Yes. It's exactly what I want."

I STOOD AT THE EDGE OF THE CASINO, WATCHING THE way everything flowed smoothly. The chips constantly tapped in the background, the music played at the perfect volume overhead, and the men possessed orderly conduct while playing for millions. There was nothing that happened in my casino I didn't know about. My need for control was constant, and if things weren't done my way, they weren't done right.

One of the dancers approached me, wearing a gold thong and bra that barely covered anything. I had minimal interaction with the people who worked the floor, even though I knew their names and their back-grounds.

My men moved in front of me, blocking her path toward me. "No one speaks to Bosco."

She rolled her eyes then looked at me. "I have a complaint."

The men pressed her back gently, getting her away from me. "There's a floor manager for that."

She raised her voice so I could hear her words as she was being pushed away. "It's that asshole, The Butcher."

The second I heard his name, I knew I needed to address this personally. "Leave her."

The men backed off right away and took their positions.

She walked up to me, a foot shorter than me even in her heels. With big hair and lots of makeup, she looked ready for her shift. "Look, I like working here. Money is good, and the security is tight. I've never had a problem with any of the sleazebags in here—because they have some manners. But this Butcher guy is a pain in the ass."

"What did he do?" I was unaffected by her obvious charms since I had a woman at home in my bed right at that very moment. If I wanted a nice pair of tits to stare at, I'd look at Carmen's.

"He tried to rape one of the girls in the bathroom, for one." She put both of her hands on her hips, strutting her attitude.

"I gave him a warning for that."

"He stares—a lot."

"Theresa." I used her real name since I knew all of my employees. "Can you blame him?" I cocked my head slightly to the side but kept my gaze on hers. "That's your job—to give them something to stare at."

"But it's not a normal stare," she argued. "It's…hostile."

"Did he threaten you?" I asked seriously. "Did he touch you?"

"No and no," she said. "But I get a bad feeling about him…"

"You know I take your safety and security very seriously, Theresa. Same goes for everyone else in this casino. I gave him a warning and told him I wouldn't hesitate to rescind his membership if he bothered you guys again. He seemed to take me seriously."

"Well, he better have. I'm not letting that asshole touch me."

"He won't, Theresa. Now get back to work."

She gave me a look full of attitude before she strutted off and resumed her post.

When she was gone, I reached in my pocket for a cigar. The Butcher was a thorn in my side, and I needed a way to lower my rage. I'd been running this casino for a decade, and while there were bumps in the road, I'd never had any serious issues. The Butcher seemed different, like there was no telling what he might do. Maybe granting him admission to the casino had been a mistake. Maybe my brother had been right. The second The Butcher stepped out of line, I would throw him out—and not refund his dues.

I was just about to light the cigar when I remembered what Carmen asked me to do. The cigar was sitting in my mouth, the tip wet from my teeth. I put the lighter back in my pocket, sighed, and then tossed the unused cigar in the trash.

Quitting would be harder than I realized.

I didn't smoke every day, just when I worked in the casino. I never lit up in my home because I didn't want my penthouse to smell. My addiction had never been so strong that I had to walk outside just to light up. But now that I was denying myself in my natural environment, I felt the kick in my side.

"Wow. Bosco Roth is turning over a new leaf." Her playful voice came from behind me. In a royal blue dress studded with diamonds, she definitely didn't look like one of the cage dancers. She was definitely more ambitious than that. She came to my side without objection since my men knew who she was.

"Ruby, how are you?" I hadn't seen her in a few months.

She was smoking a cigar, the white smoke rising from her nostrils to the ceiling. The diamonds of her dress reflected the light every time she made the slightest movement. She was rich in diamonds—and rich in every other way that mattered. "Concerned. Why did you throw away a perfectly good cigar?"

"Trying to cut back."

She shook her head slightly. "I never thought I'd see the day when Bosco Roth would listen to a woman…"

I had no idea how she knew about Carmen, but since I'd brought her to the casino, people probably talked. "Are you having a good time?"

She shrugged. "My date isn't the best gambler. He

doesn't have your poker face." She watched me as she took another drag.

"Not very many men do."

"Nope. You can say that again." She crossed one arm over her waist and propped her elbow on her hand, holding out the cigar like a cigarette. "And they don't have your other qualities either…" She gave me a cold stare, but the desire was obvious in her look.

Ruby and I'd had a short-lived fling. She was a beautiful woman who was attracted to power and money. She went from man to man, cleaning them out until she got everything she wanted. What made her different from being a con artist was her honesty. She told men exactly what she wanted before she used them, but she was so beautiful, the men didn't care. That was exactly what had happened to me. She wanted a new diamond necklace, a trip to Istanbul, and to sit on my arm for a week. We spent that week fucking and drinking until it ran its course. When she walked away, I didn't ask her to stay—even though she was good in the sack. "Keep looking, Ruby. I'm sure you'll find a good man out there." I didn't sleep with the same woman twice, but Ruby had been an exception. Though she hadn't been the kind of exception Carmen was. "Have a good night." I turned away and headed toward the elevators, dismissing the conversation without giving her a chance to respond. Ruby still wanted me because I was the most powerful man in this country. She desired nothing more than to sit on my arm forever, to roll around in my cash and retire as a wealthy woman.

But she knew that wasn't possible with me.

Ronan walked up to me, his hands in the pockets of his slacks. "I smell trouble."

I knew he was referring to Ruby. "Ignore her."

"I know I can. But can you?"

I ignored the jab. "She never meant anything to me."

"She was your longest fling before Carmen came around."

"Not comparable." We moved to a secluded table in the corner, where the men brought us a decanter of scotch and two glasses. Then they disappeared, leaving us alone together while the music played overhead.

"But—"

"I don't want to talk about Ruby anymore." She was a brief fling who never meant anything to me. She was direct about what she wanted from me, to be spoiled and fucked right. It had been a satisfying week, but I'd had no problem walking away when she clung to me too hard.

Ronan stopped when he heard the threat in my voice. He drank from his glass then licked his lips. "I hope you're in the mood to talk about Carmen, because that's my next subject."

"She's fine." The thought of Carmen didn't fill me with annoyance and dread. It was almost eleven, so I knew she would be asleep by now, spread out across my bed with the sheets pulled to her shoulder.

"I like her."

"How can you not?" She was perfect, from her pretty face to the pretty words that flew out of her mouth.

"I'm serious. She's not like the other women we fuck around with."

"No comparison."

He abandoned his drink and put all his focus on me. "I can tell she's crazy about you."

My impenetrable exterior faded slightly, even though we were still in the casino and I had to keep up my cold presence. "What makes you say that?"

"Everything. From the way she looks at you. The way she talks to you. She isn't a pushover who will do whatever you want, but she accepts you as you are. But she's not afraid to tell you off either—which is something you need."

She'd asked me to quit smoking, and she complimented me left and right. She obviously cared about me, which is a big change from how she felt about me in the beginning.

"Mom would like her."

There was no doubt about that. Mom had been an opinionated and outspoken woman, not afraid to get her hands dirty. She would admire Carmen's independence and fire. They would fit together like two peas in a pod. "I know she would."

"So I like her. You like her. Mom would like her. Hmm…" He took a drink from his glass. "Interesting."

I knew exactly where this was going. "We have an expiration date. She made that clear."

"I know. But you're the kind of man that can make things happen. So, make something happen."

My life was about gambling, booze, and women. Carmen would always have a special place in my heart because she was different. She would be a good memory, and she would be someone I never forgot about. But my life would continue forward on the path I was meant to walk—alone. "It's not gonna work out. We want different things."

"Then make sure you want the same things." Ronan handled all situations with simplicity, like everything was as straightforward as a math problem and there was only one solution. "This act isn't gonna be cute forever. When you're forty and fifty, you're just gonna be an old guy with a bunch of money."

I turned the tables on him. "You want to get married and have a family?"

He shrugged. "If I met the right woman, I'm not opposed to it."

I raised an eyebrow, surprised my heartbreaker brother would say that. "Really?"

"I'm having fun right now, but that's gonna get old after a while. If I met a woman who was absolutely perfect for me, I wouldn't let her go. I would man up and be everything she wanted—even a husband and a father."

I was still stunned.

"Come on, I just turned thirty. I'm not in my twenties anymore. You haven't been in your twenties for a while."

I never felt a particular age. I never felt rushed to do anything in particular. I figured I would live life and see where it took me. Listening to my brother say these things surprised me because he'd been a playboy for so long.

"So if Carmen really means something to you, you shouldn't let her go."

Even if I wanted those things, it didn't change anything. Even if I loved her, we still had our problems. "I'm not the kind of man she's looking for. She sees me as a dangerous criminal, not husband material.

I can't blame her. She tried to break things off with me, and I wouldn't let her. Since the beginning, I've been controlling the relationship and not giving her much of a choice. She wants an average man, safe and simple."

"So if she changed her mind about all of that, would you?" He regarded me with a serious expression, watching every slight reaction I made with my face.

"I don't know, Ronan. I've only known the woman for a month or two."

He shrugged. "They said when you know, you know right away."

I took a drink and looked away. "I'm not in love with the girl. I care about her and enjoy her company, but that's it. You're looking too hard into it."

"Maybe," he said. "Or maybe I'm making you think about things you don't want to think about."

I loosened my tie in the elevator and pulled my jacket off before the doors opened. Even though I didn't smoke, I still smelled like cigars and booze. If Carmen smelled my clothes, she might think I went behind her back and lit up anyway.

Or maybe she didn't remember asking me to quit in the first place. She had been pretty tipsy at the time.

The doors opened, and I walked into the penthouse, expecting it to be dark with the exception of a few lights. The skyline of the city was in the background, glowing with the beauty of the Italian landscape. I tossed my jacket over my shoulder and noticed the glow from the TV.

Was she sleeping on the couch again?

I crept into the living room, carefully pressing my feet against the hardwood floor so the soles of my shoes wouldn't make a gentle tapping noise. I spotted her on the long couch, her knees pulled to her chest with a blanket draped over her body. The TV was still on, but the sound was down low. Just like last time, she wasn't deeply asleep because she seemed to be aware of my presence. She opened her eyes and looked at me. "Oh…you're home." She ran her fingers through her hair then sat up, her eyes heavy with exhaustion.

"Why are you on the couch?" It seemed like every time I came home, she was crammed on this piece of furniture instead of lounging in the enormous bed with the luxurious sheets. It wasn't nearly as comfortable out here. If she wanted a TV, there was one in the bedroom. It worked exactly the same way as this one, so there was no possibility she didn't know how to work it.

"I was just having a hard time falling asleep. Too much coffee." When she stood up, she tossed the blanket over the back of the couch and walked toward me. She was in one of my t-shirts, her hair down and her skin clean because she'd washed her face before she got ready for bed. "How was your night?"

"Same as always." My hand cupped her cheek, and I brushed my thumb across her soft skin. She turned her face into my palm, letting me cradle her. I watched the subtle glow of her green eyes, the way she was tired but also wide awake. It was past one when I walked through the door, and she would leave for work in a few hours.

"So you missed me the whole time?" she teased.

I didn't smile, but my heart noticeably lightened in my chest. When I was at work, I rarely thought about anything besides money, security, and scotch. But Carmen drifted into my mind from time to time, especially when I was in my office. "You're the only woman who's ever been in my office." I'd stared at the leather couch and remembered fucking her there. We'd fallen asleep afterward, and I'd cuddled her with my body to keep her warm. She'd wrapped herself in my clothes like a blanket, and I'd acted as her personal heater.

Her playful attitude faded away, her eyes softening like that meant something to her. "Why is that?"

"I don't trust anyone down there. It's where I keep all my records and laptops." If someone wanted to steal my information, they could have a woman seduce me, and when I was passed out, she could rifle through my belongings and transfer everything to a hard drive. Ruby had tried to invite herself to my office once before, but she'd been denied. "But I knew I could trust you."

"Trust me?" she whispered, her voice shaking particularly hard on the word trust. "You hardly know me…"

We'd known each other a relatively short amount of time. I didn't know everything about her, from her favorite color to her most embarrassing childhood story, but that didn't mean I didn't know her spirit. "I do know you. I know you don't give a damn about my money. You've never been impressed by it—still aren't." My hand moved into her hair, and I felt the ache inside my chest, a sensation I didn't recognize because I'd never felt it before. With Carmen, I never had to be on my guard. I never had to look over my shoulder and wonder what her motivations were. "You're an honorable woman who comes an honorable family. You would never steal from me, not when you can accomplish anything you want on your own." Carmen was fierce and strong, more independent than most men I knew. Ruby was a man-eater looking for someone to take care of her. The women couldn't be more different. I didn't even know women like Carmen existed until I passed that alleyway. "You wouldn't betray me." She didn't owe me any loyalty, but I knew she gave it anyway. There wasn't greed in her eyes. She was afraid of my power, not obsessed with it. It allowed her to see the man under the suit. It allowed her to see me.

"No...I wouldn't." Her green eyes looked into mine, becoming more vibrant as the attachment between us intensified. There had always been powerful chemistry between us, but this connection was different. I felt it down in my office when she sat in my lap, when I told her it would be hard for me to let her go. Now I felt it again as I continued to look into her beautiful face. I didn't need to press my lips to hers to kiss her. I didn't need to touch her to sense her, to tell her how quickly her heart was racing. Somehow, I could feel everything in that moment. I'd never experienced this kind of intimacy in my entire life, regardless of how many women I'd bedded. This was different.

I lifted her into the air so I could carry her to bed. Her body moved with my direction because she could read my intentions so well. I carried her to my bedroom down the hall, our faces pressed together without kisses being shared.

I laid her on my bed, lowering with her as my jacket slipped off my shoulder and dropped beside us. My tie fell off somewhere down the hallway.

She pulled off her panties for me, too eager to wait for me to take them off. She kept her shirt on and widened her legs for me, like there wasn't time to strip down to her naked skin.

I pushed my slacks and boxers down until my cock was free. My shoes were still on and so was my collared shirt. I was too eager to take my time, so I pressed my head through her entrance, felt the notch of her body, and then slipped all the way inside. I sank in deep, hitting her at the perfect angle because her legs were wide open. I moaned once I had her, when I was surrounded by the slickness of her perfect pussy. I'd been at the casino all night, unaroused by the naked women constantly walking around, but the second I came home and saw Carmen sleeping on my couch, I was harder than steel. "Fuck…" There was nothing better than being sheathed to the hilt inside her pussy, feeling that powerful squeeze as she stretched around me.

She gripped my cheeks and dug her nails into the muscle, shivering around me because my entrance pleased her so deeply. Her nails sliced me before they ran up my back. She breathed into my face, biting her bottom lip in the sexiest way. "Yes…fuck." She was enjoying this as much as I did, like this was the first time we'd ever been together.

I started to thrust inside her, moving slowly at first but

then picking up speed. I wanted to keep it gentle to make it last as long as possible, but my hips weren't cooperating. I rammed my cock deep inside her, my balls slamming hard into her ass. I took her roughly, like I was claiming her as mine even though the world already knew they couldn't have her.

She cupped my face as she breathed deeply. "Slower…" She looked me in the eye as she gave the order, telling me exactly how she wanted to be fucked.

I'd fucked her hard many times, and she always liked it rough. She was clearly in a different mood tonight. I slowed down, still hitting her deep and hard but not scratching the wall with the bedpost.

"Slower…" She cupped my face and kissed me, keeping her legs open for me to take her. She sucked my bottom lip and released a quiet moan, her pussy tightening and relaxing around my length.

I slowed down more, obeying her command as I felt a new flood of moisture surround me. I liked to call the shots in the bedroom, to take care of the fucking while she worried about getting fucked, but I loved listening to this woman tell me what she wanted. She wasn't the least bit ashamed. Her confidence was sexy. "Like this, Beautiful?" My arms hooked behind her knees, and I slowly thrust inside her, making sure I pressed my pelvic bone into her clit. It was a move guaranteed to make a woman come. I stared at the desire in her eyes, the way she came apart for me so easily.

"Yes…" She brushed her soft lips against mine, only giving me a partial kiss because she was too swept away by my movements. Her nails clawed at my back, and her pussy was so tight it was unbelievable.

I felt like I was fucking a virgin—over and over.

She grabbed my ass and pulled me into her at the perfect pace, her moans rolling over me in loud waves. She flung her head back and writhed underneath me, putting on the most erotic show I'd ever seen.

Who knew fucking a woman this slow could be so good?

"Babe, I'm gonna come." She spoke against my lips, her whispered breath traveling over my mouth.

I almost stopped my movements because of what she'd just called me. She never called me anything besides Bosco, except for the occasional use of asshole. No woman ever called me "babe." Carmen was the first one to do it, and I was surprised how much I liked it. It was possessive, intimate, and it made me wonder if she ever called another man by that name. "Come all over my dick, Beautiful." I kissed her neck then the shell of her ear, grinding into her harder so I could make her legs shake.

She widened her legs farther as she hit her threshold, clenching around me with surprising strength. Her moans bounced off my ceiling, causing a permanent echo that would still sound long after she was gone. Her presence soaked into the walls and the sheets, her scent and spirit permanently sticking everywhere. "Yes…so good." She was a vocal lover, telling me exactly what she liked, if she wanted it faster or slower. Her tightening pussy was announcement enough of her climax, but she liked to tell me too, to broadcast it like she was proud of the high she was about to experience.

My dick thickened just a little more, prepared to explode inside her and fill her with all my come. This was the first woman I'd done many things with, from abandoning a condom to taking her down to my office. She would probably be the only woman I ever did those things with, so I wanted to enjoy it even more, treasure the time we had left together.

She gripped my ass with both hands and pulled me deeper inside. "Give it to me. Give it all to me…" She kissed me hard on the mouth as she rocked her body back into mine. "I love feeling your come inside me all night long."

Jesus fucking Christ. "Beautiful…" With my eyes locked on hers, I came deep and hard, filling her pussy with everything I had. This woman turned me on like no one else. She made my dick harder, made it bigger, and she made me dump so much come, I couldn't believe I'd produced that much at one time. I gave it to her as deep as I could, feeling all my muscles tense then relax. I softened inside her once I was finished, but my cock loved her pussy so much that he didn't want to leave. I stayed on top of her, loving how wet she was now that her come was mixed with mine.

"Perfect." She locked her ankles around my waist and gave my body a gentle squeeze. Her nails kept clawing at me and her hips bucked slightly, like feeling me come inside her gave her another small climax.

Coming inside her made me feel like I was losing my virginity again. Like this was the first time I'd ever felt the wetness of a woman. Since she was the only woman I didn't wear a condom with, it was a whole new experience. I figured I would wear a rubber every single day for the rest of my life.

Her legs released me, and she got comfortable in the bed, ready to fall asleep. She rolled over onto her side and pulled the covers around her waist. My t-shirt was baggy on her body, three times too big around her slender arms.

I got off the bed and removed my clothes, letting my slacks and boxers fall the rest of the way. I unbuttoned my collared shirt and let it fall into the pile. I'd normally wash my face and brush my teeth before bed, but the spot beside her looked too comfortable to ignore.

I turned off the light before I lay beside her, the sound of her breathing instantly different because she was already drifting off to sleep. There was no one in the world who could fall asleep quicker than she could. The second her head hit the pillow, she was out. Anytime I came home late from work, she was on the couch because she struggled to sleep, but whenever she was in bed with me, she was out like a light.

My chest pressed against her back, and my arm hooked around her waist, keeping her close against me so I could listen to her breathe. She was beside me every single night, and I'd gotten used to this beautiful woman sharing every single aspect of my life. Her hair was in my face, but I liked feeling those soft strands against my cheek. Her body made the temperature of the sheets a little warmer than I enjoyed, but I still preferred the heat over the coldness of her absence. In just a few days, she would be gone for the weekend because her brother was getting married.

I would return to sleeping alone.

My bed had been empty every night of my adult life. Women came and went. They rarely slept over, and when they did, it was uncomfortable the entire time. But Carmen was like a pillow that belonged in my bed—because she completed it.

I kissed the back of her shoulder even though she was dead asleep. "Sweet dreams, Beautiful."

CARMEN

MY DRIVER TOOK me by the café to pick up a coffee to go, and then he dropped me off in front of the flower shop. It was a cold morning, the fog thick down the cobblestone streets. I couldn't see farther than a few dozen feet.

My coat kept me warm, but my hands were freezing as I dug into my jacket to retrieve my keys. My fingers searched for the cold metal but didn't find them. Eventually, I set my coffee down on the sidewalk so I could look into my bag.

Where the hell were they?

I never changed purses, so this was the only place they could be. I must have tossed the purse in the bedroom yesterday, and the keys spilled out in the closet somewhere.

The blacked-out car stayed at the curb, Bosco's men patiently waiting until I had the door unlocked. The passenger window rolled down, revealing a bald man with thick scruff along his jawline. The men never spoke to me. They were so silent that conversation must be prohibited by Bosco. But this time, the man had something to say. "Everything alright, miss?"

"I think I left the keys at home…" I reached down to pick up my coffee again, hating myself for referring to Bosco's penthouse as home. I'd moved in to the place so easily and didn't miss my apartment at all. I loved the high countertops, the enormous mirror in the bathroom, the walk-in shower, and the spacious area his penthouse provided. I hadn't even visited the other floors because I didn't need to.

I walked back to the car, and the men immediately jumped out of the passenger door and opened the door for me.

I was surrounded by the warmth once more, the leather seats heated. We drove away from my shop, and I was annoyed with myself for being so forgetful. I always checked my keys before I left the house. Wasn't sure why I didn't this time.

It was twenty minutes back to the penthouse. I moved through the lobby, got into the elevators, and then hit the code so I could rise to the top floor. Ever since Bosco gave me his code, I could come and go whenever I pleased.

It was much better than being trapped like an animal.

The doors opened, and I walked inside. "I forgot my keys." Bosco was there before I left, so I assumed he was still in the house. He usually left around this time to work out on another floor. On rare occasions, he had to head down to the casino to do some bookkeeping.

I didn't hear a reply. "Bosco, are you home?"

No answer. He must have left already.

I headed down the hallway and went into the

bedroom. The walk-in closet contained mostly my stuff now, from the clothes I brought with me to the cocktail dresses he picked out. There were a few pieces of lingerie hanging from the rack, new additions to my wardrobe. He'd probably picked those out recently.

I knelt on the floor and searched for my keys. "Ugh… where the hell are they?"

His deep voice sounded from the living room, full of irritation. The elevator beeped when the doors closed behind him. "What does she want?"

I stiffened at his tone, knowing he was pissed about something. I rarely heard him speak that way, only when something was truly digging under his skin. I was on my knees in the closet, moving through the pile of dirty clothes that sat there. The keys must be underneath it.

"What's so important for us to talk about?" He must be on the phone because I didn't hear a second voice. He paused for a long time, listening over the line. Then he gave another response. "Fine. Let her up."

Let who up? Who was she?

I felt awkward listening to this without telling him I was there. But then I remembered how he spied on all my conversations with Vanessa like he had every right. It was petty of me to sink to his level, but since he sounded so pissed, I didn't want to interfere. What if this woman was actually a threat? I might make the situation worse.

He hung up then sighed loudly, so loudly I could hear it in the bedroom.

The elevator doors opened, and the beep accompanied it. Then the sound of heels tapped against the hardwood floor. She was walking slowly, making a subtle entrance despite the way she'd pissed him off from the lobby. Then her voice emerged, seductive, cold, and sexy —all at the same time. "You look tense."

Just from the sound of her voice, I could tell she wasn't some random acquaintance. Bosco had made it sound like the only time women came to his apartment was for fucking. Ronan hadn't even stopped by since I'd started living there. The only person I ever witnessed in this penthouse was Bosco Roth. His security detail stayed in the lobby.

His tone was clipped. "What's so important, Ruby?"

I stayed on the floor of the closet, but my curiosity was getting the better of me. I shouldn't care what this woman looked like, but my imagination made her seem like the most stunning woman in the world. She had confidence, enough confidence to hold her own in his penthouse.

That was a little scary.

I left the closet and the bedroom, creeping down the hallway barefoot so my movements wouldn't make a sound. Bosco obviously had no idea I was there because he would have called out to me by now.

I got to the end of the hallway and peeked around the corner.

I didn't like what I saw.

Ruby was in skintight jeans and heels, her legs even longer than mine. With black hair and lustrous eyelashes, she was a gorgeous woman with curves anyone would envy. Her lips were painted dark, and she wore a large diamond necklace around her throat. Her black top hugged her waist, and there was a zipper that went all the way from the top to the bottom. She propped one hand on her hip and stared at Bosco with a mixture of hatred and desire.

Skank.

I didn't like her one bit.

It would be stupid for me to be jealous, but I didn't like that woman standing in my living room like she owned it.

Well, his living room.

Bosco was in his running shorts and t-shirt. He'd obviously been on the other floor working out when his men called from the lobby. He moved his hands into the pockets of his shorts, keeping a few feet away from her. His back was to me, broad and muscular in the gray cotton.

She moved her body slightly from left to right, like she was teasing him with the subtle shake of her hips. She didn't respond to Bosco's question, holding the silence like this wasn't her first time. Without any confirmation, it was clear she'd been in his penthouse before—and definitely in his bed.

I already hated her.

When she didn't say anything, Bosco spoke again. "Ruby, what is—"

"I miss you."

I was about to rip that pretty hair off her scalp.

I couldn't see his expression, but his shoulders tensed noticeably. "Don't interrupt me again. Ever."

My heart raced, the fear mixing with the adrenaline. This woman was far more beautiful than I was, and she had the kind of attitude he liked. She had curves in all the right places, and her confidence never diminished despite his hostility.

The corner of her mouth rose in a smile. "I miss you even more…"

Bosco didn't kick her out. He stood there for another minute, their eyes locked on each other.

The pain started to throb inside my heart as I feared what would happen next. Bosco thought I was at work all day. There would be no way for me to find out about this. Would he screw her right on the couch? That was clearly what she wanted.

"If this is the only reason why you're here, you're wasting my time. You know how angry I get when people waste my time."

Take that, bitch.

Her smile disappeared when she couldn't hide her disappointment. "I'm tired of looking for the right man, a man who can spoil me…and satisfy me. You can do both. You can take me on perfect trips to Paris, but also bed me like a man who knows what he's doing."

He took her to Paris? My jealousy grew.

"And what do I get out of it?" he asked, tilting his head slightly.

I was relieved Bosco wasn't taking the bait. If he screwed her, our contract would be broken, and I would be free. But that was nothing compared to the pain I'd feel inside my chest at his deceit. He made me feel like the only woman who mattered. If he fucked her, every good feeling I had toward him would be destroyed. On top of that…I would be heartbroken. I didn't realize how much he meant to me until that moment, imagining him being with someone else, especially a beautiful woman like Ruby.

She grabbed the zipper at the top of her shirt and slowly zipped it down, revealing more of her flawless fair skin. With every inch, it showed off more of her feminine flesh, from the curves of her tits to the petiteness of her rib cage. Farther and farther she went, until the top opened completely and revealed her perfect tits on display.

Slut. Fucking slut.

Bosco didn't turn away. It wasn't clear what he was looking at, her perfect tits or her blue eyes. "Ruby, I'm seeing someone."

"So? It'll run its course." She shrugged. "Then you can have me. I can be your queen. I can be the woman on your arm. Everyone will stare at you enviously, wishing they were the man who had me." She moved into his chest, pressing her tits right against him.

I wasn't sure if I could watch this.

Bosco stepped away and moved to the elevators. "You know I don't sleep with the same woman twice."

"But you did sleep with me more than once." She turned around, still letting her tits hang out.

"And that was one time too many." He hit the button and watched the doors open. "Cover yourself up, and I'll take you to the lobby."

She took a deep breath, clearly frustrated that she was getting turned down despite being a beauty queen. "And what about this woman you're seeing? You've slept with her more than twice."

He held the door open and waited for her. "She's an exception. The only exception I'll ever make."

She finally zipped up her shirt, keeping her eyes on him. "And what does she have that I don't? I'm the only woman who can handle your world. I'm beautiful, flexible, and I don't settle for anything less than the best."

He kept up his indifferent stare, his arm still holding the door open. Even though her tits had been hanging out for the past few minutes, he didn't seem the least bit aroused. There was no bulge in his shorts, and the man was so large that it would be impossible to hide his dick in those flimsy little shorts. "She's got class. You certainly don't."

I WENT TO WORK AFTER THEY DISAPPEARED IN THE elevator, and I finally located my keys. I made my arrangements all afternoon and received a new shipment of flowers from Greece. My hands were busy, and my mind was occupied with the customers who came in to pick up arrangements for their mothers and wives.

But all I could think about was the scene I'd witnessed in the penthouse.

Ruby wanted him bad.

Bosco didn't take the bait. He was faithful to me without a struggle. She was a drop-dead gorgeous woman, but the sight of her tits didn't make him hard. Maybe he never looked at them. Maybe his eyes were on her face the entire time. Either way, he didn't fall prey to his testosterone, to the easy lay right before his eyes. Not only did he honor his commitment to me, but he also defended me.

How many other men would have done that?

Not many.

I was heartbroken watching her throw herself at him,

assuming Bosco would go through with it when there was no way for me to find out. But seeing him blow her off did a number on my heart. It made it skip a beat, made it throb in pain because his actions meant so much to me.

Only a real man could turn down a woman like that.

I was distracted all day thinking about it, unsure what I would say to Bosco when I got home. Would I act like nothing happened? Would I wait for him to tell me what happened? Was that something he would even tell me?

When the day was over, I locked up the shop and walked to Vanessa's gallery. It was a few blocks away, and even though I didn't see Bosco's men anywhere, I knew there were at least ten of them watching me, all armed and ready for a man dumb enough to cross me.

I stepped inside the gallery, seeing Vanessa closing up for the day. "How's it going?"

"Hey, girl." Vanessa rose from her desk and hugged me. "Nice to have you drop by."

I noticed the huge man lurking in the corner, watching every move I made. I glanced at him and smiled. "How are you doing?"

All I got was a quiet growl in response.

Vanessa rolled her eyes. "Carl, this is my cousin. She's cool."

He made another growl before he walked away.

When he left us alone, my eyebrows rose almost off my face. "You have to deal with that guy all day, every day?"

"He's a lot nicer when it's just the two of us. He doesn't like or trust other people." Vanessa was in black leggings and a long-sleeved dress. Her stomach was getting bigger every week, and she was deep in her second trimester. "He's actually a very nice guy...when he shows it."

"I'll just take your word for it."

"So, what's up?" she asked. "I would ask you to dinner, but I need to get home. Griffin probably already has dinner on the table. Unless you'd like to come over?"

Having Bosco's men follow me to Griffin's territory sounded like a terrible idea. "No thanks. I should be getting home."

"You mean, to *Bosco's* home," she teased.

The penthouse already felt like mine, even though it'd only been a month. The bed was far more comfortable than mine had ever been. Or maybe it was just the beautiful man sharing the sheets with me. I liked everything about the place, from the masculine furniture to the design of the bathroom. "I actually wanted to talk to you about him..." The scene I saw earlier that day had been eating me alive since I'd witnessed it. I wasn't angry at Bosco's reaction. In fact, I was incredibly touched...and that's what worried me.

"Was is it?" she asked, turning serious. "Everything alright?"

I told her the story, admitted I spied on his conversation because I'd run back to the penthouse to retrieve my keys.

"Wow," she said, her eyes wide with surprise. "First of all, who the hell is this Ruby skank?"

"No idea." I shook my head. "But yes, she's a fucking skank."

"And a snake."

"Yes." She wouldn't hear an argument from me.

"She showed off her tits and tried to get Bosco into bed?" she asked.

"Said she wanted to be his queen…basically said she wanted him to take care of her. What kind of woman just asks a man that?"

She looked away. "Well, if I said that to Bones, he'd be inside me so fast… That's like his dream. He would love it if I stayed home all day and spent his money. But at the same time, I know he loves me because I'm not like that, because I don't actually need his money."

"Thankfully, Bosco wasn't into it. And this woman was gorgeous. Like…supermodel status."

"It's pretty impressive he said no," Vanessa said. "Not all men would have the strength to resist something like that. Not just because this woman is attractive, but because she showed up to his house and basically begged him to take her. That's a fantasy for a lot of men."

"She had nice tits."

"I bet they were fake," Vanessa snapped. "Like the rest of her."

Fake or not fake, they were nice.

"It doesn't matter," Vanessa said. "He turned her down—because he's loyal to you."

That was the part that made me so confused. "I know…" I took a deep breath, feeling so much relief that I was terrified.

"If this is a good thing, why do you look so sad?" She crossed her arms over her chest, making her belly stick out even more.

There were no words to describe what I was feeling. "I

don't know…I can't explain it. I kept expecting him to grab her tits then take her clothes off, but he didn't seem remotely interested in her. Then he said I had class and she didn't. It was just…"

"Sweet?" Vanessa asked. "Romantic? Touching?"

"Yeah…I guess."

Vanessa's eyes softened as he stared at me. "Griffin used to be the kind of man that fucked anything that moved. When he met me, he stopped looking at other women. There's no doubt in my mind that he could be anywhere, at any time, and he would never mess around."

"Because he's in love with you, Vanessa."

"Exactly." She gave me a meaningful look.

I held her gaze, understanding her meaning perfectly.

"And the reason it means so much to you is because you feel the same way. You'd be devastated if he messed around. I warned you this would happen, that you would fall for the man who was supposed to mean nothing to you."

When the three months were over, I was leaving, no matter what. Regardless of how I felt, this had an expiration date. I knew what kind of future I wanted, and that would never be possible with Bosco. He was a man I would remember fondly, probably be the best sex I'd ever had, but that would be it. "Should I say something to him?"

"You would incriminate yourself in the process."

"True."

"And you would also have to talk about it…and that conversation would only go in one direction."

Bosco would tell me he didn't want that tramp. He

only wanted me. Other words would be exchanged, capitalizing on the feelings that were already in the room. "Yeah, I guess you're right."

"I wonder if he'll mention it to you."

"No idea." I had no clue if Bosco would be honest with me about Ruby. He might consider it to be none of my business. Or maybe he just didn't want to make me jealous. But knowing him, he would love the opportunity to make me admit I wanted him all to myself.

"Excited about the wedding?"

I was leaving for my parents' tomorrow after work. I'd be there all weekend, celebrating my brother's nuptials. There would be lots of drinking, laughing, and partying. But there would also be lots of sleeping alone.

I wasn't looking forward to that part.

"Yeah, I'm really excited," I said. "I've been so busy lately, I haven't spent much time with our family."

"Yes," she teased. "Very busy."

I rolled my eyes. "You'll keep my secret?" Being around all our family while they asked me a million questions would make it a little harder for her.

Vanessa gave me a fond look and shook her head. "You know I'll take your secret to the grave. But I hope when the truth comes out, you won't throw me under the bus."

"The truth isn't gonna come out."

"Ongoing secrets never stay hidden, Carmen. Especially with our family…"

"It's gonna end…in two months." A month of our relationship had already passed. It seemed to happen within the blink of an eye.

"You can say whatever you want to make yourself feel better," Vanessa said. "But I have a lot of experience in this area…and I know intense relationships like this never end. They simmer, burn, and then turn into an inferno. They may simmer once more, but the flames will never go out. They will keep going…even when there's nothing left to burn."

I CAME HOME A LITTLE LATER THAN USUAL, BUT BOSCO didn't seem surprised. His men probably told him exactly where I was when I didn't come home at my usual time. I stepped into the penthouse and saw him sitting on the couch. The smell of dinner was in the air, and it smelled surprisingly good for chicken or fish. He was on the couch, wearing his black sweatpants that hung dangerously low on his hips. He'd shaved this face after his workout, and his bare chest rippled with every breath he took.

He stared at me with that intense gaze that I could never get used to. It was dark, terrifying, and filled with so much desire, it suffocated my thoughts. To someone else, it might be impossible to figure out if he wanted to fuck me or kill me.

My purse hung on my shoulder, and my thick jacket was still wrapped around my body, hiding my curves from view. But he kept looking at me like I was buck naked and my wetness was dripping from between my legs. Ruby had put her tits on display, and he didn't tense this way for her.

Only for me.

He leaned forward with his elbows resting on his

thighs, his chiseled biceps looking thick and powerful. The cords were noticeable down his forearms, and his shiny watch was absent. His hair was slightly messy because I gathered he'd been fingering it for the last few hours. His blue eyes were beautiful, shining with unmistakable masculinity.

Time seemed to slow down, and the intense staring between us didn't fade away.

I remembered the cold way he got rid of Ruby, unaffected by her perky tits and her desperation. He could have fucked her any way he wanted, but instead, he burned the bridge and kicked her out of his penthouse. He only wanted me, didn't care about securing anything after I was gone.

I set my purse on the other couch and stripped off my jacket. It fell to the floor, and I kicked off my shoes next. I could feel the wetness in my panties, the tightness in my thighs. I'd never wanted him more than I wanted him right now. Honest, committed, and faithful, he had all the qualities a woman dreamed of.

And he had them for me.

I removed my jeans then pulled my panties down my legs.

He glanced down, seeing the pool of slickness my pussy had soaked into the fabric. I'd been wet all day, thinking about what kind of man was waiting for me at home. That hussy's tits weren't on my mind anymore— and I knew they'd never been on his mind in the first place.

I left my shirt on and straddled his waist, wanting that big cock inside me as soon as possible. I pushed his sweatpants down along with his boxers, revealing his enormous length. He was throbbing for me, bigger than he'd ever been for that skank. She couldn't even get him hard when she tried.

This man was all mine.

I kept my eyes on him as I slowly sank down his length, feeling him stretch me hard with his thick head. Once we moved past the initial notch, I slowly slid down his length until I was sitting on his balls.

He had the kind of hands built to touch a woman's body, and he gripped my cheeks with masculine force. He pressed his lips to the corner of my mouth and growled quietly, enjoying my overwhelming slickness. "You've been thinking about me all day, Beautiful."

I'd been thinking about him since the moment he blew Ruby off. All day at work, he was on my mind. I replayed the event in my head, remembering the pissed off look on Ruby's face when she was kicked out of his penthouse. "Yes…can you tell?" My fingers dug into his hair, and I looked into his eyes, seeing the most beautiful man in the world. Everything about him was perfect, from his chiseled jaw to his soft eyes. I loved the masculine lines of his face, the shadow across his jaw even though he'd just shaved that afternoon. Despite his criminal ways, I loved his integrity, his commitment to his promise.

"Fuck. Yes." He ground his hips against me slightly, feeling my wetness sheathe him all the way down to his balls. His fingers kneaded my ass as he breathed against my mouth. "You're the wettest you've ever been."

My arms hooked around his neck, and I kissed him, let him suck my bottom lip into his mouth. My hands shook as I held on to this man, feeling a burning chemistry like no other. There was more heat in his embrace than I'd felt with anyone else—by a landslide. I wondered if this was what Vanessa and Griffin felt, if this was the kind of passion people really shared. Did other people experience what Bosco and I had? Was it less? Was it more? I found it unlikely they experienced it at all.

I rose and fell on his lap, sliding his dick in and out of me at a quick speed. I wanted his length inside me, wanted as much as I could take. That stupid tramp was elsewhere, wishing she were the one sitting on his lap. But I was the one who was here. I was the only woman this man wanted.

He grabbed my hips and steadied me, his blue eyes burning into mine. "Slower." He guided my hips up and down, controlling the pace and setting it to a speed at a fraction of what it was before. His hands slid up my back until they spanned my rib cage. "Slow, Beautiful." He repeated the same words back to me, wanting that pleasurable pace I wanted the other night.

I slowed down, riding his length at such a reduced speed that it felt even better. Every movement was amplified, in addition to the sensation of my nipples dragging against his chest. My pussy grew wetter and tighter, clinging to his length like I'd never enjoyed it so much before.

"Slower." He looked me in the eye as he breathed into my face, looking like he was enjoying me even more than I was enjoying him. His thumbs spread across my belly, and he pressed into me as the desire coursed through his veins.

I ground against him, stimulating my clit with his hard

body. I finally fell into the rhythm he wanted, finally moved my body just the way he requested. I slowly rose to the top of his length then slid back down, smearing his cock with my slickness. We breathed deeply together, enjoying every single touch, kiss, and thrust.

He brushed his lips past mine like he was teasing me. Then he rubbed his nose against mine, his fingers clenching around my flesh. He gripped me tighter and tighter, only stopping when his force became too much. He pressed his forehead to mine and closed his eyes, his hands lifting me slightly to alleviate my exertion. He moaned quietly, his cock thickening inside me even more.

I stared at his lips as we moved together, our bodies so aligned, we seemed to be a single person. We lived and breathed for one another, yearned for one another. There didn't seem to be anyone else out there who mattered, not when we had each other. I always felt safe with him, knowing no one else had the power to even touch me. But I'd never felt safe from him—until now. This man would never hurt me. He would never lie to me.

And he would never break my heart.

———

WHEN I CAME HOME FROM WORK THE NEXT DAY, BOSCO was in a terrible mood. He glared at me the second I walked in the door, knowing I would grab my suitcase and then leave town to spend the weekend with my family.

He looked like he might destroy his own building.

I walked past him and entered the bedroom, doing the best I could to ignore his coldness. We'd extended our relationship for an extra three days to make up for my absence, but he was still angry about the whole thing.

I really wanted to spend time with my family since I hadn't seen them much lately, but I didn't want to leave him either. There was nothing better than sleeping in that comfortable bed with this man keeping me warm. It was hard to imagine going back to my old bed, which seemed like a cot in comparison. And there would be no sexy man waiting for me.

Bosco never mentioned his interaction with Ruby. When I came home yesterday, he behaved as if everything was normal. Maybe he forgot about her the second I walked through the door. She wasn't important enough to remember.

Or maybe he simply didn't think it was any of my business that some other woman wanted his balls.

I hated thinking about that whore.

I piled everything into my duffel bag, making sure my dress for tomorrow was on the hanger covered in plastic. My makeup, hair supplies, and sleeping clothes were packed. I wanted to bring one of Bosco's t-shirts, but my mother came into my room all the time, and she would immediately notice I was wearing a man's shirt.

His footsteps sounded behind me. Heavy and slow, they announced his ominous presence. He moved until he was directly behind me, his scent entering my nose.

I zipped up the duffel bag on the bed before I turned around to face him. He was in his sweatpants, barefoot and bare-chested. Whenever he was home, he never wore anything else. Sometimes he walked around in his boxers, showing off his muscular thighs and calves. His broad shoulders led to sexy arms, and his powerful chest led to a tight stomach that was so ripped it didn't seem like he had any fat. He was the product of a sad life, a life where there was no pizza and pasta.

He wasn't as angry as he was when I first walked in the door. Now his rage simmered, probably because he realized being pissed off wouldn't change anything. I would leave on bad terms, and that kind of departure wasn't good for either of us. He moved his hands into his pockets and sighed quietly, his nostrils flaring.

"It's really only two days if you think about it…" This man was so possessive that nothing I said would make him feel better, but I thought I would try.

"And two nights." His voice was ice-cold. "Just one night is too long."

"It'll be over before you know it."

He gave me another cold look with a hint of skepticism. "Maybe for you. I would just put my dick in my hand, but I don't think I can go back to that after having pussy like yours." The shadow across his jaw was getting thicker, highlighting the masculine curves of his face. Only a man bursting with this much testosterone could pull off a statement like that.

"How sweet," I said sarcastically. "I'll miss you too."

The corner of his mouth rose in a smile at my joke. "I really will miss you, Beautiful." His eyes turned serious again, and he pulled his hand out of his pocket to cup my face. His thumb brushed across my cheek before he gave me a soft kiss on the mouth.

"I know you will…"

His other arm hooked around my waist while his

fingers continued to glide through my hair. He didn't kiss me, just held me and caressed me at the foot of the bed. He touched me with a gentleness that didn't seem possible coming from a man like him. His affection was always territorial, but not always sexual. Sometimes, he was so delicate with me, handling me like a flower rather than a woman.

He tightened his grip around my waist and pulled me closer to him, squeezing me against his chest. He rested his chin on my head as his fingers continued to play with my hair, touching me like I was more than just a lover.

My cheek moved against his chest, and I closed my eyes, leaning on this powerful mountain. My arms circled his muscular waist, and I breathed against him, enjoying this wonderful feeling. I felt peace, like there was nothing in the world that could ever hurt me. He was as hard as concrete but comfortable like a pillow.

I squeezed him harder as the emotion overcame me. I truly didn't want to leave this man, not even to see my family. There had never been another man in my bed whom I felt this comfortable with. There was something about Bosco that made me happy, despite the fact that I disagreed with everything about his life. He was man enough for me. All the other men I dated were never this strong, this commanding. I hadn't realized how much I was attracted to power and authority until now.

I pulled away from his chest and looked him in the eye. "Make love to me before I go." I wasn't embarrassed by the request. I wanted to feel his come inside me as long as possible, to feel him deep inside me as I lay in bed that night.

He held my gaze as he listened to my request, not bothered by my choice of words. Without taking his eyes off mine, he pulled my sweater over my head. He didn't look at my tits as he unclasped my bra and let it fall to the floor. His blue eyes deepened as they looked into mine, becoming more intense with every passing second. His breathing stayed the same, but the tension between us stretched like a rope being pulled on by both ends. His hands worked my jeans next and got them loose, pushing them over my wide hips. He pulled my panties with them, getting them down my thighs.

I kicked them off the rest of the way and pushed his sweatpants and boxers down, revealing his impressive length. It stared right at me, moving against my belly. The tip was wet, already drooling at the sight of me. I kneeled down and pulled his clothes to his ankles, swiping my tongue across the head, collecting the juice before I stood up again.

Now his eyes looked even more fierce than before. His hand dug into my hair, and he guided me to the bed, laying me down at the foot. He grabbed the backs of my thighs and dragged me to the edge, my ass handing over the end of the mattress.

He planted his legs shoulder-width apart and pressed his head against my entrance. The only resistance was due to my tightness. He pushed through it with a gentle shove and then slowly dove in, sliding deep inside me until only his balls hung outside my body. His hands gripped my waist, his thumbs meeting in the middle while his fingers touched my back.

My hands gripped his forearms, feeling the tendons

and muscles shift under the skin. He could have taken Ruby like this, but he didn't want her. The only woman he wanted to fuck like this was me. His fidelity belonged to me exclusively.

He started to thrust inside me, moving nice and slow like I wanted.

I was going to be late for dinner, but I didn't care. I didn't care about anything right now, except this man who was moving so deliciously inside me. I breathed deeply as I felt him slide in and out, my body acclimating to his size like it'd never felt him before. He was a big man, and no matter how many times we fucked, my body would never mold to his magnitude. His length and girth were unnatural.

"Like this, Beautiful?" His pretty blue eyes were on mine, watching me with frightening intensity.

Everything was perfect, from the angle to the speed to his size. My nails clawed at his forearms, and I kept my legs wide open so he could continue to enjoy me so intimately. I held his gaze, thriving in the intimacy. "Yes…just like that."

His men placed my bag and dress in the back seat of the car. It'd been filled up with gas, and the oil had been changed too. Since his men couldn't drive me around for the weekend, Bosco wanted to make sure my car would get me there and back in one piece—even though my car was only a few years old.

He said goodbye to me at the curb, wearing jeans and

a t-shirt even though it was a cold evening. It'd been a clear day, so the temperature dropped an extra ten degrees when the sun set. He looked at me with both irritation and longing, like this goodbye was permanent instead of temporary. "Call me when you go to sleep." He cupped both of my cheeks and kissed me.

I kissed him back, not caring about the twelve security men who were gathered on the sidewalk. My hands felt his chest, and I noted the way his come felt inside me. He packed it deep and far, making sure it would last for at least a day. "I will."

He kissed the corner of my mouth before he dropped his hands. "My men will follow you until the halfway point. If they go any farther, it might tip off your family."

"You don't need to follow me that far in the first place."

He gave me the exact same expression. "Your safety is my responsibility, and I take that very seriously."

I'd never needed a man to keep me safe, but now that I was used to his power constantly surrounding me, I was practically addicted to it. I liked knowing I could do whatever I wanted, take a shortcut down an alleyway, and no one would ever place a hand on me. "I'll be alright, babe." The nickname flew out of my mouth once more. The last time it happened had been over a week ago. I thought I'd learned my lesson and kept my mouth shut, but apparently not.

His eyes turned darker than they'd ever been before. He suddenly moved into me again, his hand digging under the fall of my hair as he pressed his face close to mine. He spoke in a whisper so his men couldn't overhear us. "I like it when you call me that."

I wished I'd never called him that at all. It was a name people in love used. It was something exchanged between married couples, even regular couples. Now I'd said it too many times so I couldn't pretend it didn't happen.

He brushed his lips against my hairline before he kissed me on the forehead. "Have a good time. I'll be here when you get back." When he pulled away, he opened the driver's door so I could get inside.

With flushed cheeks and a racing heart, I got inside and fastened my safety belt.

He gave me one final look before he shut the door and walked away.

I didn't look at him again before I drove down the road and turned the corner. Without looking in my rearview mirror, I knew his men were hot on my tail, driving random vehicles so it wouldn't be so obvious I was being followed.

I didn't search for Bosco, not wanting to look at him again.

I kept my eyes on the road, disappointed in myself for becoming so deeply attached to this man. I melted like butter. I was at his mercy, completely and utterly. I wanted this man more than any other. I'd never been this attached to someone, this reliant on another human for my own happiness. I wasn't even a mile away yet, and I already missed him.

Fuck, I already missed him.

WE SAT TOGETHER AT THE DINNER TABLE ON MY
uncle's estate. Wine was poured, fresh bread was passed
around, and Lars made a feast that somehow topped the
last one. He even sat at the table with us and dined so he
could enjoy his evening with the rest of us.

It was obvious how happy my brother was. He smiled
a lot more than he did before. Normally, he was quiet,
saying very little unless he was trying to be a smartass. His
eyes were mainly on the woman at his side, the beautiful
brunette he'd fallen for. Luca was on his other side, fitting
in with the family like he'd always been there.

Vanessa gripped her stomach at the table and
suddenly took a deep breath.

Everyone turned silent as we snapped our heads in her
direction.

"*Tesoro*, everything alright?" her father asked, sitting
directly across from her with my aunt by his side.

Griffin had his eyes trained on Vanessa, his hand
moving on top of hers as they both felt her stomach.
"Baby, what's wrong?"

"Nothing," Vanessa said with a deep breath. "He's
kicking so hard right now." She placed his hand directly
against her stomach.

Griffin kept his eyes on her as he waited for the vibra-
tion inside her belly. His eyes narrowed slightly, a grin
forming on his lips. "He is."

"Must have liked his dinner," Vanessa said with a light
chuckle, her hand moving back to her stomach. "He does
that sometimes, just starts kicking hard for no apparent
reason. He particularly likes to do it when I'm sleeping…"

Griffin possessed the same glow as Vanessa, obviously

happy by the life growing inside her belly. He kept feeling her, his arm over the back of her chair. Like no one else was there, he concentrated on the life they made together. "He's gonna be strong."

"No surprise there," Vanessa said. "He's probably gonna be a hundred pounds when he comes out...if he looks anything like you."

Watching them together made me think of my own future. I imagined myself pregnant, my son or daughter growing inside me, healthy and happy. In the past, when I'd pictured the man who would touch my stomach like that, he'd never had a face. But now I imagined Bosco staring down at me, that sexy lopsided grin on his face.

God, this was bad.

"The doctor told you it was a boy?" Aunt Pearl asked.

"No," Vanessa said. "But trust me, it's a boy. A sweet little girl would never act like this. This is definitely Griffin's son, stubborn, restless, and too big for my little belly."

Griffin moved his hand to the back of her neck and gently massaged her. "You're sure you're alright?"

"Yeah, I'm fine," Vanessa said. "I don't think I'll be comfortable again until he's out of here. But then I'll be pregnant again...so I should just get used to this." She rubbed her belly before she took a bite out of her bread. "Sorry for interrupting everyone. Keep eating."

My mother turned to Mia and Carter. "When do you guys think you'll grow your family? No pressure," she said with a chuckle. "I'm not one of those crazy grandmas. I'm just curious."

"Let them enjoy being married for a while," Father said. "Carter, you don't have to answer that."

Carter didn't smile. His eyes flicked to Mia, who immediately frowned at the question.

I knew something was wrong, just gauging by their reactions. My brother never told me he wanted a family, but after seeing him with Luca, I assumed he wanted more children. I sipped my wine as I felt the tension settle across the table

"Well…" Carter looked at Mia, having a silent conversation with her that only they could understand.

Mia gave a subtle nod.

"You're sure?" Carter whispered.

"Yeah," Mia whispered.

My mother's face was instantly filled with regret, like she hated herself for asking a question that clearly caused both of them pain.

Carter cleared his throat. "It'll be very difficult for Mia to have more children. She…has some medical issues that we need to try to take care of."

My mother's eyes immediately filled with tears.

Father looked away, like he was angry with my mother for bringing it up the night before their wedding.

Carter continued. "She had her tubes tied…against her will."

My hand almost shattered my wineglass when I heard what he said. That monster who'd had Mia as a prisoner actually did that to her? Took away something he had no right to touch? Raping her and torturing her wasn't enough? He had to take it a step further? "Fucking piece of shit!"

Everyone turned at my outburst.

Carter remained calm. "But I'm confident Mia and I

will figure out a way to have more children. The procedure is reversible, with low odds of success. But there are other ways we can conceive, so not all hope is lost." He moved his hand to her shoulder and gave her a gentle squeeze. "And if that doesn't work out, I already have a son—so I'm happy."

My eyes watered at the sweet way my brother handled the situation, how he didn't make Mia feel inadequate for not being able to bear children naturally. He loved her anyway, didn't make her feel like she wasn't good enough. I already loved my brother, but now I respected him even more.

"Well said, baby." Mom placed her hand on Carter's and patted it.

"Yes," Father said. "Very true, son. We're blessed to have everything that we have, including Mia."

Mia's eyes watered next, touched by my family's unconditional love. I knew her son was the only relative she had in the world, and now that she was marrying Carter, she got all of us. She was getting everything she needed. "Thank you. You've all been so kind to me...I'm honored to become a Barsetti. You guys became family the second I met you. There are no words to describe my gratitude, for accepting Luca and me so openly."

"We love you," I whispered. "Both of you. And we're the ones who feel honored, Mia."

Carter's eyes moved to my face, and he gave me a look of affection I didn't receive often. He seemed annoyed with me most of the time, but now he was touched by what I said. I'd always gone out of my way to make Mia feel welcome, knowing that Carter loved her unconditionally. And if my brother loved her, then I loved her too. That loyalty obviously meant the world to him. He silently mouthed the words across the table. "Thank you."

I WASHED MY FACE AND BRUSHED MY TEETH BEFORE I went to bed. This nighttime routine usually happened with Bosco beside me, using the other sink as he snuck glances at me in the mirror.

Now I was doing it alone, my heart heavy. I wasn't sad Bosco wasn't there. I was sad Mia had been through something so horrible.

Unforgivable.

I walked back into the bedroom and pulled the sheets down on my childhood bed. The second I became an adult, I moved to Florence and worked as a waitress as I figured out how to open my shop. I saved money for a down payment, and then my father helped me with the rest. My store rent checks went straight to him since he owned the property. He didn't want to take my money at first, but when I reminded him I wanted to be treated the same way as Carter, he caved.

A knock sounded on my door.

"Come in." I knew it was Mom without even asking. She usually came into my room before bed, to stroke my hair and share a short conversation with me. I sat on the edge of the bed and watched my mother walk inside, wearing pajama bottoms and a t-shirt. Her makeup was gone, but she was still a beautiful woman. I was lucky to look a lot like her.

"I just wanted to see if you were alright." She took the seat beside me, her slender frame barely making the mattress dip. "I know that was hard to listen to…"

"No, I'm not alright," I snapped. "I can't believe that asshole did that to her."

"I know." She bowed her head and breathed a deep sigh.

"It's one thing to keep her as a prisoner for god knows how long, but then to do that? To take away a woman's happiness like that? That guy should we be dead. We should rip off his dick and feed it to a dog or something."

"I agree," she said. "But I think the best thing we can do is let it go. I know that's easier said than done, but if we don't move on, it'll keep haunting Mia. I say we forget about it and count our blessings."

"Yeah…" I still thought we should murder him.

"He'll get his in the end. They all do."

I just wished I could do the honors. "She's my sister…"

"I know." She patted my hand. "But with the medical advancements we have today, they should be able to make it work. I'm sure they'll have many beautiful and healthy children."

"Yeah, I hope so."

"We should admire Mia for everything she'd been through. She's struggled so much, but she's still got that fire. She's still strong. The worst thing we can do is look at her like she's a victim, not when she's a survivor."

I nodded in agreement. "You're right. It's just hard for me to let it go."

"I know…" She pulled her hand away. "This is a happy time for all of us. Let's not let that demon spoil it."

"Alright, Mama."

She cupped the back of my head and pressed a kiss to my forehead. "I'm so glad to have you here. I miss you."

"I miss you too."

"I feel like I haven't seen you much lately." She didn't give me a look of accusation, just sadness.

"I've just been busy with work."

"Yeah, I'm sure. I'll make more trips out there to see you. We can do some shopping for Luca."

My mother never passed up a chance to shop, and a new grandson was the perfect excuse. "Good idea."

"Love you, Carmen."

"Love you too." I watched my mom walk out and shut the door.

I got into bed and waited a few minutes before I grabbed my phone and texted Bosco. *I just got into bed.* I wasn't sure how much I wanted to talk right now, not after that family revelation. *But I'm going to sleep. I'm pretty tired.*

Instead of leaving me alone, Bosco video called me. I listened to it ring and almost didn't answer. I turned on my side and propped the phone against a pillow so it would stand up without my having to hold it. When I took the call, his face, shoulders, and chest were visible on the screen. He was sitting up in bed, shirtless and just as sexy as when I left him. "I told you to call me when you went to sleep." His aggressive nature was back in full force, enraged by my disobedience.

The sheets were pulled to my waist, and my hair was in a ponytail. My face was free of makeup, so I didn't look my best. I wasn't naked like he was, or better yet, wearing one of his shirts. "It's been a long day."

He studied me for a long time, reading the sadness in my gaze, even through a screen. "What's wrong, Beautiful?"

I wanted to brush it off and say it was nothing, but when I looked at those mesmerizing eyes, I didn't want to pretend I was okay. With him, I wanted to be completely real, not to hold anything back. He'd become my confidant, someone I could share all my secrets with. "My new sister-in-law can't have children. The reason why she can't is…she was taken as a prisoner by some psychopath. He raped and tortured her, and instead of using regular birth control, he decided to tie her tubes so she couldn't have kids."

Bosco kept the exact same expression, despite the terrible news I'd just relayed to him.

"It just…" I took a deep breath to still my rage. "It makes me so angry. It makes me so… There are no words. It just breaks my heart, and I'm having a hard time accepting it. My mother told me to let it go and count our blessings as a family…but it's hard. He should be killed for what did."

"Then why hasn't he been killed?" He hadn't blinked since I'd answered his call. He stared at me with the same intensity as he did when we were in the same room together.

"I guess he's really powerful. My family wants peace, not to fight another war…"

He took a deep breath, his eyes narrowing on my face. "What's his name?"

"I'm not sure."

"Then find out," he said harshly. "And let me know."

I stared at the anger in his eyes, seeing a look I'd come to recognize easily. "Why?"

"If my woman wants a man dead, I'll make it happen."

I stared at him blankly, terrified because I knew he was being completely honest. He never lied, not even about things like this.

"I'll bring his head to you—so you can give it to your sister-in-law. It'll give her closure."

I still couldn't believe what I was hearing. I knew he was the most powerful man in this country, so he could make it happen. He could kill this man with the snap of a finger. But it wasn't my decision to make. My family could have pursued him and burned him alive. They chose to walk away from the fight—and I would honor that. "My family just wants to let it go—"

"I don't care what they want. I care what you want. I don't want to see this sad look on your face ever again."

"It'll pass. I'm just a little shaken up right now…"

He stared at me for a long time, hardly blinking. His chest rose and fell slowly, his chiseled physique strong and tight even when he was most relaxed. He stared into my eyes like he was looking right at me instead of through a screen. "You look so beautiful right now."

His words were full of sincerity and hit me right in the heart. "My hair is pulled back. I'm not wearing any makeup, and I'm wearing a shirt that's way too big…"

"But you're so beautiful, you don't need those things. You're perfect the way you are."

This man was piercing my heart with his words, saying the most romantic things I'd ever heard. "You aren't entertaining yourself with other women until I get back, right?" I didn't know why I said that. I'd tried to deflect his intimate comment with something else.

He shook his head. "There's only one woman I want. I would much rather be alone than waste my time with a woman who will never compare to you." He ran his fingers through his hair as he stared at me, that same intense expression on his face. The only words that ever came out of his mouth were true, so he meant every single word.

But I already knew how committed he was—from experience. "I should go to bed…" I hated how comfortable this was, how we could just stare at each other and say nothing. I hated how much I enjoyed being wanted by this man, how he made me feel so beautiful, like I was the most desirable woman on the planet. He wasn't in the same room with me, but I could still feel his heat like he was right beside me.

"Can you feel me inside you?" he asked, his deep voice masculine and sexy.

I could still feel his weight deep within me, the seed he'd deposited earlier. "Yes…" I pressed my thighs together under the sheets, wishing they were hugging his waist right now.

"Goodnight, Beautiful."

"Good night, babe."

His eyes narrowed slightly, his expression intensifying at the nickname. He loved to hear that name on my lips, loved listening to me be possessive of him the way he was possessive of me. He stared at me for a moment longer before he hung up.

I COULDN'T SLEEP. I TOSSED AND TURNED ALL NIGHT, freezing cold because Bosco wasn't beside me with his searing heat. When a few hours passed, I knew it wasn't gonna happen. Just like when Bosco was at work and I was home alone, it was impossible for me to sleep without him. I usually lay on the couch and watched TV, hoping the mindless entertainment would lull me to sleep and I would know he was home the second he walked through the door.

I made my way downstairs and stepped into the kitchen. The refrigerator had an open bottle of wine, so I poured myself a glass. There were some cheese and grapes, so I stood at the counter and snacked, even though late-night eating would only hurt my waistline.

Footsteps sounded a moment later. "Couldn't sleep?" Mom came into the kitchen, looking wide awake.

Because I couldn't sleep without Bosco. "Too excited for tomorrow."

"Me too." She grabbed the bottle and poured herself a glass. "Your father is sleeping like a rock. Me…not so much."

"If you're so excited, then why do you look so sad?" I asked, popping a cube of cheese into my mouth.

She sighed before she spoke. "It's just crazy how quickly time passes. I remember the day Carter was born just like it was yesterday. He's grown into a remarkable young man, and I couldn't be prouder. It's just hard to let him go…"

I gave my mom a sad look. "You aren't letting him go, Mama. He's right down the street. They'll have more children, and you'll have grandchildren running around everywhere. It's exactly what you wanted."

"I know…I'm very lucky. I'm glad he found a strong woman like Mia. She's wonderful."

"Then we should celebrate." I clinked my glass against hers, trying to cheer her up. I knew this was hard for both my parents. They were happy, but also sad that Carter and I were getting older. In a few years, I would be married with a husband and kids too. Neither one of us would need them for anything. It was a change in roles, and soon we would be the ones taking care of them.

She gave me a smile. "Yes. We should." She grabbed a few pieces of cheese and some grapes. "So, what's new with you? How's the shop?"

"It's going well. It's been busy despite the winter season. Unfortunately, I've had a lot of funerals."

"It's the flu. It's terrible this year." She shook her head slightly. "I'm relieved your father works with grapes more than people."

"How's he like working with Griffin?"

"He's become fond of him," Mom said. "It took him a while to warm up to him, but he finally has. Says he's a good worker and he's good to Vanessa. Some beautiful young woman was setting up a distribution relationship with the winery, and she made a pass at Griffin. Apparently, Griffin lost his shit and said some pretty harsh things to her…so they lost the client."

"Really?" I asked. "Father and Uncle Crow were there and let it happen?"

"No. Your uncle called her company to follow up, and he heard the story through her."

"Man…Vanessa must have been pissed." She'd never mentioned the story to me.

"I don't think she knows," Mom said. "Your uncle never told Griffin he heard the story. Decided to let it go. He cares more about his son-in-law treating his daughter right than losing a client."

"Griffin adores Vanessa."

"He does," she said with a nod. "He's very loyal—which is why your father likes him."

Bosco was loyal too. He had a pair of beautiful tits in his face the other day, but he didn't take the bait. He threw her out just the way Griffin told that woman off. I was starting to see more similarities between the two men.

"Speaking of men… Are you seeing anyone?" My mom asked me the direct question because we talked about this stuff all the time. She'd always been open about it, talking to me like an adult. She had much more progressive views than my father and believed a woman could have the same kind of lifestyle as a man. My father knew Carter slept around for the last decade but never thought twice about it. He had very different expectations for me, so we never spoke about it.

"Not really." I felt bad lying to her, not telling her that I was in an extremely intense relationship with a man who was claiming my heart as well as my body. I used to be scared of him because of his power and his criminal life-style, but now I felt unsafe anytime I wasn't with him. My hands shook whenever I touched him, and his kisses always drove me wild. I'd never been with a man who could make me feel so good. I was starting to care less and less what he did for a living, starting to ignore the warning Griffin gave me. It seemed irrelevant when the man I knew was so loyal, honest, and kind. "I went on a few dates, but nothing stuck."

"Keep looking. The right man is out there...searching for you."

It was getting harder to believe that there was any man out there that I even wanted. I couldn't picture myself wanting someone more than Bosco. He was the manliest man I'd ever been with. "Yeah. I'm sure he is."

She finished her wine and left the empty glass in the sink. "I have to be up in two hours...hopefully I can get some sleep. We've got a long day tomorrow."

"I know..." I probably wouldn't sleep at all.

She came behind me and squeezed both of my arms as she kissed me on the cheek. "Love you, honey."

"Love you too."

I GOT READY THE NEXT MORNING, WEARING A LONG-sleeved dress with leggings underneath. The wedding was informal, a small celebration with just family and a few friends. There were no bridesmaids, just Carter and Mia and the priest who would marry them.

I went downstairs and made breakfast—French toast, bacon, and eggs. My mom had already left for Carter's place to help set up, and my father was upstairs getting ready. I made enough for both of us, even though he probably wouldn't eat anything.

"Hey, sweetheart." Father came into the kitchen wearing a suit and tie. He hardly wore anything besides jeans and t-shirts with the occasional black leather jacket. His eyes lit up when he looked at me, just like always. "Whatcha got there?"

"I made breakfast. Hope you're hungry." I set his plate on the counter so he could eat on the barstool.

"Wow. You're my guest, so I feel like I should make you something." He poured a mug of coffee and grabbed some silverware so he could eat.

"No, I don't mind." I made myself a plate and stood at the counter across from him. "You look good in a suit. Almost didn't recognize you."

He chuckled. "Your mother said the same thing. But it's only for the day. Tomorrow, I'll be back in my jeans. You look nice too. That should keep you warm during the ceremony."

"Yeah. I also have a pretty thick coat." I sipped my coffee and ate my breakfast, trying not to think about the man who was sitting at his dining table and thinking about me at that moment. My father would be disappointed if I chose to get involved with someone like Bosco. He said he wanted me to settle down with a nice guy…not a criminal mastermind.

"Good. I'm excited for your brother." He always inhaled his food because he ate a million miles a minute. He pushed his plate aside then fished out a small box from his pocket. "I got this for your brother." He opened the box and revealed a black watch. It was completely blacked out, sleek and polished. It reminded me of one of his fancy cars.

"Wow, that's nice."

"I had it engraved." He flipped it over to reveal the inscription in the metal.

To the Man I'm Most Proud of.

-Father-

"Aww, that's so sweet." I picked it up and examined it, touched that my father would be so thoughtful. He was usually erratic and rushed, rarely taking the time to slow down to have heart-to-heart conversations. "He'll love it."

"I think so too. I tried to think of something special, something he doesn't already have. So I thought he could always look at this when he's down or when he needs to remember who he is…especially if I'm not around anymore."

"Father, don't talk like that." Listening to Bosco mourn his mother made me terrified of losing my own parents. I wouldn't know what to do without them. I loved them so much.

"Sorry, sweetheart. Didn't mean to upset you." He put the watch back in the box and placed it in his pocket. He rose from the seat and reached inside his other pocket. "I know this is Carter's day, but when I saw this, I had to get it." He pulled out a small black box and opened the lid so I could see what was inside.

It was a diamond necklace, and the pendant was a rose. It was covered in diamonds, shining under the lights from the ceiling. Judging by the way it sparkled, I knew this was the real deal, something my father spent a lot of money on. The only real diamonds I ever wore were the ones Bosco gave to me. This necklace flashed just the way those did. "Father…"

"I thought of you the second I saw it. I had to get it." He pulled the necklace out of the box, unclasped the chain, and then placed it around my neck. He closed the clasp then turned me around so he could take a look. "What do you think?"

I touched the pendant with my fingertips. "I love it… it's beautiful. Thank you." I moved into his chest and hugged him.

He hugged me back and kissed my forehead. "I won't be the man who gets to buy you diamonds much longer. So I guess this is for me more than it is for you." He pulled away, affection in his eyes and a slight smile on his lips.

"That's not true. You can buy me diamonds whenever you want…not that I need them." I knew watching my brother get married was difficult for both of my parents, especially when I would follow soon afterward. It was only a matter of time. "And there will never be a man in my life who can replace you." I was lucky I grew up with two loving parents. There was never a time in my life when I had to worry if my parents really cared about me. Not everyone was so lucky—but I won the lottery.

"It's okay, sweetheart. That's how life is. You'll find a man who takes care of you, who respects and honors you, and I'll be happy to give you away. But for now, you're still my little girl—and I will treasure this time as long as I can."

EVEN THOUGH IT WAS IN THE MIDDLE OF WINTER, IT WAS a beautiful wedding. With white lilies on the grass and a great view of the Tuscan hillside, it was a special moment. It was cold, but it hadn't rained in weeks, so the soil was dry. It was just the family sitting in the chairs, and we waited together as Carter stood at the front. Luca was beside him, wearing a black suit.

He looked adorable.

Mom was already crying. Father had his arm wrapped around her as he rubbed her back.

I sat beside Vanessa, seeing her bundled up Griffin's coat because he made her wear it. It was zipped up in the front, keeping her pregnant belly warm. He had his strong arm wrapped around her, smothering her with his body heat.

It was hard not to think of Bosco.

It was a Saturday, so he was probably working tonight. I wondered if Ruby would be there. If she was, it didn't matter. Bosco didn't want her.

The harp began to play, and Mia made her way down the aisle. Though Carter had asked Conway to be his best man, Mia had made a different request. Conway escorted her, letting her rest her arm through his. They moved slowly to the music, and we all rose in our seats to see Mia float by like an angel.

In a long-sleeved white dress with her hair in curls, she

looked beautiful. She was smiling and crying at the same time, her eyes glued to Carter.

Carter didn't smile, but he gave her the same kind of intense expression that Bosco gave to me. He loved her completely and utterly—and it was written all over his face.

Conway let her go when they arrived, and he clapped his cousin on the shoulder before he took a seat with Sapphire and Reid.

Mia kneeled down to kiss Luca on the head. She gave him a big hug before she rose to her feet again.

Carter kneeled down and picked up Luca, holding him with one arm as he faced Mia. "Is it okay if I marry your mom, little man?"

Luca wrapped his arm around Carter's neck as he sat in the crook of his arm. "Yeah, Dad."

It must have been the first time he'd called Carter that, because Carter's eyes immediately softened in a way they never had before. There was a slight hint of moisture in his eyes as he kissed Luca on the head. "Thanks, son."

Mia was already crying—and they hadn't even started the ceremony.

———

My phone buzzed with emails for phone orders, so I took it out of my clutch and put it on silent before I set it on the table. There were tall heaters everywhere, keeping us warm as we sat at the tables and had dinner.

Mia and Carter danced on the back patio, swaying softly to the music for their first dance. It was just us and my maternal grandparents, who came from America to live here when my mother married my father. It was a small wedding—but it was perfect.

I sat with my mom and dad, watching them enjoy the sight of their grown son in love.

When the dance ended, they moved to their seats so they could enjoy their dinner.

"I'm going to the bathroom." I set my napkin on the table and walked away.

"Alright, honey." Mom helped pull out my chair so I could get up before she pushed it back in.

I walked into the house and down the hallway to the bathroom. The door was locked, so I stayed outside for a minute.

Vanessa came out, her hair curled and her black dress slimming despite her bump. "He makes me pee like crazy. I get up at least three times in the middle of the night."

"It'll all be worth it when he gets here." I patted her stomach gently. "How's the sex? Is he ruining that too?"

"No, as a matter of fact," she said with a smile. "Griffin actually likes it. We've had more sex now than we did before." She kept her voice down just in case there was someone in the house who could eavesdrop. "But he's also more protective, and that gets annoying."

"You have a bodyguard at work. How much more protective could he get?"

She rolled her eyes. "You'd be surprised." She walked down the hall and back onto the patio.

I used the bathroom then walked outside again. I sat in my chair and immediately noticed the way my mother looked at me. A slight smile was on her lips, and she gave me that knowing expression. It reminded me of when I was young and I tried to sneak things behind her back. She somehow always figured it out, despite how clever I thought I was.

After she held my gaze, she turned away and talked to my father, saying the wine was delicious and it was a beautiful evening.

I had no idea what that was about. That was when I spotted my phone on the table where I'd left it. What if Bosco called and she saw his name on the screen? Maybe that was what made her smile at me. Just because a man's name appeared on my screen didn't mean I was sleeping with him. He could be a client.

I tapped my finger against the screen, seeing the emails and the message that popped up.

Bosco had texted me. *Beautiful, I miss you like crazy. I'm losing my fucking mind, and I don't like it. When your ass is back here, I'm not letting you leave again. You're mine—and I don't like to share.*

My cheeks turned pale as snow, and my heart raced in my chest. I quickly locked the screen and tried to seem indifferent, like that message meant nothing to me. My ears felt hot, and my pulse was pounding in my head.

Shit. She saw it.

―――――――――

It was nearly two in the morning when everyone finally left. Luca was staying with my parents so Mia and Carter could have some alone time at the house. I caught up with Vanessa and Griffin as they headed to their truck. "Hey, can I borrow Vanessa for a second?"

Griffin started the truck and then got out. "Talk in here. I don't want her standing outside."

Being in the truck was more private anyway, so we both hopped inside. I shut the door behind him and immediately told her what happened. "Bosco texted me, and I'm pretty much certain my mom saw it when I went to the bathroom."

Vanessa's eyes widened in shock. "Shit. Are you sure?"

"She had this look on her face… I'm pretty sure she read it."

"Girl, what did I tell you? Secrets never stay secret."

"Well, I expected my secret to last a little longer than this."

"Wait…" Her eyes filled with dread. "Is his name stored as Bosco in your phone?"

"Yeah."

She sucked in a breath through her teeth. "You're even more screwed now."

I didn't even think of that. "Ugh, why is this happening right now?"

"She probably doesn't even know who Bosco is, though," Vanessa reasoned. "But if she tells your father, he probably knows who he is."

"It could still be another Bosco," I countered.

"How many Boscos are out there?" she asked incredulously. "Not many. Do you think she'll tell your father?"

My mom and I talked about my love life all the time. I even told her when I slept with someone. She never judged me for anything or criticized my actions. But she also kept our conversations private from my father, since he would go ballistic. "No. She probably wouldn't say anything."

She breathed a sigh of relief. "Then you're safe. If it stays between the two of you, then you're good."

"Yeah…"

She glanced at the window and looked at Griffin, who was leaning against the back of the truck with his arms crossed over his chest. "We should get going. Griffin is getting impatient. I can tell by the way his jaw is tightening."

"Yeah, I should go anyway. Thanks for talking to me."

"Of course. I just hope this doesn't escalate."

I hopped out of the truck and walked to my father's car. My mom had just put Luca in the back seat, and they were preparing to leave. Since I'd come with them, I got into the back with Luca.

Luca had his bag of clothes and toys, but he was already asleep against the door, exhausted since he was up far past his bedtime.

Mom stared at him from the front seat, a soft smile on her lips. "He's so adorable."

"Yeah." Father backed up then pulled onto the road. "He's a sweet kid. A lot sweeter than Carter was."

Mom chuckled then faced forward again. "What did Carter think of the watch?"

Father was quiet for a long time as he headed back to the house, the silence surrounding all of us. "It meant a lot to him…" His voice caught slightly, and he took a deep breath to cover his emotion. "*Bellissima*, thank you for giving me my children." He grabbed her hand as he kept driving. "It's the greatest gift anyone has ever given me."

AFTER MOM PUT LUCA TO BED, SHE CAME INTO MY bedroom.

I knew she would come. I also knew she would wait until my father was asleep so he wouldn't overhear our conversation.

I didn't sleep last night and I was exhausted, but I knew tonight would be another repeat. It didn't matter how tired I was; I couldn't sleep unless Bosco was beside me. It was a terrible habit I'd developed, and I couldn't break it.

Mom knocked before she came inside.

I was ready for bed, my face washed and my teeth brushed. I kept my hair down because it was too curly for a ponytail.

She sat beside me on the bed and didn't look at me. She looked at the floor, which was unusual for her. She usually looked me right in the eye.

Now I knew she definitely knew. "I'm sorry I lied before. I just... I'm not ready to talk about it."

She sighed quietly before she looked at me. "Carmen, you're a grown woman who doesn't have to talk to me about anything. Your personal life is none of my business. I've always respected you in that way, since the day you become an adult."

Ugh, the guilt trip. "I know..."

"I don't want you to feel like you have to lie to me. I

always worked hard to establish a trusting relationship with you. I've never told you what to do."

"I know that too, and you have made a good relationship between us. It's not you."

"Then why did you lie? You've told me you've been casual with men before, and it wasn't going anywhere. It just makes me worried that this is a different kind of relationship, the kind you can't get out of. You understand what I mean?"

She hit the nail right on the head.

"Because it's unlike you to lie. You never do that, Carmen. I'm just worried."

"You're right," I whispered. "It is a different kind of relationship, but not in a bad way. He's a good man. He's kind, devoted, honest, and not to mention, hot as hell."

Mom chuckled. "Okay, I feel better already. Then what is the drawback?"

"It's supposed to be a short-term thing. It's never gonna go anywhere."

"Because he doesn't want it to?" she asked.

"No…I don't want it to. I told him we have an expiration date. When that time comes, I'll walk away. He's the one who doesn't want me to leave. If he had his way…I would probably never leave."

"Sounds like he cares about you."

He's just obsessed with me.

"Why does this relationship have no future?" she asked.

"He's just…not the right guy for me. He's not what I want in a husband. I want a husband who will be a family man. I want a simple life in the countryside. This man…is way too devoted to his career. He cares more about money and power...stuff like that." I wasn't lying, but I was definitely on the edge. "But our relationship is very intense. There's this chemistry and this feeling..." I placed my hand over my heart. "I can't explain it."

A soft smile crept across her lips. "Love."

"What?" I asked, turning to her.

"That feeling you're describing"—she pointed at my hand—"is love."

I couldn't accept that fate. It was something I refused to do, something I had promised myself would never happen. Bosco was the wrong man for me. He was a demon of the underworld, and I was a flower in the sun. "No..."

She dropped her hand. "I know it's scary, Carmen. You never planned for this to happen, but it did anyway. He's not what you envisioned as the perfect husband, but having the perfect husband is overrated. True love is about loving someone because of their flaws, not despite them. You accept him for who he is, all the good and the bad. The things you don't like about him will change in time. They always do. Your father isn't the same man he was when we met. He wasn't the same man when we got married. He wasn't the same man when we had Carter. Men change...when they meet the right woman."

She didn't understand. "I just don't think Father would like him..."

She shrugged slightly. "Your father trusts your instincts. If you brought a man home, he would give him a chance. He knows you aren't going to introduce someone to him unless you're going to marry him. And if you love this man, your father is going to love him too. Trust me on that." She grabbed my wrist and gave it a gentle squeeze. "He has a hard time with you dating just because you're his little girl. But if you finally settled down with a good man, he would be very happy."

"Uncle Crow seemed to have a hard time with it…"

She chuckled. "Well, Vanessa picked the worst possible guy—at the time. That's not gonna happen for you, honey."

Little did she know that I was sleeping with the most powerful criminal in Florence. If I told her, she might have a heart attack.

She watched my expression for a while. "Do whatever you think is best, Carmen. But if this is the man you want, don't be afraid to fight for him. Don't be afraid to bring him home—even if he's not perfect. You don't want a perfect man anyway."

"Father is perfect. Uncle Crow is perfect."

She scoffed like that was a joke. "He's perfect now, sure. But he wasn't perfect in the beginning. Molding him and watching him grow into the man he is today…is such a wonderful feeling. I wouldn't change it for anything. Growing together as a couple is one of the best things about marriage." She rose from the bed and gave me a soft smile. "Good night, honey."

"Good night, Mama. Can I ask you for something?"

"Sure." She turned around at the door.

"Could we keep this between us?"

Her smile fell. "Honey, I'll always keep everything between us." She walked out and shut the door behind her.

I sat there for a while, relieved my secret was buried for the time being. I got into bed, my body stiff and tired from not sleeping, but my eyes were wide open because I couldn't sleep. I was supposed to call Bosco before bed, so I did it now. I pressed the phone to my ear and listened to it ring.

He answered almost immediately, the sound of the casino around him. "Hey, Beautiful."

"Is this a bad time?"

"It's never a bad time." The noise died away, and he was suddenly surrounded by silence. "I hadn't heard from you, so I started to worry."

"I was just busy…weddings are crazy."

"Barsettis know how to party. It's almost three."

"Yes, we know how to drink too."

He chuckled. "I like that. I like that you drink a lot but barely get drunk. Classy."

There was that word again. Classy. That was how he described me to Ruby. That word meant more to me than he realized. It reminded me of his loyalty, of his devotion to only me. "I guess I've built up a high tolerance."

"What time will you be home tomorrow?" He said the word home, like that penthouse belonged to both of us.

I considered telling him about my mother, but I feared that might upset him. I warned him not to threaten my family again, and if I had to listen to it one more time, I'd slap him so hard his cheek would be red for a week. "Around one."

He growled, like that was too late. "I want you here in the morning."

"I'm having brunch with my family."

He growled again. "You've been there all weekend. What more do you guys possibly have to talk about?"

"Wine," I joked. "We can always talk about wine."

He sighed into the phone. "I miss you. I hate that I miss you so much."

I hated myself for the exact same thing. "I know…"

He was quiet, just listening to me breathe. "You must be tired, Beautiful. I'll let you go to sleep."

Against my better judgment, I blurted out something I'd been keeping from him. It was supposed to stay a secret. I even tried to keep it a secret from myself. "I can't sleep without you…" I closed my eyes as the waves of humiliation rolled over me. I'd become so sickeningly dependent on this man. I needed him for safety, for rest, for pleasure—for everything. I kept telling myself he was just some guy I was sleeping with, but that was a lie I couldn't tell anymore.

He was quiet, absorbing my words like a sponge.

"I'm exhausted, but I won't be able to sleep tonight…"

"That's why you always lie on the couch…" He said the words to himself more than he said them to me.

"Yeah. Because I wait for you to come home."

"Beautiful…" He didn't say anything else, like there were no words to describe his thoughts.

I was embarrassed that my heart was beating on my sleeve. I used to be so cold to him, but now I couldn't keep up my poker face any longer. Now, I was just blurting things out and acting like an idiot.

He finally said something. "Now I miss you even more."

6

BOSCO

My MEN STARTED to follow her once again when she entered the city district. They kept their distance until she was far away from her family's property. The Barsettis might be living in peace and quiet, but that didn't mean they were ignorant of their surroundings. If twelve men were following a member of their family, they would notice.

My body finally relaxed once she was under my jurisdiction again. Even though there was no one in the universe who wanted to hurt Carmen, I liked knowing she was protected at all times. Since she was my woman, she was the queen of my life. She deserved to have everything a queen possessed, including my obsession, my money, and my private guard.

Now I just had to wait for her to come home.

Fifteen minutes later, my men notified me of her arrival. Her belongings were placed in the elevator with

her, and she rose to my floor. The doors gave a slight beep
when they opened, and there she was.

Beautiful.

A soft smile spread across her lips when she looked at
me, like it'd been years since we last saw each other, not
days. She grabbed her bag from the floor and carried it
inside, her pretty eyes still trained on me. She was in
skintight jeans and a dark blue sweater. Brown boots were
on her feet. Other than her beauty, the thing I noticed
most was the diamond necklace around her throat. Flawless and vibrant, those diamonds were of the highest qual-
ity. She didn't have that when she left, and I certainly
didn't give it to her. The pendant was in the shape of a
rose, which was fitting for someone as soft as a rose petal.

She unzipped her brown boots and left them on the
floor before she finally moved into me. She wrapped her
arms around my neck and then jumped up, knowing I
would catch her. Her ankles wrapped around my waist,
and she secured herself in place so she could be eye level
with me.

Both of her eyes were puffy and red, her exhaustion
bluntly obvious. She didn't sleep at all while she was gone,
her confession about her dependency entirely true. She
stared into my face fearlessly, not showing a hint of the
embarrassment she probably felt when she originally told
me her secret.

I remembered coming home from work and seeing
this beautiful woman on the couch, the TV still on and
her mind only lightly asleep. The second she heard me,
she jumped up and went to bed with me. Like a pet
waiting for its owner, she camped by the elevator and

waited for the gentle beep to tell her I was home. Unless I was by her side, she couldn't truly rest. It was ironic, considering she used to kick me out the second I fulfilled my purpose. She wouldn't even let me get comfortable because she wanted me gone right away. But now, this woman needed me, and watching her need me was the sexiest thing I'd ever seen.

She pressed her face against mine as she sat in my arms, her fingers lightly touching my hair.

This was something we did often, pressed our foreheads together and felt the intimate connection between us. It was stronger than a kiss, more powerful than making love. It was something I'd never done with a woman, let time slow down so much just to feel her. I'd never been a big talker, and I didn't have to make conversation with her. We could communicate with our silence, with this scorching chemistry that lingered in the air the second we were in the same room.

I walked out of the living room and left everything else behind. She was light in my arms, feeling like a bag full of rose petals. My hands gripped her luscious ass, and my bare feet tapped against the hardwood floor as I carried her into the bedroom I shared with her every night. I laid her on the bed and fell with her, my cock hard in my sweatpants the second I was told she was on my property.

She arched her back and pulled her sweater over her head, revealing her black bra that contrasted against her fair skin. She arched her back again to unclasp the back before she settled into the mattress once more, her perfect tits staring right at me.

This woman had the nicest rack I'd ever seen.

I pulled her tight jeans off her body, left her socks on, and then moved for the royal blue thong on her hips. I dragged it down, staring between her legs at the slit my hand could never recreate. The idea of finding new pussy to satisfy me while she was gone was laughable. There was no other woman who compared to this goddess. They all looked like hags, even Ruby, who was considered to be one of the most beautiful women in my circle. I left Carmen's necklace on, slightly distracted by the way it reflected the light from the ceiling. I wanted to know where she got it, but my cock was more interested in being reunited with its home. I pushed my sweatpants and boxers down to my knees then lowered myself between her legs. I didn't kick off the clothes entirely because I was too anxious to be inside this woman.

Her head rested on my pillow, and her curls spread out everywhere. Her green eyes were on fire, her full lips pursed and ready for my kiss. Her nipples hardened once my warm body covered hers. She bit her bottom lip in the sexiest way, preparing for the cock she'd missed so much.

My powerful arms locked behind her knees, and I settled on top of her, the head of my cock finding her opening from memory. I gently pushed inside her, breaking through her initial tightness, and then I slowly sank into her wetness until my balls gave a gentle tap against her ass.

The pleasure was so overwhelming that I closed my eyes for a brief moment, treasuring just how well her pussy fit me like a glove. It was like her slit was made for my cock, the perfect place for my dick to settle down.

She was breathing hard for me, her sexy nipples sharp.

One hand cupped the back of my head, while the other gripped my biceps. She was already on the verge of climaxing, judging by the redness in her cheeks and fireworks in her eyes. "Mmm…" Just that single sound drove me wild. So subtle and so sexy.

Jesus.

My hips started to thrust, moving at a slow speed I never used with other women. It was gentle, even delicate. I took my time as I reveled in her completely before I pulled out. I felt her again, taking the time to memorize the way her slickness coated me. I was drooling from the tip, in a place I could only describe as heaven.

She brought my face to hers and kissed me, kissed me so gently that her lips started to tremble. She kept her body still, letting me sink into her over and over again. Only her lips and fingers moved, as if too much stimulation would make her explode. "Babe, I missed you…" She kissed me harder, giving me her sexy tongue.

My cock twitched inside her, so turned on by the words she said. It wasn't dirty talk the way I usually liked. This was much deeper, confessional. Hearing her call me a possessive name and admit she missed me was the sexiest thing I'd ever heard. It was much better than anything else I'd ever heard from a woman.

She kept kissing me. "I can tell you missed me too…" She squeezed my hips with her thighs.

We were moving so slowly together, but it somehow created the best sensation between our bodies. Just being inside her was all the stimulation I needed. If this were some other woman, I would say she was boring in the sack, and I would just finish. But Carmen could lie there and do absolutely nothing, and it was still the best sex I'd ever had. "You don't even know, Beautiful."

She kept kissing me while she felt my big dick stretch her deep and wide. She kept getting wetter, wetter than she'd ever been before. There was so much slickness that my dick could barely handle it. "I'm gonna come, babe." She stopped our kiss long enough to tell me something I already knew. She looked me in the eye, her green eyes fearless.

I stopped kissing her so I could hold her gaze, witness the beautiful performance she was about to put on for me. I didn't use to care that much about watching a woman come. I didn't get off on it like most men did. But watching her enjoy me, crumble around my dick, was my favorite part of the ride. No other man had pleased her the way I had. No other man made her fall apart so beautifully. I was immensely proud of my performance, wanting this woman to get as much pleasure as she gave me.

She held my gaze as she came, sometimes biting her bottom lip and sometimes cutting her nails into my biceps. Her body shivered slightly, and her thighs squeezed me tightly. Her hips slightly bucked involuntarily, and her beautiful moans filled my bedroom and were absorbed into the walls. "God…yes." She dug her heels into my ass, keeping me pressed against her until she was completely done.

I wasn't going anywhere.

When she finished, she closed her eyes and ran her fingers through her hair. She was coated in light beads of sweat even though she was lying there taking my big dick.

She looked so perfect, fucked to satisfaction. "Your turn." She gripped my ass with her hand and pulled me into her harder.

"No." I wanted to keep pleasing her, remind her what she'd been missing while she was gone.

She pouted her lips. "I miss your come…"

Jesus Christ. A bolt of lightning struck my spine, and my cock immediately thickened at her admission. I'd never given my come to a woman before, and now it was all I ever wanted to do. I didn't just want to come so I could climax. I wanted to put my seed inside her, to know I was still within her pussy even when my dick was gone.

"Please…"

Fuck. Now she was begging for it. "Yes, Beautiful." I widened her legs so I had plenty of room to obey her orders. My cock moved through her slickness over and over, and I only needed a few more pumps until I hit the edge. I sheathed myself to the base and came inside her with a loud grunt, my hips bucking slightly as I pumped everything inside her.

"Yes…yes." She dragged her nails down my back, making my orgasm more intense from the bite of her nails. "So good."

I throbbed inside her until I finished, my seed completely pumped into her. I stayed in there for an extra moment, letting myself soften before I pulled out of her. I wanted to make sure I didn't spill a single drop. I wanted it to sit inside her as long as possible, to keep her warm and full.

I lay beside her and watched her close her eyes. She

didn't even move, still on her back. She rested her hand on her belly and the other on the sheets beside her.

We hadn't said more than a few words to each other, but it was obvious she was already knocked out. Now that she was satisfied and beside me, her exhaustion took over and she drifted off instantly. Her breathing changed until it was deep and even, and she parted her lips as she began to breathe through her mouth.

I watched her for a long time, finding her even more beautiful when she was asleep than when she was awake. She told me she needed me beside her to sleep, so I didn't move. I opened my nightstand and grabbed the book I'd been reading and got comfortable.

She suddenly turned on her side and cuddled with me, her legs tucked between my knees and her arm across my stomach. She sighed happily, still asleep.

My fingers ran through her hair as I read my book. Her smell surrounded me, and her diamond necklace pressed against my skin. Instead of reading the words on the page, I stared down at her, seeing the tranquil expression on her face. The book wasn't nearly as interesting as this woman, so I set it aside and stared at her instead.

And waited for her to wake up.

A FEW HOURS LATER, SHE WOKE UP PRESSED INTO MY side. She gave me a squeeze, her hands checking to make sure I was real. She gave a happy sigh before her eyes opened. Her lips kissed my chest before she lifted her gaze to look at me, her eyes less puffy now that she'd gotten some sleep. "You watched me this whole time?"

My fingers kept caressing her hair. "Yes."

"You didn't get bored?"

I'd never been more entertained. "No."

She gave a slight smile before she sat up and looked at the time. "I should stay awake until bedtime. Otherwise, my sleeping pattern will be totally off." She wiped the sleep from her eyes before she lay down again, as if her will to get up had evaporated.

I turned on my side so I could get closer to her. I pulled her into my chest and placed her leg over my hip. Our faces were close together, our eyes at the same level. She smelled like a mixture of her perfume and my cologne, and that was the perfect scent for a woman who belonged to me. "You were out right away."

"Well, I haven't slept in two days."

"And what did you do all night?" Imagining Carmen touching herself while thinking about me was innately arousing.

"I drank wine and ate cheese. Probably gained a few pounds because of it."

It wasn't the sexy answer I was looking for, but it made me smile. "Sounds like you had a good time."

"I did. It was nice to spend time with my family. It's rare for all of us to be together at one time. There's just so many of us now…" She stroked her fingers down my chiseled arm, feeling my biceps and triceps.

"The wedding was nice?"

"It was perfect. My brother is really happy. She's turned him into a better man."

A good woman would do that.

"And my parents are happy...but also sad. Things are changing, and watching their son get married and start his own family was a little heartbreaking. But they live right down the road, so I'm sure they'll still see him all the time."

Most of the Barsettis lived close to one another. Carmen was the only exception. It was impressive that all of them gathered that close to each other. Most family members needed a lot more space to stay sane. "I'm glad you had a good time since you won't be seeing them again for a long time."

Her eyes smiled because she knew what I meant by that. "I'm not in any hurry to leave, so don't worry."

Like I would ever let her go. Perhaps she thought I was joking, but I was being dead serious. Two and a half days was too long. I couldn't spare any more time apart. She could have lunch or dinner with them, but that was it.

My eyes glanced down to the flawless diamond around her neck. "Who gave that to you?" I tried not to get jealous, to imagine some family friend working for her affection. He could be in the wine business, some wealthy restaurant owner her father adored. He got to stare at her throughout the entire wedding and show off his wealth by giving her a beautiful and thoughtful piece of jewelry. Since my men couldn't watch her, I had no idea who was there. Carmen probably looked gorgeous in a gown with her hair done. I was sure she outshone the bride with no contest.

Her fingers gently touched the rose pendant. "My father."

All the jealousy evaporated from my blood, the relief taking over. I tried to hide the look on my face as best as I could, but I knew Carmen could read me pretty well.

"He said he won't be the man who can give me diamonds much longer...so he gave this to me before the wedding. I love it." She kept fingering it for a moment before she let it go. "My father isn't the most thoughtful man, so when he does do things like this, it's very sweet."

I was no longer jealous, but the reminder of her close relationship with her family bummed me out. She was loyal to them, and they were loyal to her. Her family would never approve of me—because they weren't stupid. I would never be good enough for Carmen Barsetti—and I knew it. "It's beautiful. Beautiful like you." My fingers moved through her hair, and I focused on her eyes, forgetting the necklace that reminded me Carmen would never truly be mine.

Her hands moved into my hair, and she kissed me, kissed me like there wasn't a load of come sitting inside her at that moment. She pressed her sexy body against mine, her nipples dragging against my hard body and bringing my cock to life. "I want more of you..."

NOW THAT CARMEN WAS BACK IN MY BED, I WAS ABLE to focus on other aspects of my life. I had a business to run, and that was impossible to do if I was thinking about pussy nonstop. I didn't have as much sex when I was single as I did with Carmen, but ironically, I craved sex even more. It didn't matter how satisfied I was—it was never enough.

While Carmen was at work, Ronan came by my penthouse. He was dressed in jeans and a t-shirt, an outfit I hardly saw him wear. The only time I saw him was at work, and he was usually in a suit like I was.

He stepped off the elevator and scanned the room. "Is your toy here?"

"She's at work." I walked up to him and embraced him with a gentle pat on the shoulder. I was working on my relationship with my brother, trying to be more than just coworkers. I couldn't remember a time when we hugged, but it seemed too soon for that. A pat on the shoulder was more contact than we'd had in years.

He mirrored the affection and did the same to me, a smile in his eyes. "Where does she work?"

"She owns a flower shop."

"Really?" he asked, grinning. "That's cute." He moved to a seat on the couch and got comfortable on the leather cushion. "Suits her well."

"It does."

"And that's pretty impressive that she owns her own business. I could tell the woman was smart, but she continues to impress me." He looked around the room, as if he was searching for something. "You got a cigar?"

"No smoking in the penthouse."

"Really?" he asked, cringing. "That sucks."

"Smoke when you leave." I didn't even have cigars because I quit a few weeks ago. After Carmen asked me to, I listened. Hearing her admit she cared about me was more than enough motivation to keep me smoke-free. "So, what brings you here?"

"They've decided to hold a high-stakes game tonight. Five players. We've got four seats filled, but they're holding the last one for you. Do you want in? Or are you going to pass?"

"What's the buy-in?"

"Twenty-five million."

I loved high-stakes poker games. They didn't happen often, at least not at my level. Men liked to play for a few million, not tens of millions. It was too enticing to pass up. I'd always been a gambling man, and I would never change my ways. Thankfully, I made so much money that my losses weren't devastating—not that I lost often. "I'm in."

He grinned. "I knew you wouldn't say no."

I had to work tonight anyway. I didn't want to stand aside and watch the others have a good time. I loved the tension, the suffocating intensity. We were constantly trying to decipher each other's moves while we were at the mercy of the random stack of cards. There was no fore-telling what might happen.

"Bringing your lady?"

I'd already brought her once, and she wasn't a huge fan of the casino. But I loved having her on my arm, loved making every man in that building hate me even more than they already did. We had incredible sex on the leather couch in my office then slept there until morning. Besides, she wouldn't be sleeping the entire time I was gone, so she might as well come with me. "Yes."

"Great. I like you better when you're with her."

"Didn't realize my company was so unbearable," I said sarcastically.

"Think about it." Ronan leaned back against the couch, getting comfortable even though he'd only been there a handful of times. "This is the first time we've connected in five years—and you happen to be seeing her."

"Our relationship has nothing to do with Carmen. I care about you whether or not she's in the picture."

"Yeah, but she softens you a bit. She makes you better."

I couldn't deny that part. I'd never felt an ounce of any kind of emotion until she came into the picture. I never talked about my mom with anyone, but I opened up to her so easily. I admitted things I'd been too ashamed to say out loud.

Ronan didn't press me for an agreement, knowing exactly what my silence meant. "So are you gonna make me lunch or what?"

I rolled my eyes and stood up. "How's salmon?"

"As long as it's food, I'll eat it."

When Carmen came home, the first thing we did was hit the bedroom. I took her from behind, holding on to her hips as I thrust into her so hard she screamed. I grabbed her by the back of the neck and pressed her into the sheets, her ass high in the air and her back curved at the sexiest angle. I liked fucking her slow and easy, but I also liked fucking her like this—like I owned her.

We had dinner afterward then watched TV on the couch. She was in my t-shirt with the remote in her hand.

I was reading a book.

"I didn't know you liked to read."

I shut the book and set it on the table, knowing I had to get ready for work. "It's a hobby I picked up late in life."

"Pretty sexy."

I turned to her, the corner of my mouth raised in a smile. "Really?"

"Definitely. But then again, I think you look sexy no matter what you do."

Good answer.

She smiled at me as she leaned against the couch, her eyes lit up and the most beautiful green color.

I rose to my feet and stretched my arms.

Her smile immediately dropped. "You're going to work, aren't you?"

"Yes." She dreaded these nights because it affected her sleep. She wasn't afraid that something would happen to me and I wouldn't come home. She just hated not having me in her bed. "But I want you to come with me."

"Tonight?" she asked incredulously.

"Yes. I'm playing in a high-stakes game tonight."

"What does that mean?" She looked so sexy in my shirt that I wished she could wear that to the casino tonight.

"The buy-in is twenty-five million."

Her jaw instantly fell open. "Jesus Christ, that's insane."

That was nothing to a man like me. "I want you at my side."

"Won't I distract you?"

"Not at all." Feeling her hands on me calmed me, made me feel more alive. Her affection would only heighten my senses—and inflate my ego. Increased confidence led to better decisions. Better decisions led to better wins. "Come on."

"I feel like I don't have a choice in the matter."

The context of our relationship hadn't changed. She was mine for three months. She did what I asked— because she had to. I didn't say that to her, letting my intense stare do it for me. "You won't be sleeping while I'm gone, so you might as well." She would lie on this couch with a blanket draped over her legs, listening for the sound of the elevator.

She couldn't deny my reasoning. "I guess you're right…"

MY ARM HUGGED HER WAIST AS WE WALKED THROUGH the casino together. She was in a short dress with a slit up the side. There was a cut in the fabric over her hip, showing her gorgeous bare skin. She wore the diamond necklace her father gave her, but the rest of her diamonds were from me. Her hair was curled and pinned to one side, showing her slender neck and the earrings that hung from her lobe.

She was stunning.

Smoke filled the room, and the sound of the moving

chips reached our ears. It was loud enough to be audible above the music. Dancers moved in the cages that hung from the ceiling, most of them in just their thongs.

Carmen stuck tight to my side, moving in a little closer once we were surrounded by the criminals that roamed the streets at night. Thieves, murderers, and gang members were everywhere—but no one would fuck with me. Not just because I was surrounded by men who could kill them in less than a second, but because they would be ejected from the casino. That was the last thing they wanted, lack of access to a place to gamble their killing money. It was the only thing strong enough to bring peace to a group of the most volatile men in the country.

I didn't look at her when I spoke. "You never have to be scared, Beautiful. You're just as invincible here as you are anywhere else." My fingers rested on her bare skin, feeling the warm softness of her flesh.

She turned her face toward mine. "I know."

At any point in time, my men had eyes trained on me. Every inch of the casino was covered, and there was nowhere I could stand without at least ten men guarding me. I walked to the corner table, moving through the smoke and the low lights to the green table. It was stationed away from everyone else, having a bit of privacy. The other players were already there.

Including The Butcher.

After I gave him my warning, he seemed to have toned down his behavior. There hadn't been another incident of harassment since. The worst thing he did was stare, and I couldn't punish him for enjoying the sight of a naked woman. With six scars along his face, he was a grotesque man. Beefy and covered in tattoos, he looked as threatening as he seemed.

I didn't flinch when I came into his presence.

Carmen did. She moved closer to my side and made sure not to look at him.

The other men were different kinds of criminals, the kind that defrauded the government and lied about stocks. They took money from the exceptionally wealthy and made themselves insanely rich. They looked normal, wearing their suits and ties. The Butcher stood out.

We took our seats.

The dealer stood at the head of the table. "The buyins have already been placed." He nodded to the chips in the center.

I tapped my lap, indicating for Carmen to take a seat.

She hesitated for a moment before she listened. She sat across my thighs and crossed her legs, small in comparison to my large size. Her arm hooked around my neck, and she stayed close to me.

Some of the other men had women at their sides. The Butcher was alone.

We started the game.

"Cigar, sir?" One of my men handed me a fresh one along with a lighter.

I raised my hand and silently dismissed him.

Another man brought two glasses of scotch, remembering that was Carmen's choice of drink as well.

She stayed still and looked at my hand as I played, keeping up a poker face so she wouldn't give me away. She rubbed my chest and gave me the affection I liked, soothing me and keeping me calm despite the rising tension at the table.

When I looked at The Butcher, his eyes were always on Carmen. He was hardly paying attention to his cards, more distracted by my woman than the cash on the table.

The whole reason why I brought her with me was so men could be envious of me. Not only was I the richest and most powerful man in that building—but she was the woman I was fucking. No other man could have her— because she was mine.

The game continued as we were dealt more cards, tossed some, and then raised our bets. The bet started at twenty-five million, but we quickly escalated to fifty million. One of the men folded right away, probably because his hand was just too shitty to stand a chance.

The Butcher's eyes were still on Carmen. He probably looked at his pile of chips before he raised his bet because he was too distracted by her.

Carmen ignored him, her attention only on me.

More of the men folded, leaving The Butcher and me alone in the round.

His stare never ceased. He was only halfway in the game, most of his brain thinking about the woman sitting on my lap.

The moment came to throw down our hands.

I had four aces.

He had two pairs.

The dealer pushed the chips toward me. "Bosco Roth wins the hand."

Millions of dollars in chips were pushed toward me. The other men didn't hide their annoyance at the fortune

I'd just won. I put in twenty-five million but made three hundred million in profit—within fifteen minutes.

Carmen was still, probably shocked by the transaction that had just happened right in front of her.

Like The Butcher hadn't just lost a fortune, his eyes were still on Carmen.

I started to get angry, feeling like he'd crossed the line from appreciation to obsession. I turned my gaze on him and stared at him for several heartbeats, the tension rising with my anger.

When he felt the hostility, he turned his gaze on me.

I didn't say a single word, but I didn't need to. The threat in my eyes was more than enough. Women were obviously a weakness for him. He couldn't keep his hands to himself and his dick in his pants—even when they said no. It was one thing to harass a dancer or let his stare linger too long. It was another matter when my woman was involved.

The corner of his mouth rose in a smile before he finally looked away.

I watched him a moment longer, making sure he wouldn't make the mistake of turning back to her.

He didn't.

7

CARMEN

BOSCO WAS A PHENOMENAL POKER PLAYER. He won most of his hands, and he always walked away from the table with the biggest winnings. It was all luck, so I didn't know how he managed to be so good at a game that was unbiased.

It must be that poker face.

If I were home right now, I would be sitting on the couch waiting for him to come home. I wouldn't be able to sleep until that elevator beeped with his arrival. It had nothing to do with security, knowing I was invincible with him there. There were a dozen men in the lobby who guarded his fortress.

I just missed him.

When we were sitting at the table, there was a terrifying man who didn't seem to belong there. With six scars across his face, he was hideous. They looked like purposeful cuts he made with a knife, shaving off the skin until he flattened the surface. With a fat nose and a bulky physique, he looked like the devil himself.

I wasn't too proud to admit he scared me.

If I saw him on the street, I would immediately turn the other way. I didn't need to know who he was to understand he was lethal. He was a threat to every single person on the planet, especially with that sneer.

He wouldn't stop staring at me.

He looked at me the entire time, hardly paying attention to the game because I was more fascinating. The only reason I didn't walk away was because being next to Bosco was the safest place in the world for me.

But I didn't like it.

Finally, something scared him off because he looked away and never turned back.

Bosco probably did something.

When Bosco was finished with his hands, he handed his chips to one of his men then approached Ronan on the floor, his hand around my waist.

Ronan addressed me before his brother. "Carmen, you look lovely." Unlike the rest of the men in the casino, he seemed to be a gentleman. He leaned into me and kissed me on the cheek. "And my brother looks a lot better because you're with him." He grinned then turned his gaze on Bosco.

Bosco obviously trusted him because he wouldn't let another man touch me otherwise. "She makes the casino look better too."

"No arguments there." He slid his hands into the pockets of his suit. "So, I hear you cleaned up pretty well."

Bosco shrugged, remaining humble despite his immense winnings.

Ronan chuckled. "Carmen really does make you better." His statement seemed to refer to a previous conversation they'd had when they talked about me in private.

Bosco didn't challenge the statement. "I know she does." He pulled me closer into his side.

The room smelled like cigars and booze. I was glad I didn't wear any of my own clothes to the casino because the smell would never come out of the fabric. Bosco was the only one who didn't smoke. I wasn't sure why he'd suddenly cut back.

One of Bosco's men approached him, in a black suit with a visible earpiece. He leaned toward Bosco and spoke quietly so only Bosco could hear.

Bosco nodded then turned to me. "There's someone I need to speak to. My brother will keep you occupied until I return." He kissed me on the corner of my mouth before he walked away with the man who approached him.

Most of his men stayed behind with me, discreetly surrounding the two of us. Ronan watched his brother walk away before he turned his gaze on me, his blue eyes the same color but not filled with the same intensity and longing. He stepped closer to me so we could speak easily over the loud noise around us. "Still not a fan?"

"Of what?" I asked.

He nodded to the floor. "All this."

"It's impressive, but not for me."

"I don't blame you. Women are treated as second-class here, unfortunately. Not you because you're with

Bosco, but that's the mentality around here. Anytime a woman is in here, she's usually topless. That's what the men expect."

Well, they weren't going to see me naked anytime soon. "One of the men at the table wouldn't stop staring at me. I was relieved when the hand was over."

His eyes narrowed, his gaze turning serious. "The one with the facial scars."

"Yes." It looked like that man stuck out like a sore thumb too.

"Don't worry about him. Bosco would never let anything happen to you. Neither would I." He gave me an affectionate look. "You're the best thing that's happened to my brother. He used to be a robot, but now he acts like a human being again. You're putting him back together... piece by piece."

My eyes softened at the sweet words. "He's a good man."

"I know he is. But I think he forgot for a while." He gave me a smile that was friendly. He was far more approachable than his brother, not having the dark intensity that fueled Bosco. "I see the way you look at him. You're crazy about him."

I wanted to deny the claim, but I couldn't. My heart had completely melted for the man. I was weak in the knees and head over heels. This man had made me weaker than anyone else, had affected me more deeply than anyone ever could. I'd never come close to feeling this way about any other man. Not even at all. "We have a connection." I wasn't going to put my heart on the line in front of his brother, not when I wouldn't even tell Bosco how I felt. I was still determined to walk away from this relationship at the end of our arrangement.

He smiled. "Alright, I'll stop grilling you about it. But in case it wasn't as obvious to you as it's been to me…my brother is crazy about you too."

I already knew that, based on the way he looked at me every single morning, afternoon, and night.

"He told me you own a flower shop."

I was relieved with the change of subject. "Yes, I've been running it for a few years."

"That's really cool," he said. "What made you get into that?"

I shrugged. "I love flowers. I've been making arrangements since I was little. My brother and cousin both went to university, but I was never interested in extending my education. I always knew being a florist was what I wanted to do."

"Not too many women own their own business. That's awesome."

"Well…my father helped me a lot." I couldn't pretend I did it all on my own. Without his money, it wouldn't have been possible. He was the one who believed in me and put his money on the table. Now I was paying him back, month by month.

"But you're the one who handles it every day by yourself?'"

"Yeah."

"Then that sounds like you're running the business —he's not."

"But he gave me the money."

"Then he's an investor," he said. "Don't downplay

your qualities. You're one cool chick. I liked you the moment I heard you tell off my brother."

I grinned. "You would have liked anyone for telling off your brother."

He smiled but shook his head. "No, I'm loyal to my brother. If someone talks shit to him, I've got his back. But you're a special exception to that—because everything you say is true. You've straightened him out. This is the first time I've seen him happy in over five years."

"How do you know he's happy?"

"That's easy," he said. "The guy actually smiles—once in a while."

Just when I smiled, I spotted a woman in a dark blue dress pass in the background. In sky-high heels and with black hair, she walked across the room like she owned the casino. Covered in diamonds similar to mine, she looked like a beautiful queen. I recognized her right away—Ruby.

Ronan followed my gaze and glanced at her before he turned back to me. "Do you know her?"

"Do you?" I countered, feeling the jealousy spike in my muscles. I hated that slut. Just looking at her pissed me off all over again. She had a prominent cleavage line because her girls were on display for everyone to see. I was certain there was only one man she was trying to attract —mine.

"I see her around."

"Who is she?" I asked. "A member? A stripper?" She was the only woman on the floor who wasn't in a cage. She dressed like she had money and power. She didn't seem to fit into any category.

"Neither," he said with a chuckle. "She's a gold digger."

That sounded about right.

"She likes bedding rich and powerful man in exchange for a luxurious life. She takes her spoils then moves on."

"So she's basically a prostitute?"

Ronan shrugged. "I guess, but not quite. She's pretty selective." He studied my face, seeing the rage in my eyes. "You really don't like her, huh?'"

"No. I'm not a big fan of skanks."

He laughed. "Bosco must have told you about her. You don't seem like the kind of person to tear down another woman for no reason."

No, Bosco never had. "I know he slept with her for about a week."

"It was his longest fling before you, but it was still very short. I wouldn't look into it too much."

Easier said than done. "She came to his penthouse and practically threw herself at him." I kept staring at her, wanting to rip that pretty hair out of her scalp. "Bosco told her he was seeing someone, but she didn't care. She unzipped her shirt and let her tits pop out. If that's not slutty, then I don't know what is."

Ronan raised an eyebrow. "When did this happen?"

"A few weeks ago…" I probably shouldn't have said anything since Ronan might mention it to his brother, but I was too angry looking at her to care. If I had to see her down here at the casino, then I wouldn't be able to keep my cool. Imagining Bosco screwing her again after I was gone filled me with such dread I felt sick to my stomach.

"What did he do?"

"Told her to leave. Said she didn't have class…like I do."

"Wow." Ronan watched her for a moment before he turned back to me. "I guess that doesn't surprise me. He's so hung up on you, why would he care about her? Besides, she only wants him for his power. You seemed to want him despite his power."

That was true.

"So don't let her bother you. He doesn't care about her. He only cares about you."

WE CAME HOME AFTER TWO IN THE MORNING.

I was exhausted from being up so late. I had to wake up in a few hours, so I quickly washed my face and brushed my teeth before I got out of the skintight dress that reeked of cigars.

I got into bed without waiting for him, putting on one of his t-shirts before I slid under the sheets.

He joined me when he was finished with the bathroom. "Did you have a good time?"

I was basically a trophy that he paraded around. My only job was to look good in the dress he bought for me. "I really like your brother." I lay on my side and faced the other wall, relaxing because his bed was so comfortable.

He spooned me from behind, not smelling like the casino anymore because he'd shed his suit and washed his hands. His face pressed into the back of my hair, and he circled his thick arm around his waist. "I hope you mean that in a friendly way. I would hate to murder my only family member."

"You already know the answer, Bosco." My arm rested over his, and all the rage I felt for Ruby faded away when I remembered he was sleeping with me, not her. He could have had her if he wanted her, but he didn't. "He says a lot of nice things about you."

"You never lie to me, so don't start now."

I playfully bucked against him. "I'm being serious."

He chuckled against the back of my neck, his lips touching my hair. "He's a good guy."

"He said the same about you."

"What else did he say?"

I considered telling him that Ronan said Bosco was crazy about me, but I decided to keep that to myself. "He asked me about the shop." I didn't mention Ruby either, electing to pass on the topic.

He kissed the back of my shoulder, his hard dick smothered right between my ass cheeks. He slightly ground against me, telling me he was going to fuck me at some point before we went to sleep.

"You seemed to have a good time. You won, like, a bazillion dollars."

He didn't say anything in response.

"How did you get so good at poker?"

"I've played for a long time. And I have a face that's impossible to read."

"I can read it," I countered, knowing exactly when he was angry, aroused, and playful.

"You're the only person who really knows me. You know me better than Ronan."

I stared at the other wall in the darkness, my breathing changing because his words were surprisingly sweet. He confided his personal thoughts to me, sharing more than just his vast wealth. "You know me better than anyone else too…" My family knew me well, but Bosco knew me in the most intimate ways. He had a piece of me that no one else would ever have.

He kissed my neck. "I know, Beautiful." When he smothered me with his affection, I knew there was no place I would feel safer. Even when that terrifying man stared at me, there was nothing he could do because Bosco was there, flanked by guards all across the casino.

"That man with the scars…do you know him?"

Bosco flinched at the question, his hand gripping my arm a little tighter than usual. "You noticed him?"

"Well, he was staring at me the entire time. Ronan told me not to worry about it…"

He propped himself above me but said nothing, letting the silence grow in intensity. "He was right. Don't worry about him."

"He's a bad man, isn't he?" Judging by the way both of them dismissed him without giving any information, they were protecting me from something.

"He won't look at you again. I took care of it."

"Then you don't know him?"

"I know all my members. But I don't associate with all of them. They call him The Butcher."

"Oh…what a wonderful name."

"But like I said, he won't bother you. So don't worry about him."

Regardless of who that man was, he was powerless

against Bosco. There was nothing he could ever do to either of us. "Alright."

He rolled me onto my back and gazed down at me, looking possessive because of the delicate nature of our relationship. He positioned himself on top of me, separating my thighs with his muscular ones.

I didn't take off my shirt, and he only pulled down the front of his boxers. When he was this close to me, I couldn't smell the cigar smoke on his breath the way I used to. When he came home from work, it was sometimes potent if he didn't brush his teeth. "When did you stop smoking?"

He halted on top of me, our bodies close together. His cock rubbed against my clit, stimulating me with his hardness. He looked down at me with a slightly bewildered expression. "A few weeks ago."

"Oh...good." Smoking was so unhealthy. I wanted Bosco to live for a long time, so I was glad he quit the terrible habit.

He kept watching me, like he saw something in my eyes. "You don't remember."

"Remember what?" My head rested on his pillow, and I sank into the mattress, his weight pinning me underneath him.

"You're the one who asked me to quit." His hand moved into my hair, and he cradled my face close to his. "You said you wanted me to live as long as possible..."

I didn't remember that at all. "Oh..." But then again, I said a lot of stupid things I should keep to myself. I admitted most of my secrets to him because I couldn't keep them bottled inside. Since I didn't remember it, it must have happened the night we had pizza and beer at the dining table. I drank too much, and the rest of the night was a blur. "Well…I'm glad you listened to me."

He rubbed his nose against mine. "And I'm glad you asked."

A STORM HIT FLORENCE, SO IT RAINED FOR THREE DAYS straight.

I still went to work because the shop needed to stay open, but customers were scarce. On the third day, I considered closing early because not a single person had come in all day. My arrangements were placed in the window, and the front door was shut because the streets were flooded. Hardly any cars passed.

I wondered if Vanessa was having the same luck.

I stood behind the counter and stared at the pouring rain, watching it drip down the windows. My shop was on the corner, and the walls were made entirely of glass. I leased one of the newer buildings in the city so my flowers could be on display everywhere. It was the best way to get customers to walk inside right off the street.

The street was pounded by the raindrops, and the clouds were so thick not a single ray of sunshine could pierce through. I didn't mind the rain, but when it drove all my customers away, it was a bit of a strain on my business.

I was tempted to go home and get back into bed with Bosco. Warm and dry, it was the most comfortable place in this city. I hadn't been to my apartment once since I'd moved out. I had no idea what kind of shape it was in.

Just when I decided to close up for the day, I grabbed my bag and umbrella and put all my essentials in the safe in the back. I returned to the front of the store and grabbed the keys off the counter. Bosco's men didn't need to be notified that I was leaving, because they would show up the second I walked outside.

I walked to the front door with my key at the ready. Something made me look up, whether it was to check the rain or something else I saw. My hand froze on the door because I spotted his shadow right away. Lurking like a gargoyle, he stood on one of the balconies of the apartment across the street, staring down at me with complete disregard for the rain. His clothes were soaked, but he remained absolutely still, not caring that my eyes were on him. He held my gaze with the same expression he wore the other night.

With the same six scars on his face.

The memory of my attack in the alleyway came back to me. I felt helpless then, but I felt even more defenseless now. This man was stalking me, obviously because he hadn't stopped thinking about me since he saw me at the casino a few nights ago. He didn't care about Bosco's men. He didn't care that I would tell Bosco I'd spotted him.

He didn't care about anything.

My palms were sweaty, and my heart was racing. He was too far away to do anything, and it didn't seem like he wanted to shoot me. He just wanted me to know that he was there—that he was watching me.

I couldn't stay inside the shop forever, so I stepped out

into the rain, locked the door behind me, and thankfully, the black car appeared to take me home. They opened the back door for me and ushered me out of the rain before they took off.

I was surrounded on all sides as I was taken away from that psychopath, but my heart still wouldn't slow down.

I felt like he was still watching me…even when I was miles away.

MY HEART HADN'T SLOWED DOWN. BLOOD POUNDED IN my ears during my rise in the elevator. I wanted to get into Bosco's arms as quickly as possible because that was the only place in the world I would be safe.

I'd known there was something wrong with that man. I'd felt it the second I looked at him.

How long had he been watching me? Had he been there every single day that week? And I just didn't notice him until now?

The elevator doors opened and I stepped inside, my feet finally hitting the hardwood floor of his apartment. "Bosco?" I couldn't hide the fear in my voice. It erupted so naturally because I couldn't keep myself under control. This was worse than the alleyway. This man was specifically seeking me out. I didn't take the wrong turn at the wrong time.

"Beautiful?" His voice sounded down the hallway. His feet thudded against the floor a second later as he came toward me. He appeared around the corner, his hair still slightly damp from the shower he'd just took. He was in only his boxers, his powerful legs looking thick under the fabric. Once his gaze settled on me, he knew there was something wrong. "What is it?"

Now that we were in the same room together, I moved into his chest and clung to him, finding comfort in his strong chest and broad shoulders. This was my safe place, the only place in the world where that man couldn't touch me.

"Carmen, you're scaring me." He grabbed my shoulders and pulled me back so he could look into my face. His eyes shifted back and forth as he looked into mine, reading all the warning signs my body was emitting. "I've never seen you like this."

My hands held on to his arms, and I found strength in the power I could feel in his pulse.

"What is it?" he demanded. "Tell me." His tone showed his impatience. I was taking too long telling him the problem, and he didn't like to wait.

"I was closing up the flower shop when I saw him. He was standing on one of the balconies of the apartments across the street. He was just standing in the rain… watching me without blinking. He didn't care that I saw him. It was like he wanted me to see him…wanted me to be scared."

His arms slowly lowered to his sides, and he stared at me with a look of rage I'd never seen. "Who?" The vein in his forehead was throbbing. The cords on his arms were tightening. His entire body tensed as it prepared for the battle about to ensue. Instead of comforting me, he moved away because the fury was too much for him to control. "Who did you see?"

"That man from the casino…with the scars on his face."

Bosco heard my answer, but he kept up his stare like he hadn't. His chest rose and fell at a quicker rate, and redness flooded his face. He moved back from me again, his hands forming fists. He didn't ask any other questions, but his eyes lit up like small bombs went off in each one.

I stayed quiet as Bosco wrestled with his rage. I didn't know what else to say. I didn't want to calm him down because I was still losing my mind. I was scared, and I didn't have the pride to pretend I wasn't. Seeing that man stand in the rain and watch me like prey was one of the most disturbing moments of my life. I couldn't keep Bosco calm when I was this terrified.

He didn't ask me if I was certain of what I saw. He took my word for it right away. He stepped away and pulled his phone out of his pocket. He called someone and pressed the phone to his ear. "Double the perimeter around the building. I want twelve more guys for the next shift. The Butcher is stalking my woman, and I want him shot on sight if he gets within a mile of this building." He hung up then made another call. "Ronan, stop what you're doing because we need to talk. The Butcher is stalking Carmen." He paused as he listened over the line. "He was sitting on the balcony across from her shop—in the pouring rain. He was watching her." He listened to his brother before he responded. "I have no idea how long this has been going on. Carmen just noticed him. The second he walks into that casino, I want to know about it. He's going in the ring—and I want to be the one to do it."

HE LAY BESIDE ME IN BED, THE SHEETS PULLED TO HIS waist. His boxers were on because I wasn't in the mood for sex. I was still terrified by what I'd witnessed.

His anger had started to fade a few hours ago. Now, he seemed more concerned about the way I was feeling. His fingers ran through my hair, and he kept his gaze on me the entire time. "I understand you're unsettled, but there's nothing to worry about."

"He was just standing there in the rain…"

He tucked my hair behind my ear before he trailed the backs of his fingers down my arm. "He's going to be dead soon."

"When he saw me look at him, he knew I would tell you. So he's not gonna show his face again."

"There's nowhere for him to hide. I have every criminal in this city by the balls. When I put out a notice to find someone, I always get them within twelve hours. This will be no different. He'll be dead by this time tomorrow."

Until that moment came, I wouldn't be able to relax. I wouldn't be able to sleep even with Bosco beside me. That psychopath was out there, and he wanted me—with terrible intentions. He was no different from the men in the alleyway, except he wanted to be the one to enjoy me. A man who had no problem pissing off Bosco Roth either had to be crazy or more powerful than he let on.

When I didn't say anything, Bosco cupped my face. "Beautiful, look at me."

"I am…"

"Really look at me."

There was a haze in my eyes because I kept thinking about that gargoyle in the rain, ready to feast on my flesh. I concentrated on the man blanketing me with affection and security, trying to forget about the monster that wanted to prey on me.

"I would never let anything happen to you." His thumb softly grazed my cheek. "My men wouldn't have let anything happen to you. He would have to go through all my security and me before he came anywhere near you. Those are impossible odds. I would die before I'd let that happen." It was a sweet confession, something that would touch my heart if I weren't still disturbed by what I'd witnessed that afternoon.

I stared at his handsome face above me, seeing the concern burn in his eyes. My fingers felt his powerful shoulders and his thick arms, remembering that this man had complete control over the city. Regardless of what trick that horrible man had up his sleeve, he wouldn't be able to overpower Bosco. "I know…"

"Then stop looking at me like that."

"Like what?" I whispered.

"Like you're scared." He kissed the corner of my mouth. "Where's the fighter in the alleyway? Where's that woman?"

"I am a fighter," I said quietly. "If someone comes after me, I'll hold my own. But that's not what happened, Bosco. That man perched on a balcony and stared down at me like a bird preparing to swoop down on his prey. He's stalking me. He's obsessed with me. He wants me— and he wants me to know that. They call him The Butcher for a reason. He's a psychopath, unpredictable and impossible to understand. He was like an animal playing with his food. Yes, I'm scared…and no one would judge me for being scared." Fear was a survival instinct, and my body was telling me this was serious shit. "Maybe I should call my father…" My family managed to overcome everything. Maybe I should get them involved.

His gaze saddened as he listened to me. "Do what you want, Beautiful. But I promise you, he'll be dead within twenty-four hours. There's no reason to get anyone else involved. There's never been an enemy I couldn't defeat with the simple wave of my wrist. This guy is no different."

"Then why would he blatantly act that way? He's obviously not afraid of you."

He tilted his head slightly as he tried to think of an answer. "This man is different from most. They say he's out of his mind. His actions can't be predicted because there's no logical motivation. He clearly has mental issues. He probably acted on instinct without understanding the full consequences of his actions. Ronan discouraged me from admitting him to the casino, but I didn't listen. I just wanted his money—and that was a mistake."

"Great…so he really is a psychopath."

"A psychopath that will be dead very soon." His fingers touched my chin. "I'm a man who keeps his promises. I promise you he'll be dead within a day. You can see the body yourself. Do you trust me, Beautiful? Do you believe me?" He gave me a desperate look, like he wanted me to place all my faith in his hands. He wanted me to feel safe, to believe in the reputation he'd built for himself.

This was the same man who'd asked for compensation for saving my life, the same one who'd showed up at my shop and my apartment. He cornered me then asked for more, securing me for three months. It would be easy to say he was a dangerous man, but that didn't change anything. I trusted him more than anyone else on this earth. "Yes…I trust you."

I STAYED AT THE PENTHOUSE THE FOLLOWING DAY, NOT going to work even though my shop was supposed to be open. It was raining anyway, so there probably wouldn't be many people stopping by for a visit.

Bosco stayed home with me, doing all his work via his laptop and the phone.

The Butcher hadn't appeared yet.

Bosco said he would be dead in twenty-four hours, and the deadline was fast approaching. I was concerned that he hadn't been located yet, that this monster had managed to slip through Bosco's men posted all over the city. I didn't mention him as the day passed, not wanting to talk about the freak that loomed over me in the rain.

I could only assume he wanted one thing from me.

And I didn't want to think about what that one thing was.

Bosco and I sat on the couch together, his arm draped over my shoulders as a blanket lay in my lap. We hadn't had sex since I'd come home yesterday because I wasn't in the mood. All I could think about was the moment that man would finally be dead.

Bosco's phone rang, and he fished it out of his pocket. "Ronan, did you find him?"

Ronan's voice was audible because the phone was close to my face. "He just walked in."

Bosco was quiet for a few seconds, clearly shocked. "Seriously?"

"Yeah. He just hit a poker table."

"And he's pretending everything is normal?"

"Seems that way," he responded. "What do you want to do?"

"Grab him and throw him in the ring. Don't start until I get there. Who else is on the waiting list?"

"That guy who stole a few million from one of our members. Can't remember his name. But he has a tattoo of a dragon on his chest. Beefy guy."

Bosco seemed to know exactly who that was. "Good. The Butcher won't stand a chance." He hung up.

I was relieved this was finally over.

"Get dressed." Bosco left the couch and headed to his bedroom.

"Wait…what?" I stayed in my spot, my blanket wrapped around me.

"You're coming with me." He turned back to me. "I want you to see the body. It'll help you sleep tonight."

"But he's not dead yet…" I didn't want to be in the same room with him while he was still breathing.

Bosco gave me a terrifying scare, like he wasn't in the mood to be delicate anymore. "There's nothing he can do to you. Walk in there with your head held high and show every man in that casino what happens when they fuck with Carmen Barsetti. Now get your ass up and change.

Don't make me ask you again." He turned around and marched off, making good on his word not to give me another warning.

His tough love invigorated me, made me realize I shouldn't be afraid of a sick man like that. I should show him that he couldn't treat women that way—that he would pay for his actions.

BOSCO WAS VISIBLY ANGRY, HIS ARMS SWINGING BY HIS sides and his shoulders tense. He usually took his time when he walked across the casino floor, drawing attention to himself as well as his majestic prestige. But now he didn't care. All he wanted to do was get to the ring as quickly as possible.

The casino floor wasn't nearly as full as it usually was. There were only a few tables operating, while the others remained vacant and the dealers stood there idly, having nothing to do since there were no players. The women danced in their cages even though hardly anyone was watching.

"It's quiet tonight." I kept up my stride beside him, feeling uncomfortable when his hands weren't on me.

"They're all underground." Before he arrived at the elevator, his men hit the button and the doors opened. He stepped inside with me at his side. The men stayed outside, and the doors shut, bringing us into solitude. The elevator shifted then began its descent. He slid his hands into his pockets and stared at the metal doors, his jaw clenching in rage. He looked like he wanted to fight The Butcher himself.

"What happens if The Butcher wins the fight?"

He didn't answer, keeping his eyes straight ahead. He was so pissed off, perhaps he didn't hear me.

I didn't dare ask my question again.

The elevator came to a halt, and the doors opened to pure pandemonium. Men were yelling at each other, making bets. There was a ring in the center, lifted up so everyone could see well. It looked like the kind of ring they had in Vegas where professional fighters duked it out on live TV. Men sat in the bleachers that rose up toward the back so everyone had a good view.

Cash was being exchanged between men, and dealers were going around taking bets.

Two men sat in the ring at opposite corners, hand-cuffed and shirtless. They only wore their jeans, their shoes and socks removed.

The second I looked at The Butcher, I was scared all over again.

Bosco must have felt my fear because he grabbed my hand and pulled me with him. His men made a path through the crowd, and we ascended the steps to a special platform with a few chairs. "Sit." He commanded me like a dog.

I would have told him off for it normally, but now wasn't the time.

He turned to walk away again.

"Where are you going?" I blurted out. I was guarded by six men, but I preferred Bosco's protection over anyone else's.

He turned back to me, still looking livid. "Getting the execution started." He moved down the steps and stepped into the ring, wearing his fitted black suit and matching tie. The second he stepped through the ropes, every man in the audience cheered.

I couldn't believe what I was looking at. It was an underground fight club, a place where criminals fought to the death. All the men cheered as they put their money on the line, gambling on life and death.

My heart was racing so fast. This was unreal.

Bosco walked up to The Butcher and kneeled down so they were eye level. They exchanged a few words, their eyes locked on one another. It was impossible to figure out how the conversation was going because it was so loud in the concrete room.

Bosco finished what he needed to say and stood up. He moved to the center of the ring, and once his right hand moved into the air, everyone turned dead silent.

If there were crickets, we would be able to hear them.

Bosco lowered his hand, his shoulders stiff with the power that ran through his veins. He surveyed the men in the room, the members of his casino. He was in charge of this building, of the entire city. He was the only one with the strength to organize a community of murderers, traitors, and thieves. "Bets are closed." He indicated to the man in the corner, the one The Butcher would have to fight. "Mango is sentenced to the ring for stealing from a fellow member. Two and a half million dollars was swiped off the table and into his pocket. The punishment fits the crime."

Everyone in the audience booed.

Bosco turned to The Butcher. "The Butcher is sentenced to the ring for his crimes against me." The men had started to cheer, but once they understood the severity of the crime, they turned quiet once more. "He tried to steal something that belongs to me, something more valuable than all the cash on my casino floor, all the jewels in my vault, all the cars in my garage. For his crime, he will be sentenced to death."

The crowd booed once more.

The Butcher stared at Bosco, and slowly, a grin spread across his face. It was more of a sneer than a smile, and his scars stretched across his face as his muscles pulled his skin tighter. Like this was all a game, he grinned at Bosco fearlessly.

I was fifty feet away, but the distance wasn't enough. If The Butcher won The Brawl, I didn't know what Bosco would do. Perhaps he would take him to the curb and shoot him on the sidewalk. Either way, I wouldn't be able to sleep that night until he was dead.

Bosco raised his right hand again. "Let The Brawl begin."

Thunderous cheers erupted, so loud I could barely hear myself think.

Bosco left the ring and moved back to the platform where I sat. The men were released from their handcuffs so the fight could begin. Bosco moved to the seat beside me, and like everything was normal, he crossed his ankle over his knee and rested his hands in his lap. His affection was absent, probably because he was so angry that touching me wasn't appealing.

Ronan took the seat beside him, dressed in a gray suit.

I crossed my legs and appeared as indifferent as possible, even though it seemed like I was deep in the underworld. I wore a skintight black dress and the diamonds Bosco asked me to wear. My hair was pulled back, and I had on the tallest heels I'd ever worn in my life.

The men came loose from their holds, and that's when the fight began.

IT WAS BLOODY. IT WAS INTENSE. IT WAS ALMOST TOO much to watch.

The two men pounded their fists into each other's faces. Since there were no rules, the men didn't hesitate before they poked each other in the eye and slammed their heel into the other guy's knee.

Blood smeared across their cheeks, and their muscles bulged with the adrenaline. Both of their lives were on the line, so they gave it everything they had.

Bosco was silent as he watched the fight, still as a statue and his eyes unblinking.

Ronan leaned forward with his elbows on his knees, watching every single kick and hit. "What did you say to him?"

Bosco didn't look at his brother. "That he will die for coming too close to my woman."

I heard what he said, and I was slightly touched by the way he referred to me.

"Let's hope it works out that way."

The fight kept going, and it seemed like they were both tiring out.

I just wanted it to end. The only reason I kept watching was because I wanted to be respected. If I looked away, people would think I was weak.

Things took a turn for the worse when The Butcher punched the guy so hard he flew down onto the concrete floor. Then he grabbed his leg, and with his bare hands, snapped his knee, breaking it with enough force that the crunch was audible in the entire room.

"Shit," Ronan muttered under his breath.

I felt a little vomit rise in my throat.

The man screamed out in pain, holding his knee because the agony was too much. He started to crawl away while The Butcher looked down at him. Then The Butcher raised his gaze and looked right at me, that same look on his face that he wore the other night. He purposely provoked me, tried to get under my skin.

I held his gaze with an indifferent look, refusing to cower under his intimidation.

He turned his gaze to Bosco than slammed his foot on the man's head. He kept slamming down until his skull caved in, and he lay lifelessly on the floor, limp as a dead fish. Blood was smeared everywhere.

Men cheered when they won their bets.

This wasn't how I wanted the fight to go, and I hid my disappointment as best I could.

The Butcher walked to the edge of the ring, looked at Bosco, and then took a bow.

Wow, he was one smug son of a bitch.

Bosco's expression didn't change.

Ronan was silent.

I waited for Bosco's men to pull The Butcher out of

the ring so he could be shot in an alleyway, but nothing happened.

Bosco stood up then loosened his tie.

My eyes moved to him, unsure what was happening.

Bosco stared at The Butcher as he pulled off his tie and dropped his jacket onto the chair.

My eyes snapped wide open. "What the hell are you doing?"

Bosco unbuttoned the front of his shirt then dropped that on top of his jacket, standing shirtless on the platform.

The Butcher grinned like this was his lucky day.

Ronan stood next to his brother. "I don't think this is—"

"Shut up." Bosco silenced him with his hostility.

This couldn't be happening. I moved to my feet next and stood right in front of him, forcing him to look at me instead of The Butcher. "Bosco, this is stupid. You could just shoot him later."

He pulled his shoe off next. "I want to do this. Now sit down." He spoke calmly despite the intensity of the situation.

"No!" I grabbed both of his wrists. "I won't let you. What if he kills you?"

He kept his indifferent expression. "He won't."

"That man just crushed the other guy's skull!"

He slowly pulled my hands off his wrists. "Carmen, I made a promise to you. I keep my promises."

"Then shoot him! Have someone else do it. Don't do this!" I was entering a full-blown panic attack. "You can't do this. I won't let you. Please stay. Please." I pressed my hands against his chest, begging him to listen to me. Tears burned in my eyes because I was terrified of losing this man. I'd come to care for him so deeply that I wouldn't be able to go on if I lost him. I didn't want a single scar on that beautiful face. "Don't do this to me. I can't lose you…"

That lopsided grin stretched across his face. "Beautiful." His hand cupped my cheek, and he wiped away a tear. "As much as I'm enjoying this, I have to go."

"Why?" I demanded. "This is stupid—"

"This man will suffer for what he did. I will keep the respect of my men in the process. Men will be too terrified to even look at you. This is my world, and this is how I run things. I'm the executioner—and I will kill him with my bare hands."

I was crying harder now. "Babe, don't leave me…" I used his nickname, desperate to make him listen to me. "I'm begging you…"

"I know," he whispered. "And I love watching you beg. But I never make a promise I can't keep. I promise I'll come back to you."

"You can't make a promise like that!"

"I can. And I will." He cupped both of my cheeks and kissed me on the mouth. It was soft and short. He abruptly pulled away and slipped off his other shoe and socks before he moved to the stairs. "Ronan, keep her back."

Ronan stood in the way so I couldn't chase after him. He gave me a sad look, like he didn't like this either. "There's nothing we can do now. He can't turn back."

My face was stained with tears, and my makeup was smeared across my face. Every time I tried to breathe, I couldn't get enough air. "This can't be happening…this can't be happening."

Ronan grabbed my hands and guided me back to the chair.

The crowd went wild when Bosco approached the ring. They were even louder than before, men whistling and screaming. More bets were made as people gambled on the biggest brawl that had ever taken place.

Ronan sat directly beside me, sighing loudly under his breath.

"Why is he doing this?"

"Because he made a promise to you. The Butcher will dead in twenty-four hours." He looked at his watch. "And he's only got an hour left."

I didn't know what else to do because I was so scared, so I grabbed Ronan's hand and squeezed it, squeezed it so hard it was like I was going into labor. "I can't lose him, Ronan. I just can't. That man is everything to me…"

He squeezed my hand back. "He's everything to me too."

BOSCO STARED AT THE BUTCHER FOR A LONG TIME, HIS arms by his sides with a calm look on his face. He sized up his opponent with his poker face, hiding every thought deep below the surface. He slowly moved as he circled The Butcher.

The Butcher grinned like this was the happiest day of his life. He was already bloody and covered with sweat, but he seemed rejuvenated to see Bosco face him himself. "When you're dead, she's mine."

The second part of that threat didn't scare me. Only the first part. I didn't care about myself in that moment because all I cared about was Bosco getting out of there alive—and without a broken knee.

Bosco's expression didn't change even though a comment like that would normally make him snap.

"I'm not sure if I can watch this…" I covered my cheek with my hand, uncertain if I wanted to cover my eyes or keep watching. "If Bosco is about to lose, will you intervene?"

Ronan shook his head. "I can't. It's against the rules."

"But this is your brother—"

"Trust me, he wouldn't want me to."

Bosco was the first one to rush in, moving quickly with his lithe and ripped physique. He slammed his fist into The Butcher's face and another into his stomach, making him stumble back from the force.

Bosco quickly stepped back and pulled his fists toward his chin, just as a boxer would. His slacks hung low on his hips, and his muscled physique gleamed from the sweat he'd already produced. He wasn't nearly as large as The Butcher, but he was definitely quicker.

The Butcher recovered then laughed, like that hit did nothing. "That's all you got?"

Bosco remained silent, refusing to react to his taunts or make some of his own. He was fully focused on the fight, not distracted by his hatred.

I kept squeezing Ronan's hand. "I want this to end."

"It won't be long."

The Butcher charged Bosco suddenly, moving his head down like ram trying to destroy a boulder.

Bosco moved out of the way then slammed his knee into The Butcher's face.

The Butcher fell to the ground but quickly got up.

"Bosco knows how to fight?"

Ronan nodded. "Martial arts, boxing, and street fighting. He's conserving his energy, only taking the hits he knows he'll land."

I was relieved Bosco knew what he was doing.

When The Butcher got up, he was angry. His nostrils flared like a pissed bull, and he went after Bosco again, moving quicker. "When I get my hands on that little bitch, I'm gonna fuck her in the ass so hard—"

Bosco slugged him in the stomach then slammed his face down into his knee. He somehow remained calm even though The Butcher was saying all the right things to get a rise out of him.

The Butcher snapped and threw his fists, landing three in Bosco's face and one in the gut. He came at him with every bit of his strength, slamming all of his weight into the punches and beating Bosco until he was bloody.

"No!" I covered my face, unable to watch.

"Come on, Bosco," Ronan said under his breath.

More cheers and boos erupted as the fight went on.

Listening to it was just as bad as seeing it, so I looked up again.

Bosco's face was dripping with blood, but so was The Butcher's. They were both breathing hard, becoming exhausted by throwing the punches as well as taking them.

Bosco's left eye was already darkening, and blood streaked from both nostrils.

"And when I'm done fucking that bitch, I'll slit her throat and leave her on your mother's grave."

I held my breath at the comment, knowing that would get to Bosco.

"Shit," Ronan said.

Bosco's eyes widened, and he moved in, slamming his fists into The Butcher's face.

The Butcher covered himself with his arms and laughed, laughed loud enough for everyone to hear. "Finally found a button." He slammed his fist up, hitting Bosco underneath the chin.

Bosco fell to the ground.

"No!" I brought Ronan's hand to my face as I started to tremble.

"Get up, Bosco," Ronan said.

Bosco stayed down, seeming to be unconscious.

"Oh my god...oh my god..." I covered my face and started to sob. "No...please."

The Butcher started to speak. "The king has fallen. Now it's time for me to break each bone. One at a time —" His words died in his mouth, then there was a loud smack as his heavy body hit the pavement.

I opened my eyes again, seeing Bosco on his feet and standing over The Butcher. He slammed his bare foot right on the other man's throat, making The Butcher cough loudly. Then Bosco snapped his elbow, breaking it with an audible crack.

The Butcher didn't cry out, but he tried to get up with

his single working arm, falling over onto his stomach instead.

Bosco jumped into the air then landed right on The Butcher's lower back, making another cracking noise that was unmistakable.

He broke The Butcher's back.

This time, The Butcher screamed. He tried to move his legs, but he couldn't. He tried to crawl away with one arm, but he was too heavy. The panic entered his eyes, and it was so apparent it was almost hard to look at.

Ronan breathed a sigh of relief. "Bosco has the best poker face in the world."

Bosco stepped away from The Butcher and walked to the edge of the ring, raising both arms in the air in victory. He was covered in blood and sweat, but he looked more kingly than ever before.

The crowd went wild.

Bosco moved to each other side of the ring and did the same thing, getting all the men riled up and louder. He kept throwing his arms in the air, getting them to scream at the highest level.

The Butcher had given up. He lay there, unable to walk and barely able to move.

"What do you mean?" I asked Ronan about his comment.

"He used The Butcher's arrogance against him, made him think he had the upper hand. In reality, he never did. He was waiting for the perfect moment to pull that stunt. The comment about our mom didn't make him angry—he just let The Butcher think that. And when he dropped his guard…that's when Bosco came to life."

Bosco walked back to The Butcher and stared down at him, standing strong and proud as the unquestionable victor.

The Butcher managed to flip over so he could look at the man who had defeated him. His arrogance was gone, and now all that was left was a crippled man. He stared at Bosco, breathing deep and hard. "Mercy."

Bosco stared down at him without blinking.

"What does that mean?" I asked.

"He's surrendering and asking for a quick death."

"Does Bosco have to comply?"

"No, but he will."

"Really?"

He nodded. "It'll prove to everyone he has absolute power, but he's also fair."

Bosco raised his hand and motioned for one of his men to approach the ring, a pistol in his hand.

"Look away," Ronan said. "You don't want to see this."

I closed my eyes and looked down, waiting for the gunshot to announce it was finally over. "Where's he gonna shot him?"

"Right between the eyes."

I was glad Ronan told me not to look.

The sound of the crowd grew louder. The tension rose as everyone waited for The Butcher to meet his end. With my eyes closed, I could feel all the energy in the room, feel Bosco's power even fifty feet away.

Then I heard the gunshot.

The Brawl was finally over—and Bosco was the winner.

BOSCO WIPED DOWN WITH THE TOWEL HIS MEN GAVE him, getting the sweat and blood off his body. He wiped his face clean, only a few spots of blood coming out of his nose. His eye was already turning black because he'd been hit so hard in the face.

The Butcher had been taken away and placed in a body bag. Who knew where the corpse would end up.

I wanted to rush down the stairs and into Bosco's arms, but Ronan kept me on the platform.

"Wait for him to come to us." He held on to my wrist for a second before he let go.

Bosco spoke to a few men before he finally made his way up the stairs. After winning such an intense fight, he seemed perfectly casual like nothing had happened. The men in the crowd were paying their loses and pocketing their wins before they filed out of the room.

I should let Ronan greet his brother first, but I was too anxious to be considerate. The second he was on the platform, I moved into his chest and touched his searing skin, feeling his strong heartbeat and muscled frame. I held on to him and kept my face against his body, immediately sobbing once I finally had him back. The fear of losing him had nearly driven me insane, and knowing it was really over made me so emotional, I didn't know how to cope. "I'm so glad you're okay..." My tears stuck to his skin and slid down his stomach. "God, I was so scared."

His hand moved into my hair, and he rested his chin on my head. "I know, Beautiful. But here I am—in one piece." He kissed my forehead and squeezed me against his chest, giving me the comfort I craved. "I keep my promises."

I pulled away so I could look at him. "What the hell were you thinking?" I knew I sounded like a nagging wife, but I didn't care. "He could have…" I couldn't even finish the sentence.

His eyes narrowed on my face, watching me fall apart even though he was perfectly okay. "I won't apologize. It was worth it to see you put all your cards on the table." He cupped my cheek and kissed me before he turned to his brother.

What did that mean?

Ronan gave him a disappointed look and shook his head. "You're fucking crazy."

Bosco shrugged. "So you shouldn't be surprised, then."

"You're right, I shouldn't be. But I am." He clapped him on the shoulder. "Let's not do that again. You've made your point to The Butcher and every member of the casino. They'll be telling this story for a long time."

"Good. It's a great story."

"Are you alright? Need to see a doctor?"

Bosco didn't bother answering his question before he turned back to me. "Let's go home, Beautiful." He wrapped his arm around me and pulled me close so he could speak into my ear. "I want you on your belly, my fingers gripping your neck, and my cock deep inside you." He brushed his lips against my cheek before he grabbed his clothes from the chair. He put each piece on, securing the buttons of his shirt before he put on his tie. His jacket came last, and despite the black eye on his face, he looked as good as new.

He took my hand and guided me down the stairs. His men already respected him, but now he parted the crowd with his presence, like a god who was unanimously praised by all his subjects. He even had a subtle glow, like the world was at his fingertips and he had the power to guide us and destroy us at the same time.

WHEN WE ENTERED HIS PENTHOUSE, HE WAS STILL IN the same aggressive mood. He tossed his jacket on the floor then yanked off his tie. "There's lingerie in your closet. Pick one and lie on the bed, stomach flat and knees together." He ordered me around like I was a whore rather than a woman.

"Aren't we going to talk about this—"

He flashed me a look that made the words die in my mouth. "Tomorrow. Tonight, I fought for you and won. I want to enjoy my victory by fucking you senseless." He moved to the bar and poured himself a glass of scotch. "Now, do as I say." He turned his back to me and took a drink, his open shirt loose around his body.

I knew there was still a jolt of adrenaline in his body because of the battle he just fought. Testosterone was pounding in his blood, his masculine nature taking over every other aspect. He'd returned to the man I'd originally met, the dangerous man who called off those men in the alleyway. He was cold, aggressive, and controlling.

This was the second time he'd saved me, and this time,

he got his hands dirty. He punished the man for terror-izing me, for stalking me outside my shop with the inten-tion of raping me and killing me. Instead of sending his dogs to take care of it, he did it himself. I was his woman, so he fought like he was my man.

That was why I didn't talk back. That was why I obeyed. I walked into the bedroom and found the lingerie in the closet. I'd noticed it before but hadn't tried anything on. I picked a black bodysuit with a crotch that unfas-tened. Black and lacy, it was sexy and graceful at the same time. I noticed the tag along the seam.

Barsetti Lingerie.

I doubted that was a coincidence.

I fixed my hair and makeup in the bathroom. I'd cried so hard when Bosco stepped into that ring. I was terrified I would never get him back, that he would lose his life defending me. My heart broke in two, and seeing every hit he took made me feel worse. My mascara had been destroyed, and my foundation had run off with my tears. I reapplied everything, setting my face back to normal and hiding the puffiness around my eyes.

I put on the black ensemble then followed his direc-tions. I lay on the bed, my stomach against the sheets with my knees together. I turned down the lights to accompany his dark mood and waited.

His bare feet sounded a moment later. He took his time as he stepped inside, knowing I would wait as long as he wanted me to.

I kept my eyes on the headboard, waiting for him to take me.

His knees hit the mattress, and he slowly moved up my

body. His hands glided over the bare spots on my back, and he touched my hair with his fingertips. He felt the curve of my ass with his palm, moving over it gently.

He grabbed one of the pillows near my head then stuffed it underneath my hips. He tilted my ass to the ceiling and made my back curve at a deep angle. Then he unfastened the lingerie over my pussy and made the body-suit pop open to reveal my slit.

Instead of shoving his dick inside right away, he gave me his mouth instead. With gentle slowness, he licked the area, giving it soft kisses before he moved his tongue deep inside me. He sucked my clit into his mouth and gave it a little nibble, making my entire body tense.

I felt my body relax and tense at the same time, the arousal kicking into my bloodstream and making my pussy wet. I held myself up on my elbows and closed my eyes as I enjoyed what he did to my body, enjoyed the soft strokes of that experienced tongue. Quiet moans escaped my throat, and I gripped the sheets underneath me, my breaths becoming louder and deeper.

Bosco pulled his mouth away then positioned himself on top of me. With his knees on either side of mine and his hands on the mattress beside my hips, he pressed the head of his cock against my wet entrance. Once he was inside, he gave a forceful thrust and shoved himself the rest of the way, making my hips slam against the pillow propped underneath me. He halted as he enjoyed the way his dick felt inside me, a groan coming from his lips.

I moaned when I felt his enormous size inside of me.

He grabbed the back of my neck just the way he promised, and then he fucked me harder than he ever had before. His hips slammed into me, and he hit me deep and strong at a profound angle, making my body tense over and over. "You." He thrust hard. "Are." He thrust again. "Mine."

My body shook forward every time pounded into me. I gripped the sheets and felt them slide under my sweaty palms. I bit my bottom lip as I felt him destroy my pussy, fucking me harder than I'd ever been fucked in my life. Sometimes he squeezed my neck a little too tight and I struggled to breathe, but despite his aggression, I loved his dominance. High on the adrenaline rushing through his body, he took it out on me. The blood lust got to his head, and this was all he wanted to do, to celebrate his victory by fucking the pussy he'd just fought for.

"Fuck." His loud groans filled the bedroom as he fucked my cunt mercilessly. He breathed deep and hard, getting covered in streaks of sweat just as he did during the battle. His cock was harder than it'd ever been. His pumps increased, and he groaned even louder, coming inside my slit with a victorious moan. "Fuck yes." He grabbed the front of my neck and squeezed me, keeping me in place as he dumped every single drop inside me.

Listening to him explode inside me fueled my own climax. He always waited for me to come first, but tonight, he clearly was in a different state of mind. I was the prize he'd won, and he wanted to enjoy me selfishly, to keep fucking me until all his adrenaline was finally out of his system.

He softened inside me, but that didn't stop him from thrusting. He was still big enough to make an impact, and his cock moved through his own come inside my cunt. A minute later, he was back to full hardness, and he thrust into me forcefully, grinding me and my clit hard against the pillow. He pressed his hand against my lower back to keep my body at the angle he liked. Then he pressed farther into me, making my clit drag against the pillow he slept on.

I knew I was about to come. I could feel it in the way I tightened around him. His cock felt so good when it was this big and this aggressive. I was powerless underneath him, subjected to his cruel thrusts and groans, but I liked it. He'd just fought a man with his bare hands and got off on killing him. I could feel it in the way he handled me, like he was a wild animal that had chased off an opponent so he could mate with me. The Butcher wanted to be the one lying on top of me right now, but he couldn't outmatch Bosco.

I came, turned on by his aggression, his come, and the way he'd killed a man to protect me. It was a powerful climax, the kind that made me scream and bite my bottom lip at the same time. I ground my own clit against the pillow, getting off on the image and the huge cock in my pussy.

"I own you." He spoke directly into my ear, feeling my pussy contract all around him. He kept slamming into me, his sweat dripping onto my back. "I paid for this cunt with my fists, my blood, and my power. It's mine. Say it."

"Yes...my pussy is yours."

He growled into my ear. "You are mine. Say it."

"I'm yours."

He dragged his tongue down my neck and gave me a gentle bite. "I'm your protector, your lover, and your man.

No one looks at my woman and gets away with it. No one comes close to her without my permission." He kept moving hard, his endurance never breaking. He closed his fists against the bed and kept thrusting, groaning at the same time. "I will fight for you. I will die for you. Because that's what a real man does for his woman." His lips grazed against my ear as he spoke.

I grabbed his ass and pulled him deeper into me, getting off on the words he yelled into my ear. I came again, just when I least expected it, and I squeezed his cock so tightly I probably bruised it just like his face. "Bosco…"

He groaned a moment later, exploding inside my pussy for a second time. He dropped more come between my legs, adding another load to the first pile. Our orgasms overlapped, and we moaned together and clawed at each other as we both enjoyed it.

He paused when he finished, breathing hard against my ear. "Let's see how much come this pussy can hold." He started to move again even though he was still soft.

I gripped his wrists on either side of me, using them as an anchor to keep myself still as he thrust into me. "Give it to me, babe. Give it all to me."

8

BOSCO

BY THE TIME I woke up the next morning, the rage had finally subsided.

I was high off ecstasy, blood lust, and adrenaline. I killed a man I despised, made him pay for what he did, and then I shot him right between the eyes. My hand didn't flinch when I pulled the trigger, but it shook immediately afterward, giving me a surge of power that my body couldn't metabolize. I saw his blood stain the concrete, watched the light leave his eyes the second the bullet pierced his skull.

It was like taking a hit of the best drug.

I couldn't see straight because the sensation was so powerful. Even when I returned to Carmen, I couldn't shake it off. I put my life on the line to save her, a woman who would walk away from me in six weeks, but I didn't hesitate before I made my decision. She was the most important thing in my life right now. When I saw him stare at her like a piece of meat, I knew what I had to do.

I didn't look back.

In hindsight, it was probably stupid. It could have ended quite differently. But I'd promised Carmen I would have him dead in twenty-four hours, and if I didn't take his life in those next thirty minutes, I would have broken my promise. Not once in my life had I broken a promise, and I wasn't going to start now.

Besides, I wanted to prove my point—that there was nowhere safer in the world than by my side.

She was dead asleep when I woke up the following morning. I went into the living room and made some breakfast because I was starving. After the night I'd had, I skipped the lighter breakfast options and went for pancakes, bacon, and eggs. I cooked everything before I sat at the dining table and ate, knowing Carmen could be asleep for a few more hours.

Ronan called me, his name appearing on the screen.

I answered. "Where did you dump the body?"

"In a landfill. The rats and insects will eat him until there's nothing left but bone."

"Good." I'd considered giving him a grave just so I could piss on it.

"The whole city is talking about what happened last night."

As they should be.

"How's Carmen?"

She enjoyed the rough way I took her last night, so she seemed to be in good spirits. "She's fine."

"Bosco, she was terrified. She grabbed my hand so hard, she almost broke it."

A slight surge of jealousy moved through me, but I

dismissed it because it was unwarranted. Carmen only held his hand because she was scared—scared for me. "I noticed."

"She was in tears the whole time. Told me she wouldn't know what to do if she lost you."

I forced myself not to smile even though that was exactly what I wanted to do. Watching that woman cry for me was the biggest turn-on ever. She put her emotions out in the open, admitted the depth of her feelings without even realizing it. Knowing she cared so much gave me another jolt of energy throughout the fight. She cared more about my safety than her own. "Yes, she's hung up on me."

"I'd say it's more than that."

The last time we'd spoken about it, Carmen was still determined to end our relationship once our three months were finished. Now I wasn't sure if that would happen anymore. The time we spent together had solidified our commitment to one another, had deepened the connection so powerfully that I was certain it was more than just lust. She couldn't sleep without me, she couldn't stand the sight of me getting hurt, and she missed me whenever we weren't together. "Yeah, you're probably right."

"It meant a lot to her that you didn't fool around with Ruby. She hates her, by the way."

I stilled in my chair and stopped eating, that information registering in my brain as brand-new. "What?"

"She said Ruby practically threw her tits at you."

How did Carmen know about that? I didn't even tell Ronan it happened. The second Ruby was gone from the building, I forgot about it entirely. It took me a moment to figure it out how that was possible.

She must have been in the penthouse. She must have witnessed the whole thing and never told me.

"Yeah…it happened a while ago."

"Well, my best advice is to keep Carmen away from her. She might give her a black eye."

Imagining Carmen being jealous was always a turn-on. I heard the sound of her steps down the hallway as she approached the living room. I glanced in her direction and saw her run her fingers through her hair, wearing my gray t-shirt better than I ever did.

She crossed the room then came to the table, her eyes immediately lighting up when she saw what I made. "Oh, thank god. I need some real food after last night." She leaned down and kissed me on the neck before she walked back into the kitchen.

I almost forgot Ronan was still on the phone. "I'll talk to you later." I hung up.

Carmen came back with a plate full of food and took the seat across from me. She had a mug of coffee, three pancakes, and plenty of eggs and bacon. She immediately started to eat, starving just the way I'd been that morning.

I sipped my coffee while I stared at her.

"This is good." She shoveled another bite of pancake into her mouth.

I hadn't finished my breakfast, but now I was too distracted by her to eat. I sipped my coffee as I stared at her face, loving the way her hair naturally framed her face and how my shirt slipped down over one shoulder. She was perfect, regardless of the time of day or what she was wearing.

She met my gaze, knowing I was staring at her. "What?"

I was tempted to confront her about Ruby, but there wasn't much to say. Whether she was intentionally spying on me or she happened to be in the wrong place at the right time didn't really matter. Remaining faithful to her was the easiest thing I'd ever done. Why would I want some gold digger when I could have her? She shouldn't be surprised by my actions. But it did mean something to me that it meant so much to her, that my fidelity made her happy. That meant if I'd fooled around, it would have broken her heart.

I decided to keep the information to myself since it seemed so pointless to share out loud. It was obvious why I was immune to Ruby's charms, even though she was good in bed with a beautiful body. It was obvious why I put myself in the ring and fought a psychopath with my bare hands. It was obvious why I did everything when it came to her. And it was also obvious why her reactions were the same in every single instance. "Nothing."

"How's your pussy, Beautiful?" I lay on top of her on the bed, our naked bodies grinding together.

She rubbed her clit. "I can tell it's a little sore…"

That was to be expected since I viciously pounded into her like she was a toy. "I would apologize, but I can't since I wouldn't mean it." I widened her legs then lay on my stomach on the bed. "But I can do this." I cupped her thighs with my hands then kissed her softly, being delicate after the harsh way I'd taken her last night. I took my time as I tasted her tartness, circled her clit with my tongue, and then slipped inside her slit. I kissed her just the way I would kiss her on the mouth, with deep softness.

She relaxed on the pillows and moaned, enjoying the way my mouth pleased her so gently.

My cock was hard underneath my body, but he had plenty of fun last night. He could wait until she was ready again.

She dug her fingers into my hair and slowly ground against my face, loving the way my mouth and tongue were pleasing her. Her sexy moans became louder, and when her nipples hardened to the sharpness of diamonds, she came against my face. "Bosco…" She ground right against my mouth, bucking slightly because the pleasure was so intense.

I loved pressing my face between her legs, feeling her clit vibrate with her orgasm. I loved the way she reached for more because my moves satisfied her. I didn't go down on my flings very often, only on rare occasions, but I loved being settled between her legs like this.

Best pussy ever.

I pulled my mouth away then moved back on top of her, knowing my cock would settle down after a few minutes. I held myself on my arms and looked down at her, finding her the most beautiful woman that had ever been in this bed. It took a long time for her to give me a real chance, and now that she had, my life felt complete.

This woman completed me.

With satisfaction in her eyes and a slight smile on her lips, she fingered my hair. "You're good at that."

"I just like eating your pussy."

"Really? I've never had a guy do that to me before."

Because none of them had been man enough. "They were pussies. That's why."

"Well, they tried. I just never let them."

"Why?"

She shrugged. "Seems too intimate for a fling."

"You let me." And this was still defined as a fling.

"But we both know you're different." She cupped my face and brushed her thumb across my cheek. "I still can't believe you did that last night. You have no idea how scared I was."

I turned my head into her palm and kissed it. "I do. I saw your tears."

"But you did it anyway."

"Because I had to. I wanted to kill him with my bare hands. That's how much I hated him."

"You could have died."

I shook my head. "Not when I had so much to live for." I hooked her leg around my waist. "You're my woman and I will protect you, even if that means getting my hands dirty once in a while. You should never feel scared with me ever again. I'm the most powerful man in this city—and I hope I proved that to you."

Her eyes softened. "You proved it a long time ago."

"Then I'm the best choice in a man." There was no one else who could compete with me. Carmen deserved the best—and I was the best. I wanted to ditch this contract we'd set up and start being real. I knew how she felt about me, and there was no way she couldn't figure out how I felt about her.

She widened her legs then locked her ankles around my waist. "Give it to me slow…"

"I thought you were sore."

Her arms wrapped around my neck, and she pulled me closer. "I don't care."

9

BONES

I'D BEEN DROPPING Vanessa off at work and picking her up every night at the end of the day. The storm that swept through the middle of the country had been drastic. The roads were flooded and dangerous, and since she drove a small car, I couldn't let her commute to work alone.

Even if my son weren't growing inside her.

I pulled up to the curb in front of the gallery and then escorted her inside.

Just the few short feet into the store left us both soaking wet. Her private security was already there, giving me a slight nod in acknowledgment. He didn't talk much, but that was why I liked him.

"You really don't need to drive me every day," Vanessa said. "I always drive slow——"

"Our arguments always end the same way. I disregard what you say and do what I want. So let's skip the beginning and the middle."

Any other woman would slap me for talking that way.

Vanessa accepted me, saw through my coldness and saw the love behind the statement. "Well, thanks for bringing us to work."

Us. There were two of them now. Two people I had to love and protect with my life. I moved my hand to her stomach even though he wasn't kicking. I still liked to touch her belly, to feel it while I slept at night. Whenever he started to kick, my heart did the strangest thing…it did somersaults. "Call me if you need anything." She was almost at her third trimester. We were more than halfway into her pregnancy, and the doctor said everything was going well. So far, it seemed like my wife and son were both healthy.

"I know." She rose on her tiptoes to kiss me. "I love you."

"I love you too." I still got chills when I heard those words from her. Sometimes it was hard to believe that this was real, that we got the future we'd always wanted. She was my wife, my family. And pretty soon, I would have someone who shared my blood. I wouldn't be the only member of my bloodline. Soon, I would have a son. "I'm going to check on Carmen before I head out."

"If she needed something, she would call."

"I'm here anyway. May as well. We both know she's not the kind of woman to ask for help."

Vanessa's smile fell immediately.

I suspected there was something going on between the two of them, but since Vanessa didn't tell me about it, I assumed it wasn't my place to know. "I'll be back in a few hours."

"Alright." She rubbed her belly, suddenly looking stressed.

I stayed still, knowing she had something else to say to me. "What is it?"

"It's about the baby. I've been thinking about names…"

I hadn't given it much thought. I assumed we would wait until he was born before we figured it out. It was only recently that the doctor confirmed he really was a boy. Vanessa's assumption had been correct. "Alright."

"You can say no if you want. I completely understand, and I wouldn't be angry about it…"

I already knew what she was going to ask. "If that's what you want."

Her eyes narrowed in confusion. "You don't even know what I'm going to say."

"Baby, I always know what you're going to say. You're the one who's growing my son inside this little belly." My hands cupped both sides of her stomach. "So you have a lot of say in the matter. If you want to name him that, we can. I know it's important to you."

Her hands moved over mine. "What do you think I want to name him?"

It was obvious, written in her eyes full of love. "Crow."

Her eyes immediately softened when I got it right. "You did know…"

I knew everything about my woman, from her thoughts to her moods. She and I shared our bodies as well as our souls. We existed as almost a single person.

"You would really be okay with that?" she whispered.

I'd come to respect her father. I didn't like him initially, but he wore me down. Now I saw him as a father figure, as someone that I even admired. "Yes." I would do anything to make her happy.

Her eyes watered. "That's so sweet…" She gripped my hands and moved into me. "Thank you."

I pressed a kiss to her forehead.

"When we have our next son, I want to name him Griffin." She looked up into my gaze. "Because you're the other man I admire more than anyone else in the world. There's nothing better than that."

I wasn't expecting that. "Really?"

"Yes. I want him to carry your name when we're gone, to know there's a piece of you still out there. It's an admirable name. I love it."

The thought hadn't crossed my mind to name my son after me. I knew she was named after her aunt, so naming children after our relatives was common for them. "We can talk about it when the time comes."

"Alright."

I kissed her on the forehead again before I turned away and walked out. I ignored the rain and got into the truck before I drove a few blocks away to the flower shop. The second I pulled up to the building, I knew something was wrong. All the lights were off, and the place looked closed. There wasn't a note on the door with an explanation.

I drove away and headed to her apartment next, checking to see if she was home. Maybe she didn't open the shop because of the weather. Or maybe she walked to work but never made it.

I went to the second floor and arrived at her door. I

knocked loudly, so loud there was no chance she didn't hear it.

No answer.

I knocked again then pressed my ear to the door, listening for the sound of the shower. But there was no water on.

That was when I started to panic. I pulled out my phone and called her.

No answer.

My old ways came back to me, and I picked her lock before I stepped inside. All the lights were off, and it seemed like there'd been no one there for a long time. The flowers on the table had died a long time ago, and the stench was potent in the air. I opened the fridge next and saw nothing but expired and moldy food.

She hadn't been there in a long time.

I explored the rest of the apartment and discovered the same thing.

I locked her apartment before I left and tried to call her again. I'd just seen her at the wedding, and everything had appeared to be fine. It didn't seem like she was in any trouble, but she obviously hadn't been staying at her apartment in that time frame.

I made it to the lobby and picked her mailbox lock while I listened to the phone ring as I called again.

She answered this time. "Hey, Griffin. How are you?"

When I opened her mailbox, it was so stuffed with mail that I couldn't even get anything out. She obviously hadn't checked it in weeks. I didn't bother looking through it before I shut it and locked it again. "I dropped off Vanessa at the shop then stopped by your flower shop to see how you were doing. But it's closed." I didn't accuse her of anything, choosing to read her tone of voice and all the other signs I could gather from her demeanor.

"Oh, yeah." Her voice turned a little higher, indicating that she was lying. "I was getting no customers because of the rain, so I stopped bothering. When the weather clears up, I'll open again. Besides, I don't want to go out in the rain anyway."

That sounded plausible, but she seemed slightly flustered over the line, making me assume there was something I was missing. "Then where are you now?" She obviously hadn't been home in a while.

"Oh, I'm at home," she said. "Just sitting in my pajamas."

She lied to me. She didn't seem to be in any kind of danger, so why would she lie?

"Thanks for checking on me, though. But I'm just taking it easy."

She was definitely hiding something, but what could it be? "Of course. I'll let you go." I hung up without waiting for her to respond.

I stayed in the lobby as I thought this through. If she hadn't been home in months, that meant she was staying somewhere else. She couldn't afford to have two places, so that meant she was crashing with someone, probably a guy.

But what guy would she stay with for two months?

She hadn't told anyone that she'd been seeing someone, and if she was living with someone for two months, then the relationship must be serious. That meant she didn't want anyone to know about it.

But why?

Then it hit me.

Bosco.

She was staying with Bosco.

Vanessa must know about it. That was why they were so secretive all the time. Carmen must not be in any real danger. Otherwise, Vanessa would intervene. And that could only mean Carmen chose to be with Bosco.

But that was just as good as being his prisoner.

10

BOSCO

I CAME home from the casino and spotted Carmen on the couch. She was wrapped in my t-shirt with a blanket draped over her legs, her hair all over the place and the TV on low. Like an obedient pet, she waited by the front door so she would know the second I was home.

I liked it.

I liked having a woman wait for me.

She was dead tired, because when I scooped her up in my arms and carried her into the bedroom, she didn't wake up. I set her on the mattress and pulled the sheets over her shoulder before I stripped off my clothes. My suit had absorbed the smoke in the air, and my lips tasted like whiskey. I tossed everything in the bin and shut the lid so the maid could take care of it in the morning. I set my shoes on top so they could be properly shined.

I got into the shower next and closed my eyes as the warm water dripped down my body. The second I'd stepped into that casino tonight, there was a ripple of silence that was pregnant with respect. The Butcher was a formidable opponent, but being the honorable king I was, I'd executed him myself. I'd accepted him into the casino, and it was my job to eject him. The men didn't say a single word to me, but I knew exactly what they were talking about.

Ronan told me everything.

The men practically bowed to me.

Ruby made eyes at me all night long, wanting my dick even more than she had before. I risked my life to protect my woman, and Ruby would give anything to be that woman. She wanted the security, the protection, and the jewels I could offer.

All of that belonged to Carmen.

It was ironic. I wanted to give all those things to Carmen because she didn't want them in the first place.

I scrubbed the smell out of my hair with shampoo and let the suds fall around me. The door opened and closed behind me, and then a moment later I felt soapy hands on my body. She rubbed the soap across my hard body, her soft hands feeling the grooves between my muscles. Her fingers rubbed my back too, massaged the muscles deep and hard.

I closed my eyes as I enjoyed it, enjoyed this woman's touch in so many ways. I shared my space with her completely, and our time together was so perfect I stopped worrying about the weeks we had left together. After everything we'd been through, I knew that contract didn't matter anymore.

She wasn't going anywhere.

She belonged right here with me.

My life had changed drastically since I'd passed that dark alleyway. Now my bed carried the scent of a single woman, someone I would risk my life to protect. I was faithful to her, not getting hard for the most beautiful woman who frequented the casino. I was immune to other tits and curves because Carmen was the only woman I wanted. I'd turned into a pussy-whipped man who wore his heart on his sleeve.

But I was okay with it.

She wrapped her arms around my waist and squeezed me, her tits pressing into my back. She rested her cheek against me, her hair sticking to my skin.

My hand rubbed her arm over my stomach, and I stayed still, absorbing her affection. The sound of the water filled the space around us, shutting out the outside world. It was just the two of us together—man and woman.

When I thought about my mother, I knew she would have adored Carmen. She would have respected her because Carmen respected herself so much. My brother thought she was wonderful. I never viewed women as people, just objects. But when Carmen came along, she straightened me out.

I needed to be straightened out.

She broke the silence. "How was work?"

I slowly turned around and let the water hit my back. "It was work." My hands slid around her soapy waist, and I looked down into her beautiful face, seeing the clean skin from the lack of makeup. Her eyes were full of sleepiness but also excitement since I was finally home.

"Anything different?"

"The men are serious around me. A little more afraid. Have a little more respect."

"That sounds like a good thing."

"It is. I suspect no one will break the law for a while, not when that memory is fresh in their minds."

She rested her face against my chest and held me under the water. She wanted to touch me so much that she couldn't wait until I joined her in bed. She preferred to get wet with me then wait until I was dry. "You should try the day shift."

I chuckled. "No such thing, Beautiful."

"Well, you should come home earlier. Three in the morning is rough."

I couldn't change my hours, not even for her. I needed to make appearances often, to maintain the power over the floor. My schedule was never predictable, so it was impossible for men to plot against me. "You could just go to sleep. Let me wake you when I get home."

"You think I haven't tried?" she asked with a weak laugh. "I just lie there, tossing and turning."

I loved knowing she needed me so much. It was better than listening to one of my lovers beg me to fuck them. "Why is that?"

"I'm not sure," she said quietly. "I guess it's everything. I'm freezing cold without you beside me to keep me warm. I don't feel as safe without you, even if there are twenty-four men in the lobby. I'm worried that you're okay, being surrounded by all those murderers. And I'm used to listening to you breathe when I fall asleep. The sound of the TV isn't nearly as similar, but it's the next best thing."

It was the sexiest confession I'd ever heard. She'd told me she didn't need a man for anything, but she'd just poured her heart out to me, basically admitted that she was helpless without me. She needed me by her side just to sleep. It was the strongest form of dependency.

She stared at me as her fingers trickled down my arm, like she expected me to say something.

"All I ever wanted was for you to give me a chance—and you did."

I MADE LOVE TO HER IN MY BED, MOVING SLOWLY between her legs until I made her thighs squeeze around my hips in pleasure. Her hair was spread across the pillow, and she moaned in my face as her pussy squeezed me like a boa constrictor. Her fingers dug into my hair, and she bucked against me, her green eyes bright like they were on fire.

I moved deep inside her as I came, pumping my seed into her where it would remain all night long. We were skin on skin, and feeling her warm, wet flesh was the most erotic experience of my life. I couldn't wear a condom again, not with her. Releasing inside her was the most intimate experience I'd ever felt. There was only one woman I would do it with—Carmen Barsetti.

When I finished, she immediately went to sleep. Feeling safe and satisfied, she finally let her mind slip away. The sheets were pulled to her shoulder, and her lips immediately parted with her deep breathing.

I kissed the back of her shoulder and got comfortable in preparation to drift away, but then my phone rang on the nightstand. No one would call me at this hour unless it was important, so I grabbed the phone and walked down the hallway. The screen showed Drake's name, the head of my security team. I took the call. "What is it?" I'd just slaughtered The Butcher, so I didn't expect to have any issues for a while.

Drake didn't waste my time and got right to the point. "I think there's something you should know. We've been keeping a close eye on him, and I'm certain he doesn't know we're following him. I have ten guys on him right now, so if you want us to pull the trigger, we will."

This sounded like bad news. "Who?"

"Bones."

I stopped in the center of the living room, hearing his name loud and clear. I hadn't given him much thought after Carmen and I became more serious. Her family had never been an issue because she kept our secret so well. But the second I heard his name, I knew there would be a problem.

"What's he doing?"

"He went to Carmen's flower shop yesterday. Stopped outside for a while even though it was closed. Then he went to her apartment, broke the lock, and went inside. He was in there for a while before he left, then checked her mailbox. He didn't take anything. Then he made a call."

My heart started to race in my chest, thud like a drum. Bones was an adversary I didn't want to cross, not because I was afraid of him, but because he was Carmen's family. If he told the Barsettis, he could make life difficult for me. Keeping our relationship a secret had made Carmen relax and give me a real chance. When she'd stopped worrying what her family would think of me, she'd finally looked past the deplorable way I made a living. The best solution to this problem was to kill him before he had a chance to say anything.

"He's still in the city. You want me to take him out?"

"Why is he still here?"

"He's been watching her apartment. I'm guessing he's trying to figure out where she really is."

Shit. He was a smart man, and he would figure it out soon enough if he hadn't already. "Has he called Carmen?"

"He called her yesterday. The conversation only lasted a minute. The transcript showed that he asked where she was, and she said she was at her apartment. At that time, he knew that wasn't true."

"He didn't say anything to that?"

"No. He also approached the jurisdiction line but didn't cross it. Looked at your property from a top of a building. We think he was looking for her car. It's parked outside, so he probably saw it."

The only reason he wouldn't confront her was because he'd already figured it out. And if he saw her car, that was evidence enough.

"My guys have a clean shot at him. He's alone."

I was tempted to do it. We could make it seem like an accident, like he drank too much and lost control of his truck. It would make all my problems go away. But when I thought about how devastated Carmen would be, I knew that wasn't an option. It would break her heart. Even if she never figured out I was the one who ordered the hit, she would be upset for a really long time. "Leave him be."

"You're sure?" Drake asked in surprise.

"Yes." He had a wife at home. He was just trying to protect Carmen, and I couldn't hate him for that. "I'll take care of this myself."

I STOOD OUTSIDE THE LARGE GATES TO HIS PROPERTY and made the call. In the countryside, it was particularly dark, especially when the stars were obscured by heavy clouds. A thin fog had rolled into the area, making the cold bite all the way down to the bone. In my jeans and leather jacket, I was fine. But Carmen wouldn't survive.

Heavy footsteps approached, the sound of a beefy man coming toward me in the darkness. Even with the metal gate separating us, I could feel his rage as it grew stronger and stronger.

The gates were nearly twenty feet high, tall enough that they would be extremely difficult to climb. Cobblestone walls surrounded the property, lush ivy growing over it. The place was a fortress as well as a historical landmark. The reason he bought it was because of his unique protection out here in the middle of nowhere.

The gates unlocked, and the light flicked on along the wall, illuminating the area near the road.

That's when I saw him, his blue eyes fierce as he pointed a gun at my face.

I glanced at the barrel pointed at my chest but didn't react in alarm. "I'm unarmed. And alone." I nodded to the black car parked on the other side of the road, a two-seater that wouldn't be able to fit an army or a cache of artillery. "If I wanted to kill you, my army would have destroyed your home and your lives before you even woke up."

Bones was just as threatening as his reputation claimed him to be. Muscular, tall, and with a hint of sadistic rage in his eyes, he was the murderer people paid millions to hire. Covered in tattoos all the way up to his neck, he was a nightmare most never wanted to witness in person. He lowered the gun and emptied the barrel of the bullets before he tossed the gun on the grass. "And I prefer to kill a man with my own hands."

I gave him a lopsided grin. "What a coincidence. I just did the same a few days ago. Good times."

Bones didn't drop his hostility, furious that I was on the outskirts of his property. "You crossed a line coming here. This is where my family lives." His tone deepened. "Don't come near my family." Both of his hands tightened into fists like he wanted to break my face cleanly in two.

"I have no interest in hurting your wife. I don't care about her. You're the only person I want to see."

"Then we could have had this discussion elsewhere."

"Secrecy was the utmost importance. And like I said, I'm unarmed. I don't go anywhere without my hundred-man army. But I left them behind—as a show of good faith." I indicated the wide-open spaces around me. "We're alone, Bones."

He was still livid, and nothing I said would dim his rage.

"You know why I'm here."

He didn't confirm it or deny it.

"Have you told her family?" I'd never met either of the Barsetti brothers in person, but I knew them by reputation. I was certain they knew me by reputation as well. They wouldn't like me sleeping with one of their own, not when I was rumored to be the cruelest man in the center of the country.

"No."

"Good choice. I don't need to tell you they're no match for me. I've warned Carmen what I'd do to her family if she ever got them involved. I'm not the kind of man that kills for sport. I kill for a reason. And the Barsettis have respectable blood that has reigned in these parts for generations. I don't want to kill them—but I will."

His eyes narrowed slightly, his blue eyes looking like piercing shards. "Carmen is my sister. She's my family. I will protect her at any cost. You may be a powerful man, but don't forget who you're dealing with."

I'd always admired Bones. Unlike other men, he didn't pretend to be unafraid. He truly was unafraid. "Yes, you're a very talented killer. But you don't own the world like I do. It's an unfair match, and we both know it. Round up your boys, and you're still outnumbered a hundred to one."

"You're my only target. Once you're dead, I don't need to worry about anything else."

The threats were rising, the testosterone was brimming. The situation escalated so quickly because neither one of us would back down. "I'll be frank with you, Bones. I don't want to hurt any of you because it would hurt Carmen. She loves all of you very much."

"I know she does."

"Then the best way to keep the peace is to keep your mouth shut."

"I've never been much of a talker, but that's unlikely." His kept his arms by his sides, only wearing a t-shirt despite the nearly freezing temperature. Vapor escaped his nostrils and rose in the light. "Is she a prisoner? Do you hurt her?" He tensed his jaw as he waited for me to answer, preparing for the worst but hoping for the best. Despite our illegal backgrounds, we were both honest men. Truly formidable adversaries never told a lie because they were never afraid of the repercussions.

The questions were fair, but they offended me anyway. "I would never hurt her. Her safety is my priority. I protect her, take care of her, and adore her." I held his gaze as I gave him the answer, unafraid of the depth of my feelings for this woman. "And she's not a prisoner. We agreed to a three-month arrangement. She insists I'm not the right man for her, that I'm not the man who will give her a marriage and four children. When our time is over, we'll walk away from each other."

Bones's anger slowly decreased. "You'll let her go when that time comes?"

I was a man of my word. "Yes."

He couldn't hide the relief that swept across his face.

"But I don't think it will come to that. As hard as it is to believe, that woman wants me. She loves my protection, my power, and my wealth. I'm the kind of man she's always wanted but never found. I'm the only one who has proved I'm worthy of her. When the time comes, she won't leave."

His anger flared up again. "You'll never be good enough for Carmen Barsetti. I warned you to stay away from her, but you didn't listen to me."

"We both know I don't listen to anyone," I said coldly.

"Even if she wanted to stay, her family would never approve. I'm sure you've noticed how close they are by now."

"And yet, they accept you." It was a low blow, but also a valid point. "You killed people for a living. I just make money."

Bones didn't rise to the insult. "You're surrounded by the monsters of the underworld. As long as she's involved with you, she'll never be safe. My occupation and my personal life were distinctly separate."

"But your wife was captured and taken to Morocco."

Bones didn't ask how I knew that. "Don't talk about my wife again."

Clearly, Vanessa was his only hot button. "I'll cut to the chase. Are you going to be a problem?" Bones wouldn't lie to me because his reputation was founded on his honesty.

"Since it's going to be over soon, I'll keep it to myself. As long as you aren't hurting her and she has a way out, then I don't see the necessity of involving her family. It'll lead to a war, and lives will be lost. It's better this way."

I was glad he wasn't going to be difficult. "Like I said, she's not going to leave me."

"She's a smart woman. She knows staying with you isn't an option."

And he didn't know she was in love with me. "We'll find out soon enough."

11

CARMEN

Now that the storm had passed, I opened the shop again. I got a new shipment of flowers and put together arrangements so they could sit in the window. Thankfully, the customers started to flock inside now that the sun was out again. A lot of my clients were restaurant owners, buying fresh arrangements to put on their tables and into their pots outside. They already ordered wine from my father, so naturally, they came to me for their floral needs.

Around lunchtime, things started to slow down. Instead of working the register constantly, I trimmed the flowers and made new arrangements at the island in the middle of the shop. My shop was a workplace as well as a store. When people passed on the sidewalk, they saw me working inside, and that gave the place more character.

The door opened, and someone stepped inside.

I looked up, expecting to see a stranger's face. "It's nice that the rain finally stopped, huh?"

Griffin stared me down, his blue eyes so cold they

looked hot. Smoke was practically erupting from his nostrils, and he looked like a wild bull about to charge me. He was still as he stared at me for a while, and then he finally crossed the tile floor to my table.

He didn't need to say a single word to tell me what was on his mind.

He knew everything.

His hands gripped the edge of the table, his powerful shoulders shaking with ferocity.

I was still, actually afraid of him. "You're scaring me."

"Good." He spoke with a tense jaw, his softness no longer present like it was when Vanessa was around. "You should be scared because you're in the most dangerous situation of your life."

Yes. He definitely knew.

I set down the flowers and the shears and removed my gloves. He'd called me a few days ago to check on me. That must have been when he'd figured everything out. He must have dug a little deeper and finally discovered the secret I tried to keep hidden.

Shit.

He kept staring at me with that terrifying expression, reminding me of my father when he was disappointed in me.

I didn't know where to begin. It seemed like anything I might say would piss him off even more.

When Griffin realized I wasn't going to say anything, he did. "I warned you about him. I told you to stay away from him. I specifically told you to tell me if he bothered you ever again. So what the hell happened? You just ignored everything I said?"

Thankfully, there was no one else in the flower shop to witness this conversation. I knew Bosco's men were posted everywhere, probably watching us through the windows. But they would never hurt Griffin, not when he was my family. "It didn't happen like that."

"Then how did it happen?"

"It's a long story…"

"I've got all day." He slammed his fist down. "Tell me how my favorite Barsetti made the worst mistake of her life."

The word mistake didn't resonate with me at all because that wasn't how I felt about Bosco. My life had changed so much, and as bad it sounded, I was actually happy. "He asked me to dinner, and that's where it all started."

"And you didn't say no?"

"I did in the beginning…"

"And then he made you?"

I shrugged. "Not exactly. It was supposed to be purely physical. That's how it was for a while, but when I realized how deep I was getting, I tried to end it."

"Tried?"

"He wouldn't let me," I whispered. "Said he wouldn't let me go."

"Fucking piece of shit—"

"But then he changed. He agreed to three months and promised he would let me go when that time came."

"And you believe him?" he asked incredulously.

As hard as it was to admit, I trusted that man deeply. "Yes. He's a man of his word."

Griffin stared at the counter as he gripped the edge. "This is a fucking nightmare."

"Griffin, I know you don't like him—"

"Don't sit there and list off his qualities. The man is dangerous, lethal, and not good enough for you. You really want to be involved with a psychopath like that? That man only cares about one thing—power. He exploits it, abuses it, and gets off on it. I realize I'm not the perfect man Vanessa dreamed about, but I'm a dramatic improvement over him."

I'd never seen Griffin act this way, raise his voice to shake the windows with his baritone. I felt bad for Vanessa anytime they had a fight. "He's not the same man that he was before. He's different now. At least, he's different with me."

Griffin rolled his eyes. "You're smarter than this."

"I know him better than you do, Griffin. I'm not saying you're wrong about everything you just said. But there's a lot more to him than you realize. He's kind, generous, protective, and—"

"Psychotic? You tried to dump him, and he wouldn't let you. He thinks the rules don't apply to him."

"And you know what?" I challenged. "I'm glad he didn't let me walk away. He said he wanted a real chance with me, and once I gave it to him, he showed me that he's sensitive, loving, and gentle. He's not just the monster you perceive him to be."

"Fuck, this is worse than I thought." He rubbed the back of his head, his chest puffing up with the deep breaths he took.

"Please tell me you didn't tell my father about any of this?"

He looked me in the eye and shook his head. "No. But that's because Bosco told me you asked for an expiration date."

So they'd actually spoken to each other? "When did you talk to him?"

His eyes narrowed in ferocity. "The man showed up to my house at four in the morning—where my pregnant wife sleeps."

My heart fell in my chest. "I know he would never hurt either of you..." I refused to believe Bosco would intimidate my family with his army of men.

"He came unarmed and alone," Griffin said. "But I don't give a shit. He crossed a line, Carmen."

"And what did he say to you?"

"He threatened me to keep my mouth shut."

The disappointment rushed through me.

"He said he doesn't want to kill us, but if we move against him, he will. So he encouraged me not to tell your father and your uncle. The only reason I agreed is because of your agreement. When your time is over, you can walk away."

That deadline was only a few weeks away now. I couldn't believe how quickly the time had passed. Now we only had a month left together. I agreed to this contract because it gave me everything I wanted—time to enjoy him and an escape route. But the idea of leaving him behind and marrying someone else filled me with unexpected sadness.

"You will walk away, right?" Griffin moved closer to

me, examining my face with an intense expression. "When your time is over, you will leave him and move on? Tell me that so I can let this go."

That was the plan, but the idea of actually going through with it sounded horrible.

"Carmen?" he pressed. "I need to know this is gonna end. Once I do, I can relax. If he's going to remain a dirty secret that only we know about, then I can keep your secret. But if he's gonna be a part of our lives forever...I can't betray your father and uncle."

"Even if that were the case, who I'm sleeping with is none of their business."

He looked pissed again. "When you're fucking the most dangerous man in the country, it is their business." He held my gaze without blinking, drilling his thoughts deep inside me. He pressed his finger to the counter. "By fucking him, you're endangering all of us."

"He would never hurt any of you."

"If we became a problem, yes, he would. He said it to my face."

"I know him," I said with confidence. "He would never hurt you—because it would hurt me. He puts on an act for everyone else, and I'm sure he means it at the time, but when it comes to us, he's different. As long as you don't tell my father, there will never be a problem anyway—"

"Are you going to leave him or not?" He slammed his hand down on the counter. "Answer me."

I had to remind myself that nothing had changed. Bosco and I might have developed a deeper connection, an intimate relationship that I would never find with anyone else, but that didn't change what came next. There was no future with this man. There was no marriage, children, or dinners with my family. If Griffin was this upset about it, my father's behavior would only be similar. I would probably never find another man who would make me forget about Bosco entirely, but at least I would have the other things I needed. I dreaded the moment I would pack up my things and leave, saying goodbye to a man I'd given myself to completely. But the ending had been written before we even began. I'd told Bosco what would happen, that I wouldn't change my mind about my decision. He would let me go because he was a good man who kept his word. And that would be the end. "Yes. I am."

WHEN I CAME HOME FROM WORK, BOSCO ACTED LIKE nothing had happened. In just his sweatpants, he kissed me when I walked through the door. His fingers moved into my hair as he cupped my neck, and he lavished me with the same intimacy he showed me every night before we went to sleep. He sucked my bottom lip gently before he let me go. "Beautiful." He rubbed his nose against mine before he stepped away.

I was so mesmerized by that kiss I nearly forgot about my uncomfortable conversation with Bones. I watched him walk away, the powerful muscles in his back shifting underneath his tight skin.

"I made dinner. Are you hungry?"

Bosco did most of the cooking, so that was a nice change from my single life. But most of the time, it was greens with some kind of non-fatty meat. It was too healthy to my liking, and I'd already dropped five pounds since I moved in—not that I was looking to shed weight.

Everything felt so normal that I almost ignored the elephant in the room. "Bosco, we need to talk."

He stilled with his back to me. A quiet sigh filled the space before he turned around and faced me, his affectionate look gone. Now he looked irritated, annoyed that we were going to have this conversation. "Alright."

"Griffin came to my shop today—"

"I'm aware."

"He didn't appreciate you showing up on his doorstep like that."

"I didn't appreciate him sticking his nose where it didn't belong." The kind and affectionate man I was used to had disappeared. Now the cold ruler was in the foreground, cruel and defensive.

"He's just looking out for me."

"And I'm looking out for you too. Nothing good would happen if he told your family about our affair. I made sure that didn't happen—because I don't want to kill the people you love."

I'd warned him not to threaten my family again, but he'd crossed the line once more. My eyes narrowed, and I suddenly felt twice as big, twice as bold, and twice as pissed. "This is over." All the affection I had for this man disappeared when he crossed the line. It didn't matter how much I cared about him, how much I'd fallen for him. My loyalty would never change. I was devoted to my family, my bloodline, and I wouldn't put up with someone threatening to touch even a single hair on their heads.

He couldn't hide his surprise as well as he usually could. "What—"

"We. Are. Over." I turned my back on him and marched off.

His footsteps sounded behind me. "Carmen." When I didn't turn around, he grabbed me by the arm.

I twisted out of his grasp the way my father taught me, spun around, and then slapped him hard across the face.

He turned with the hit, but his body remained perfectly still. He clenched his jaw noticeably, his blue eyes filling with irritation. He slowly turned back to me, his skin slightly red from my palm. "You're the only woman who's ever pulled that off."

"And I'll pull it off again if I have to." I wasn't afraid of this man anymore. I wouldn't let him have the power a second longer. "I'm getting my stuff, and I'm going home."

"This is home," he said, his eyes brimming with rage. "You belong to me."

"Not anymore. I told you not to threaten my family again, but you did it anyway. Our agreement is off. I won't sleep with a man who speaks about my family like that. I love them more than anything in the world, and if you ever think my loyalty to them will change, then you don't know me at all." I turned away, determined to grab my stuff and get the hell out of there.

He followed me into the bedroom. "Carmen."

I grabbed my suitcase and started to shove everything inside.

He raised his voice. "Carmen."

I ignored him.

"Goddammit." He grabbed me by the arm again and yanked me toward him. "I'm sorry." He released me right away so he wouldn't get slapped again, his nostrils flaring with his frustration. It was the first time I'd ever heard him apologize for anything—and it seemed like he meant it. "Stay."

I knew the power had changed in the relationship because he gave me a choice. He didn't phrase it as a question, but I definitely had the option to leave.

He kept staring at me, a slight look of fear in his gaze. "Beautiful…I said I was sorry."

I believed he wouldn't hurt my family because he was a fair man. But now I wanted to know with absolute certainty. "I want you to promise me you will never, ever hurt a member of my family under any circumstance. And I never want you to threaten that you will, not to me or to any of them. Those are my terms. Take them, or I walk." I was negotiating with a man who didn't need to negotiate. He had all the power and could do whatever he wanted. But I was going to try, to use my leverage over this man.

He was quiet for a long time, like he was actually considering what I asked. "Alright."

I couldn't believe I actually got my way. "I want you to promise me."

Anger flashed across his eyes. "I'm a man of my word."

"You said you always keep your promises. I want this to be a promise."

"And what if they attack me?"

"That would never happen."

"You really think so?" he asked coldly. "A father will do anything for his daughter if he thinks she's in danger."

"My family would never hurt you."

"Why?"

"Because I would never let them, okay? Now, promise me."

He sighed before he finally gave me what I wanted. "I promise."

All the fight left my body once I'd secured something so important to me. Now I never had to worry about it again. Bosco would keep his promise to me—because he'd proven it a million times over.

"Can you forget the suitcase now?" His body relaxed slightly now that the worst was over.

"Yeah…" Now that my rage had evaporated, I knew I didn't want to walk out the door. This was exactly where I wanted to be—with this man. "Why did you show up on his doorstep like that?" I resumed our previous conversation.

"It was the best time. I didn't want anyone to see us together. I didn't want there to be a history of me on his phone. I wanted to come unarmed so he would know I wasn't a threat to him or you."

"He doesn't like anyone coming near his wife."

"I wasn't there for her. Couldn't care less about her."

"It was still rude. You never show up on someone's doorstep like that."

"It's done," he said. "The conversation is over. Let it be."

"Why did you do that in the first place?"

"I already told you. I wanted to make sure this would

remain a secret. It would make both of our lives difficult if it didn't stay that way. I've never met your family, but I know they wouldn't be happy if they knew we were together. It would cause a lot of problems, and since I'm happy with the way things are, I didn't want to disrupt that." His muscles were still tensed, his shoulders rigid and his abs tight. "He didn't leave me much of a choice since he was snooping around everywhere. He knew exactly what the repercussions would be, but he did it anyway."

"Because he wants me to be safe."

"The safest place in the world is by my side. He knows that."

Carmen knew Griffin couldn't disagree with that statement.

"He yelled at me for a bit but finally let it go."

"Good."

"Since this is gonna end in four weeks, he said he would let it run its course."

Just a second ago, he was angry then apologetic. But now he wore a new expression. His eyes fell slightly, the beautiful blue color fading. His muscles stopped tensing and immediately went slack. His breathing changed as well—becoming nonexistent. It was the first time he'd dropped his gaze, breaking eye contact with me like my face was too much for him. "Yeah…let it run its course."

IT WAS TENSE FOR THE NEXT FEW DAYS. IT TOOK TIME for us to recover from the difficult conversation we'd had.

He wasn't angry or bitter. He was just cold, not nearly as affectionate as he used to be.

Sex was to the point. Conversations were short. Life turned bleak.

We sat together at the dining table and had dinner, a boring meal of fish and vegetables. The only reason we had rice was because I demanded it. Shirtless across from me, he looked at his food instead of me.

I wasn't sure what had pushed him away. Whether it was the promise I forced him to make or the reminder that our relationship was almost over. The second one wasn't a surprise, so it must have been the first one. But I wouldn't apologize for protecting my family. Not now. Not ever.

His phone was sitting on the table, and it started to ring. Ronan was usually the person who called him, but today, there was a different name on the screen.

Ruby.

AKA the biggest skank ever.

He glanced at it before he hit the button to ignore her call.

My blood immediately boiled at the sight of her name. I despised that woman, wanting to throw her in the ring myself so I could rip her hair out of her skull and punch her in the boobs. She was like a shark circling her prey, waiting for the moment I was gone so she could have Bosco to herself.

Bitch.

Bosco acted like nothing happened. He kept eating, as if he forgot about her name the second after he saw it.

Something snapped inside me. I had no idea what it was. I wasn't angry at Bosco because he didn't do anything wrong, but I was pissed that Ruby kept wanting him without even being subtle about it. I guess I was jealous...super jealous.

I grabbed his phone and called her back.

Bosco stopped eating. He stared at me while he held his fork, his eyebrow slightly raised because he had no idea what I was doing.

Her seductive voice was as slutty as it was when I heard it in person. "Bosco, I knew you'd come around. Perfect timing because I'm buck naked on my bed, only covered in diamonds."

I seriously wanted to knock her out. "Listen up, skank. Bosco Roth is mine. I'm living with him, I'm fucking him, and it doesn't matter how nice your tits are, he doesn't want them. His hands are already full with mine." I hung up and slammed the phone down, still livid that this woman had such audacity to call him in the first place.

Bosco didn't take his phone back or got upset that I told off one of his regulars. He kept holding his fork as he stared at me, his eyebrows slowly returning to their normal place. He didn't ask me why I did that or how I knew about her tits.

I avoided his gaze, embarrassed that I'd let her get under my skin. I shouldn't be jealous. I shouldn't be angry that she wanted to fuck him the second I was gone. Bosco was gonna fuck someone. It didn't really matter if it was her or not. But the fact that she wanted him when he was still mine pissed me off.

Silence continued.

Bosco resumed eating, not wearing a smug smile like he normally would during moments like these.

I felt like I should give an explanation, but I didn't know what to say. "I'm sorry…" I would be pissed if he called someone with my phone, and I shouldn't have done that to him. When I was angry, I couldn't think clearly. "I shouldn't have done that."

"You can do whatever you want, Beautiful. I don't care about her."

"Ever since I saw her throw her tits out at you, I've hated her. I just can't stand her."

He stopped eating but didn't seem surprised by what I'd said.

That meant Ronan must have told him. "I wasn't spying on you. I forgot my keys, so I came back to get them. By the time I was done, her tits were out, and you were having a deep conversation."

"I wouldn't care even if you were spying on me. I have nothing to hide." Bosco had always been transparent from the beginning, never ashamed of any of his qualities. It was refreshing to be with a man who truly didn't care what anyone thought.

"I was surprised you didn't do anything." I'd expected him to palm her tits before he fucked her on the couch. We hadn't been together very long, so he didn't have a reason to be loyal to me. She was drop-dead gorgeous. No matter how much I hated her, it couldn't change that fact. I was sure Bosco enjoyed fucking her in the past.

He set his fork down and held my gaze, his expression darkening. "Why would I want her when I have you?" He said it with sincerity, his words coming from his heart as well as his mouth.

"But she's got perfect tits, enough confidence to just

show up on a man's doorstep and demand sex, and she's—"

"Nothing compared to you." He didn't blink the entire time he held my gaze. "She could be the most beautiful woman in the world, and my dick isn't going to respond. You could never find out about my infidelity, and it still wouldn't change anything. I love you, Carmen Barsetti— so I'm never going to want anyone else but you." Without a hint of shame, he continued to hold my gaze, unapologetic. It didn't seem like he cared what I said in response. He spoke his mind, confident in his statement and unafraid of what I would say in return.

The second I heard what he said, my body tensed noticeably, all my muscles getting tighter and uncomfortable. His words didn't surprise me, but they caught me off guard anyway. Bosco Roth just declared his love for me, and now he stared at me so hard, like there would be consequences if I didn't say it back.

A full minute of silence passed, and not once in that minute did he blink.

I tried to find the right words to say, but nothing popped into my head. I was still determined to walk away from this relationship when our time came to an end, but he'd just thrown a curveball at me. Saying those words would make our breakup nearly impossible. I refused to say it back, and I refused to accept the love he just confessed. "Bosco—"

"Don't act surprised. I didn't have to jump into that ring and kill the man who bothered you. I have hundreds of dogs on my payroll who could have handled that for me. I put my life on the line and snapped his arm and broke his back—because you're my woman. I'll gladly get my hands dirty in your honor. If that's not a declaration of love, I don't know what is."

There was nothing I could say to that because he was completely right.

"You're the safest woman in this city because I protect you. I protect you because you're the single most important thing in my life. You aren't just the woman I'm sleeping with. You're the one who sleeps beside me all night, the one who has dinner with me, the one I'm completely committed to. Ruby is a beautiful woman who knows her way around a bedpost, but she'll never be more than a good lay. You, on the other hand, are the only woman I've ever loved. You're the only woman I've ever skipped the condom with. You're the only woman who makes me apologize, forces me to make promises, and turns my hardness into softness. Let's not pretend that my love isn't written all over my face, written all over every little thing I do. I didn't expect this to happen, but now that it has, I'm not afraid to say it. So you'd better not be afraid to handle it."

I listened to every single word, no longer shocked by the sudden confession, but by the aggressive way he forced me to accept it. He wasn't ashamed in the least, and he wasn't angry that I didn't say it back. He only wanted to prove his point further, to show that his confession was amplified by his actions.

Now he stared at me, silently demanding that I repeat the phrase back to him.

I refused to do it.

He sat back in his chair, his eyes filling with disappointment.

"I told you I'm leaving when this is over."

"Even though you're in love with me?"

"I never said I was."

"Cut the bullshit." He pushed his plate aside and leaned over the table closer to me. "You can keep lying to yourself, but that's not gonna last long. And you can't lie to me at all—because I see it written all over your face. I see it when I'm buried deep inside you, when you're crying because you're worried about my safety, when you sleep on the couch as you wait for me to come home at night. I've always admired you because of how strong and real you are. You've never been afraid to be honest, to tell the truth exactly as it is. But now…you're weak. You're too weak to face me like a real woman. You're too scared to own up to the truth. That's not the Carmen I know. The woman I know, the woman I love, has a much stronger backbone than that."

12

BOSCO

I DIDN'T NEED to go to the casino that night, but I went anyway.

Because Carmen had pissed me off.

After I checked on the floor and talked to security, I took the elevator down to my office underground. It was the quietest place in the world, the one location I could truly be alone without being bothered. The only person who could get down here without my prior knowledge was Ronan—and he hardly ever did.

I sat in my leather chair with a glass of scotch in my hand. I stared at the wall, my elbow on the desk and my fingertips lightly pressed against my cheek. My thoughts kept going back to Carmen, the one who came into my life so unexpectedly. Now she was ruining my life because she wanted to leave.

It was a bunch of bullshit.

I knew she loved me. She just didn't want to love me.

Too fucking bad.

Hours passed, but I was in no hurry to head home. Carmen would be on the couch because she couldn't sleep without me. This was my cruel way of showing her exactly how dependent she was on me.

Just in case she forgot.

The elevator clanked as it descended to my floor, and heavy footsteps thudded against the concrete as someone came down to join me.

It could only be one person.

I stood up and poured another drink. "All I got is scotch. Drink up." I set the glass at the end of the desk and sat down again.

Ronan grinned before he picked it up. "Do you ever have anything else?" He took a drink before he sat down on the leather couch, the couch where I'd fucked Carmen that one time.

"Good point." I swirled my glass before I took another drink. "Is there something you need?"

"No. Drake told me you'd been down here a long time. Wanted to see if everything was alright."

"I'm fine." The words weren't convincing, even to me. I came down here to get away from Carmen, not to think and talk about her.

He took a long drink before he wiped his mouth on the back of his sleeve. "Look, it's late. How about we cut the bullshit and just get right to the point? I know there's something wrong, and I'm guessing it has something to do with Carmen. If you don't want to talk about it, fine. But not let's pretend."

I didn't want to talk about it, but I didn't want to coldly dismiss my brother when he was only trying to be supportive. I'd pushed him away already, and it was a miracle he was still there. I wouldn't take him for granted again. "You're right. It's about Carmen."

"Yeah? What happened?"

"I told her I loved her. She refused to say it back."

Ronan's eyes opened wider, just as surprised by her reaction as I was. "You know she's lying, right?"

I rested my fingertips against my temple. "Yes." There was no way a woman could kiss that good, could fuck that good, and could cry that good without meaning it. I saw the way she used me as a crutch, the way I made her feel safer than anyone else in the world.

"Now the question is, why is she lying?"

"A lot of reasons. The biggest one, she wants to break up in four weeks."

"Really?" he asked. "Doesn't seem like she wants to leave."

"I think she'd rather move on than try to make it work with me. I'm still not what she wants in a partner."

"What does she want, exactly?"

"A family." She wanted four kids, one right after another.

"And that's not something you're willing to do?"

I shrugged. "She's never asked. That's what makes me angry. She already ruled me out with even bothering to find out. She's never given me a chance to be what she wants—even though I keep proving her wrong over and over."

"Maybe you should tell her that."

"No. I've been bending over backward for this woman

for too long. She needs to meet me halfway. She needs to tell me how she feels."

Ronan didn't disagree with me. "She'll come around, Bosco. It's only a matter of time. She's been crazy about you since the beginning. Maybe she can lie to you for a while, but she can't lie to herself. It won't last long."

"I hope you're right. I'm purposely lingering, knowing she's sitting on the couch, waiting for me to come home. She told me she can't sleep without me. I'm reminding her how much she needs me…just in case she forgot."

WHEN I CAME HOME, SHE WAS EXACTLY WHERE I expected her to be.

But this time, she was sitting upright with her knees pulled to her chest. Her hair was in a ponytail, and she was watching an old sitcom on TV. It was almost five in the morning, and even though she was supposed to wake up in forty-five minutes, she'd stayed awake the entire time.

Point proven.

I ignored her as I walked inside and headed for the bedroom. I stripped off my clothes and tossed them into the bin before I put my shoes on top.

She helped herself into bed, getting under my sheets and closing her eyes.

I got on my side of the bed, but just because we were in this rut didn't mean we weren't fucking. I pulled her panties down her ass and legs and then rolled her to her stomach. Even if she didn't want to participate, she was getting fucked. That pussy would be stuffed with my come regardless.

She barely had a chance to say a single word before I shoved myself inside her.

"Don't say a goddamn thing." I thrust hard, pressing her into the mattress as I ground against her with all my weight. I was pissed at this woman, but no matter how angry I was, it didn't change my needs. I could have stopped by Ruby's place and gotten my dick sucked, but I only wanted this come—even when I was angry.

She moaned with my thrusts, her body shaking with the intense way I drove into her.

I wasn't in the mood to please her, so I didn't care about getting her off. All I cared about now was driving myself into a climax so I could go to sleep.

But she came anyway.

I pounded hard and fast, making her ass cheeks shake because I thrust into her so hard. I fucked her pussy like a toy and moved through the cream she made for me. With a groan, I came. Come exploded out of my head and entered deep inside her, exactly where it belonged. I kept thrusting as I enjoyed the last of my orgasm, turned on by the way I was stuffing her.

When I finished, I rolled off her and moved back to my side of the bed, purposely putting space between us. If she didn't want to be loved by me, I would show her exactly how that felt. I would show her what it was like to mean nothing to me.

She moved to her back and stayed on her side, her breathing still heavy in the darkness. She usually fell asleep almost instantly, but now she seemed to be wide awake.

She looked at the ceiling with the sheets pulled to her waist.

I turned on my side and purposely looked away from her.

I wasn't tired and neither was she, but neither one of us would speak. Practically oceans apart, we pretended the other didn't exist.

13

CARMEN

I WAS LOW.

I turned down Bosco's feelings and pretended he didn't mean anything to me. I told him I was leaving when this relationship finished its contract, but I failed to mention how much it would hurt when that moment came. I could see the future, the pain I would put my parents through. I could see the drama, the fights, the guns that would be pointed at each other. It took six months for Crow to accept Griffin—and it almost didn't happen.

Bosco wouldn't be any different.

They would never approve. He would be a wedge in my relationship with my family. He would never be a father or a husband. He would always be the king of the underworld, the man of mass destruction.

I had to leave. I had no other choice.

It didn't matter how I felt. It didn't matter how many tears I shed. It didn't matter that he was the only man I'd ever allowed to come inside me. All the feelings that existed between us, the connection, the intimacy...they didn't matter.

It wouldn't work.

So I stayed strong and didn't utter the words he wanted to hear. I let the distance between us linger. I let him fuck me like I meant nothing to him—and I still came anyway.

He purposely came home late every single night, forcing me to lose sleep because I was wide awake until he walked through the door. He knew it—and that was exactly why he did it. He just wanted to prove his point.

And he did.

The days passed, and there were no signs of improvement. I was afraid this was how we would spend the last three weeks together, having meaningless sex and no conversations. He would avoid me by staying at work all night, and I would continually be sleep deprived every single day.

He was too stubborn to let it go. I knew his behavior wouldn't change until I told him what he wanted to hear.

That I was madly in love with him.

I worked at the shop all day, and when closing time arrived, I piled all my cash into a leather pouch and locked the doors. I walked to the bank down the road, the place where I had my business accounts. Since I was the only employee, I didn't even consider myself to be a small business. I was simply a one-woman show.

There was a long line at the bank, so I stepped inside and pulled out my phone. Griffin hadn't contacted me since our last conversation, and since Vanessa hadn't called me either, I wondered if she knew anything about it. It didn't seem like something Griffin would keep from her, but maybe he didn't want to scare her.

I heard the doors behind me slam closed.

Then the gunshots went off.

I dropped my phone on the ground as the four armed men stormed across the floor of the bank. They pulled men and women from their booths and dragged them onto the floor, pointing guns at their faces and ordering them to stay down.

Jesus Christ, I was in the middle of a robbery.

I dropped to the floor like everyone else and kept my head down.

The men secured the doors with thick cables so no one could get inside. The windows seemed to be bulletproof because the gunshots didn't make the glass shatter.

That meant Bosco's men couldn't get to me.

Shit.

Two men went down the line and started ordering people to hand over their belongings while the other two hit the tellers and demanded them to open the drawers.

When one woman refused to hand over her wedding ring, they shot her.

Now I was scared. Truly scared. I could keep calm in intense situations and find a way out, but this time, there was no escape route. All the doors were secured with cables, and I couldn't jump out of a window.

I was stuck.

The man kept going down the line, taking people's phones, wallets, and anything else valuable, from jewelry to expensive shoes.

I didn't care about any of my possessions—except my necklace. My father gave this to me, and there was no way I was letting them have it. I tucked my necklace inside my sweater then covered my shoulders with my hair.

The man's face was covered with a black mask, and he held a pistol. He pointed the gun right between my eyes.

It was the second time that had happened to me—and I was getting tired of it.

I dropped the leather pouch in his bag along with my phone and wallet. I was wearing cheap rings that weren't sentimental, so I threw those in there too, just so he would understand I was cooperating.

"Anything else?" he asked, pressing the barrel right into my skin. The metal of the gun was cold.

"No." I kept my voice stern, knowing Bosco's men would make it inside the building any second. It'd been nearly three minutes since the robbery began. The police hadn't even arrived. The men would probably take off any minute now if they wanted to get away.

"Then what's this?" He reached into my sweater and yanked on the chain, revealing the rose made out of diamonds. "Bitch, you want to die?"

I wasn't giving up my necklace, not when my father gave it to me on my brother's wedding day. "Fuck you." I kicked him hard in the knee, making him fall back and shoot his gun by mistake. He shattered a light in the ceiling.

My instincts kicked in, and I lunged for the gun.

"I don't think so, bitch." He grabbed me by the shoulder and yanked me back. He pulled his arm back and punched me hard in the face.

It was a powerful hit, but I had enough adrenaline to keep me going. I punched him in the throat and forced the air from his windpipe.

"What the fuck?" One of his comrades finally came to his aid and pointed the gun at me. "If you don't want to die, I suggest you sit still." He nodded to his accomplice. "Get the necklace and let's go."

"Just shoot her."

"Nah, she's too sexy. We've got her wallet, so I'll hunt her down later."

Why were all men such pigs?

The man moved on top of me and grabbed my necklace.

Now there was nothing I could do but let him take it.

An explosion sounded behind me, accompanied by breaking glass and the sound of shards hitting the bank floor.

I knew exactly who it was. "Thank god."

The man abandoned my necklace and ran for his gun.

I kicked it away. "Take that, bitch."

Men rushed in, firing weapons right away, shooting three of them but leaving the fourth one alive.

Then Bosco arrived, his face red and the cords in his neck twitching. In jeans and a t-shirt, he was dressed casually, but he somehow carried all the power befitting his persona. A pistol was in his right hand. "Which one?"

Two of his men grabbed the man who had punched me in the face.

The guy struggled at first, but then stopped when he realized he was outnumbered, his comrades lifeless behind him.

"Him?" Bosco tossed his gun to one of his guys then pulled out a knife.

Oh my god.

"Shit! No!" The guy tried to twist away.

Bosco was on him fast, stabbing him over and over, hitting him in the chest, neck, and stomach. "You fucking touched my woman."

It was so violent, I had to look away. I didn't get a sense of revenge out of the sight. I felt weak and sick. I lay down, trying to tune out the horrifying sounds the man was making as he was being stabbed to death.

I kept my eyes closed until it was finally over.

Bosco dropped the knife then came to me next, not a drop of blood on him. "Beautiful." His powerful arms surrounded me, and he brought me close, examining the black eye that was already forming on my face. He sighed in despair, his eyes full of heartbreak. "I'm so sorry." He pulled me into his chest then kissed my neck and cheeks, giving me kisses and love everywhere. "Fuck, I'm sorry I wasn't fast enough."

I rested my face against his shoulder and closed my eyes. "Babe, I'm okay."

His arms shook as he held me. "No, you aren't. I promised no one would ever touch you."

"It's my fault. He tried to take my necklace, and I fought him."

"Doesn't matter." He kissed my forehead then ran his fingers through my hair. "The men couldn't make it through the doors, so we had to bring in an explosive. If the windows weren't bulletproof—"

"Babe, I'm fine." I pulled away so I could look him in

the eye. "It takes more than a black eye to slow me down." I cupped his cheek, seeing the harsh pain in his eyes. If he hadn't come to my rescue, I would be dead right now. On top of that, those men would have come back for me with worse intentions. "You saved my life."

His fingers felt the swelling and the bruising around my eye before he kissed it.

It was the third time Bosco had saved my life. I went to this bank on a daily basis to deposit my profits. Not once had anything like this happened, and if it happened some other time, I probably wouldn't have survived. There were a lot of things I wouldn't have survived if this man weren't looking out for me, constantly protecting me. Maybe it was the adrenaline or maybe it was the gratitude, but the words came out of my mouth. "I love you."

The pain was still in his eyes from my injury, but they softened just a bit. "I know you do."

"I was scared to say it. But I shouldn't be because everything you said was right. You've proven your love for me a million times over...and you're the only man in the world who deserves me." All a father wanted for his daughter was a man who could protect her. Bosco fit the bill perfectly, even coming to my aid in person because he wasn't afraid to put his life on the line. Bosco had other poor attributes, aspects that would be difficult to look past, but I knew the man underneath the money and power. He was kind, protective, and devoted. Admitting my feelings out loud made our situation so much more complicated, but it was already complicated.

Bosco watched me as his men cleaned up the area. They grabbed the dead bodies and dumped all the belongings that were in the bag so everyone could have their stuff back. But he seemed only to be focused on me. "Let's go home."

BOSCO SAT BESIDE ME AT THE DINING TABLE, PRESSING ice wrapped in a towel against my bruised eye. "You're sure you don't want to see a doctor?"

"I'm fine."

He continued to hold it there, sighing quietly under his breath. He looked torn up inside, as if he could feel the injury on my face himself. He lightly pressed the ice against my cheek before he moved again. "I could get you something stronger."

"I don't need anything." I could tough it out for a few days. The swelling would go down soon, and then the purple color would slowly fade away.

He set the towel down and fished out my necklace from his pocket. "This belongs to you."

I didn't care about my purse or the money from the shop. All I cared about was this gift my father gave me. It was probably worth more than all the money in my leather bag, but that wasn't why I fought for it. It could be worth a quarter, and I still would have taken a black eye for it. "Thank you." I clasped it back around my neck and felt the pendant with my fingertips.

Bosco stared at it for a while before he cleared his throat. "What are we going to do?"

I knew my father would be livid with the man I'd chosen. He would be even worse than Uncle Crow. My father was the one who punched Griffin in the face just for looking at me too long. His heart was in the right place, but his emotional outbursts made him impetuous and unpredictable. We never talked about my personal life, but that was because my father wanted to pretend I didn't have a personal life. In his eyes, I was a virgin waiting for my husband to arrive, and until I brought that man home, he wouldn't think about it.

He wouldn't like Bosco at all.

With Griffin adding his opinion on the matter, there was no hope. Vanessa warned me this would happen, but I was too stubborn to realize she was right. My heart wasn't as strong as I thought it was. I thought I could resist Bosco, and maybe I could have if he'd never confessed his love for me. "I don't know…"

"You don't know?" he whispered, staring at me with his head slightly tilted. "That doesn't sound promising."

"Just because I love you doesn't mean anything has changed."

His eyes immediately fell in disappointment.

"I already know how my father is going to feel about this, not to mention the rest of my family…"

"Your family isn't the one who's in this relationship. It's you. You're a grown woman, and it shouldn't matter what they think. You're so independent and free. It's one of the reasons I fell in love with you. Submitting to their opinions goes against everything in your nature."

"And if this were about me riding a motorcycle or traveling the world alone, I would agree with you. But Bosco, this is about…" I didn't want to finish the sentence because it would make things more complicated. I refused to talk about marriage and kids this soon. "This sort of thing is a big deal in my family. And since my family means so much to me, I don't want to ruin what I have. I have something everyone envies me for. I have two fathers and two mothers, and I have cousins who are siblings, and siblings who are like friends. It doesn't matter how much I love you, I love my family more." That was probably a hurtful thing to say, but I had to be honest.

He didn't flinch at the statement. "You're getting ahead of yourself. Let's start at the beginning and see where it goes."

This man had just saved me—again. I didn't want to hurt him. I didn't want to take a swing at his heart when he adored me. "Regardless of how we feel about each other, nothing has changed. We're from two different worlds…and I see no scenario where they mix." I couldn't look him in the eye as I said it, all my courage stripped away. Maybe I loved this man and he loved me, but at the end of the three weeks, it would still be over.

He stared at me and patiently waited for me to meet his gaze.

But I refused to comply.

"So in three weeks, you still want to leave?"

I swallowed, my heart in so much pain I didn't even notice the pain over my eye. "Yes."

He gripped the towel, the cords on the back of his hand flexing all the way up his forearms. "Fine."

My eyes turned back to him, shocked that he agreed so easily. I expected him to get angry, to tell me off for not giving him what he wanted. But instead, he accepted my decision without complaint. Something wasn't right.

He held my gaze then pressed the towel back over my eye.

"And you're just okay with that?" I whispered, refusing to believe he let me off the hook so easily.

He softly pressed the coldness against my swollen eye. "We both know you aren't going to leave, Beautiful. I won't stop you if you want to try, but there's no way you're gonna walk out that door. You love me too much. You need me too much. And more importantly, you can't live without me."

ALSO BY PENELOPE SKY

The story concludes in…

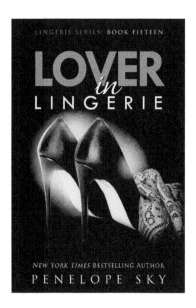

Order Now

Printed in Great Britain
by Amazon